Praise for The Shopkeeper of Alsace

"A literary tour-de-force rich in love, history, and heartache. Laura Knoy expertly puts to page the timely and unforgettable true story of a woman who carried her family through two world wars." — Miranda Hardister, editor and bookseller

"The giant events of the 20th Century become intensely personal through this story of a thoroughly relatable, real-life heroine, Sarah. *The Shopkeeper of Alsace* is a deeply satisfying immigrant saga of love, family, war . . . and hope." — Suzanne Rico, award-winning journalist, and creator of the nationally acclaimed WWII podcast *The Man Who Calculated Death*

"A beautifully conceived depiction of endurance, determination, and bravery in a time of wartime peril. *The Shopkeeper of Alsace*, inspired by real-life individuals and lesser-known events of World War II, combines detailed history with an engaging and moving human story. In her impressive debut novel, Laura Knoy offers an insightful depiction of the struggle to survive." — Margaret Porter, award-winning author of 15 historical novels, including *Beautiful Invention: A Novel of Hedy Lamarr*

THE SHOPKEEPER OF ALSACE

THE SHOPKEEPER OF ALSACE

Laura Knoy

Bink Books
Bedazzled Ink Publishing Company • Fairfield, California

978-1-960373-76-2 paperback

Cover Design
by

Sapling
Studio

Bink Books
a division of
Bedazzled Ink Publishing
Fairfield, California
http://www.bedazzledink.com

To Annette

MAP OF KEY CITIES IN
THE SHOPKEEPER OF ALSACE

Prologue
ALSACE, FRANCE
MAY 1940

IN THE GREY stillness of early morning, I padded into my sons' bedroom. I brushed each boy's cheek with a kiss, their faces still smooth but already hinting at the men they would soon become. At my touch, both mumbled something like "goodbye," before rolling back into the profound slumber of adolescence. I then slid down the hallway to my eight-year-old daughter's room, and gazed at her from the doorway, memorizing how her tangle of auburn curls fell over her face. I didn't risk entering; she might startle and wake, beg me not to leave, ask me questions I couldn't answer. Guilt jabbed a finger into my ribcage. *What kind of a mother are you, Sarah?* it asked. *Perhaps the worst kind,* I answered. I closed my daughter's door, put on my shoes, picked up my suitcase, and left.

Then I plunged into a war. Again.

I was a teenager when the Great War erupted, a conflict that would later be named "World War One." Poland, where I was born, was a battleground, a long-disputed territory coveted by all the combatants. Polish Jews like us were pawns, sometimes courted for political and material support, other times scapegoated and targeted as traitors. At age fourteen, I learned that war isn't just what happens at the battlefront. Behind the lines, it's poverty and hunger. It's frantically gathering your belongings and fleeing when the night is its blackest. It's soldiers who take what they want. Your food. Your business. Your home. Your body.

But as traumatic as my girlhood was, it also prepared me for right now. And this time, I was no untested teenager. I was a mother, a wife, and a successful businesswoman with everything I loved and had built at stake. I was ready. Poland taught me how to survive: to plan, to move, to hide, to lie. I could do it again.

Chapter 1
AMSHINOV, POLAND
MARCH 1915. THE GREAT WAR

THE CELLAR WAS dank, but I dared not move to find a blanket. I sat, stiff and still, on a lumpy bundle of assorted items gathered in a stained sheet. I tried to breathe quietly, just shallow sips of air that smelled of old dirt. Voices filtered down from the shop floor above me: my father's, calm and courteous—the others, harsh and demanding. They had returned, they wanted something—and I feared it might not be anything we sold at our store. The chill around me seeped inside, a swirling fog of unease that filled my chest and stomach.

If only I could erase what happened yesterday. What I'd started.

THE MORNING HAD begun with promise. The icy drizzle of the evening before had lifted, and the brown and grey stones of our village's central square shone in the early spring sunshine. Perhaps this first glimmer of warmth would entice more customers to venture out, despite the columns of soldiers often passing through town these days and the occasional, far-off thud of a cannon. Plus, it was Market Day, always our busiest and most profitable time of the week.

Our shop was the most popular in Amshinov, all due to my father. Berek Elkshutz had the soul of a shopkeeper; he knew just the right way to cater to everyone's needs, country dwellers and townsfolk, Jews and Gentiles. But it wasn't just what he sold, it was how he did it: with kindness, fairness, and a genuine concern for his customers. Owning the village's most prosperous store was a position that could have created envy, even dislike. Instead, my father drew respect and affection from everyone.

The whisper of spring did draw more people that day, in fact it was our best Market Day since the war had begun a year ago. After the peasants sold their crops or livestock at the village's open-air market, they came into our store, stomping their muddy boots and shouting hearty greetings. They were poor farmers, but on Market Day, their pockets jangled, heavy with coins. They would buy nails, tools, and bullets for hunting, flour, millet, and canned fish. These essential purchases completed, some took a moment to browse the shelves, gazing longingly at items I knew they couldn't afford: musical instruments, elegant coats from Warsaw, and soft leather boots. These would be bought by our wealthier customers, the families who ran Amshinov's distilleries, taverns, and the village itself.

By midmorning, we'd had so much business that the floor was covered with mud. I handed a mop to my little sister, Zofja, and a broom to one of our young cousins, telling them to clean up as best they could without disturbing customers. But just as they took their first swipes at the dirt, the shop's wooden door flung open with such force that splinters flew off. Half a dozen Russian soldiers barged in, their dull khaki uniforms in contrast with their cheeks, which blazed red from the cold and, I guessed, early morning drinking.

Customers screamed. Those close to the door fled, while others cowered in a corner. I held Zofja's shoulder with my left hand and my cousin's shoulder with my right.

"Don't you dare move," I warned them.

The jovial chatter of moments ago ceased. The soldiers' leader strode to the counter, the clanking of his canteen against his belt now the only sound. Despite the leanness of wartime, he had a wide girth. He scanned the room, assessing the shelves, the jars behind the counter, the barrels on the floor.

"The mayor was right. This is a fine place for us to replenish ourselves."

Not again. My grip on the children's shoulders tightened, to control myself as much as to control them. For the past year, when soldiers passed through town on their way to and from the battlefronts, they'd ask the mayor where the Jewish shops were, in exchange for a promise to leave the Christian shops alone. Our store was often their first target.

With a wave of his meaty arm, the officer directed his men to help themselves to whatever they wanted. I bit the insides of my cheeks, willing myself to stay quiet, while furiously watching as they stuffed socks, tea, onions, and apples into the satchels they wore at their sides. My father always ordered us not to react, that looting was a cost of war we simply must learn to accept. I managed to find some grim satisfaction in knowing that they couldn't take everything we had. Much more was stored in the cellar below, hidden from their thieving hands.

We'll be all right. We can recover from this.

Their bags bulging and our shelves now bare, the soldiers eyed their commander, awaiting an order to leave. Instead, he strolled to the cash register and pointed to my father, who was behind it.

"Empty it," he said.

All those coins that we had just earned that morning.

Don't do it, Papa. Don't give it to them.

I strained to catch my father's attention, so focused that I didn't notice a small shoulder slide out from my grasp. My cousin, a feisty eight-year-old boy, had escaped my hold and, in an attempt to prevent this final act of theft, thrust his slight frame between the hard rail of the counter and the man's soft stomach. It took the Russian less than a second to place his Mosin rifle on the boy's skinny chest.

I didn't think—about their guns, their absolute power over us, how many of them there were. I leaped forward, grabbed my cousin, and thrust him aside.

"Leave him alone. Take what you want. And *go*," I said.

The rifle then landed on my own chest, its cold bayonet point poking through my woolen dress. I stared down the long, wooden barrel, into the face of the man holding it—a professional killer. *One finger is all it would take.*

Instead, the group of Russians sniggered.

"She's a saucy one," a thin muskrat-like soldier said to his commander. "You like that in a girl."

The heavy officer pulled his thick lips back, like a bullfrog trying to smile. His teeth were brownish-grey, stained with tobacco. He lowered the rifle, appraising me.

"Yes, Sergeant . . . you're right. She *is* saucy."

He grabbed my chin with his grimy hand and lifted my face to him. My nostrils filled with the fetid scent of body odor and vodka. I stared at the floor, resolving not to give him the satisfaction of eye contact again. Several long seconds passed. The officer dropped his hand. With a jerk of his head, he indicated to his men that they should go. They left the cash register alone.

THE FOLLOWING EVENING, my father and I were by ourselves at the store, refilling the shelves from our hidden cellar stocks while having the same disagreement we'd had for months now: whether to leave our village. I wanted to go. Other Jewish families had already departed, tired of the looting and the constant threat of war. Amshinov had changed, they said—it was no longer the comfortable haven it had been for so long. I felt it, too; a shift in how people talked, walked, and especially how they looked at one another; their eyes unsettled, their voices lowered, their pace more rapid than before. But Papa always insisted we stay. *This is home.*

We heard the Russians before we saw them, guffawing and singing as they approached our shop door.

Papa grabbed my arm. "Down to the storage room. Quickly."

He opened the trap door, cut into the floor behind the counter. I clambered down the ladder, scraping my shins in my haste. I knew there'd be blood but couldn't risk the noise of searching for a cloth or rag. I sat in the dim light that leaked through the trap door, settling myself among hefty bundles containing clothes, shoes, pots, and farm tools whose sharp edges poked me. My mother always said that to be Jewish in Russian-controlled Poland meant you must always be packed and ready to go. Even in Amshinov, a town known for its long, peaceful coexistence between Jews and Christians.

Amshinov is a tolerant sibling, but Russia is still the parent. Remember that, Sarah, my mother would say. My father would lovingly protest. *Now, now, Lea . . .*

Whether to trust non-Jews was a common point of disagreement between them. My mother had grown up elsewhere in Poland, where outbursts of antisemitic violence could ignite from nowhere. Her own family had escaped multiple pogroms, their homes burned, their livelihoods destroyed. As a girl, she'd heard the screams of women being dragged off for rape; she'd run from the crazed mobs intent on killing. My mother's family had fled to Amshinov when she was a girl with nothing.

But my father's childhood was idyllic. He was born in Amshinov in 1870, a full century after the town's Christian fathers had granted Jews unusually broad rights, in recognition that they'd saved it from financial ruin. Jews could live in almost any neighborhood they chose and work in almost any profession they wanted. Some Jewish men even served as town burghers. But even in this unusually friendly atmosphere, Mama had insisted we maintain our hidden stocks. As she became more ill, and more aware that my father would soon be alone with five children, she often ordered me to check the cellar, to swear to her that yes, there was plenty. I know she thought Papa was too confident, too optimistic that our solid, prosperous life would continue.

You were right, Mama. I shuddered alone in the cellar.

At least she would have been impressed by how much more we had salted away now, thanks to our steady stockpiling since the very first days of the war. But where would she have chosen to be at this moment? Here in the cellar with me? Her warm, work-hardened arms around my trembling shoulders? Or behind the counter with my father, preparing to confront the Russians?

I heard Papa greeting them, up above. I shivered more deeply, remembering their smell of alcohol and sweat . . .

"Gentlemen, you're back so soon . . . may I help you?" my father asked.

"*Dah.* You *can* help us."

It was the commander.

"We've come back to remind you that you owe us a favor, after that little dramatic scene we tolerated here yesterday. You're lucky we didn't kill that little boy. No one would care if we did, and maybe we should have, because we know what you people are up to."

"I don't understand . . ."

"Don't pretend. You and every Jew in every Polish village are helping the Germans. They're fortified with your food. They fire bullets from your shops. They know our troop movements thanks to information from your spies." He growled louder with each accusation.

The thunk of boots taking a few steps—then a thud, or a crash. Had the officer thrown Papa to the floor? What should I do? I knew my father would want me to sit still; after all, I was a small, unarmed fourteen-year-old girl. But every fiber in my being compelled me to check. I would not stay hidden and helpless in a cellar while my father was threatened. I crawled up the ladder and lifted the trap door just an inch to peek out.

Papa was unhurt. The officer had merely bumped into a samovar, a big, metal tea set. I lowered the trap door lid, but it was too late. The Russian had seen me. He leaned over in an exaggerated bow.

"Ah, it's our fierce little she-wolf from yesterday . . . what a delightful surprise. Come up, come up, my dear . . ."

I emerged, reading the contorted emotions on my papa's face: furious that I'd taken such an outrageous risk, but also the suffocating fear of a father sensing that something terrible could happen to his daughter and that he might be powerless to stop it.

Papa took my hand. His palm was warm, the blood pumping fast, although outwardly, he remained composed, as if the three of them had been discussing the price of cabbages. Still the smaller, subordinate officer seemed less interested in my presence than in lecturing my father.

He shook his finger in Papa's face. "*Dah*, as my commander says, we are not at all fooled. We know which side of this war you people are on. And it is not on *our* side. So . . . to make up for you Jews' lack of loyalty to the Tsar, we'll stay at your inn tonight. We've heard it's quite comfortable."

Papa exhaled, and I felt his pulse slow. Was this all they wanted? When times had been better, our parents had bought a small house near our own home to run as an inn. Along with the shop, it had been a successful family enterprise. Then came the war, no one was traveling, and military officers were our most frequent "guests." Of course, they never paid—yet another cost of war that my father told us we had to swallow.

"Yes, of course," he said. "We'll make it ready for you. We have hosted many of the Tsar's soldiers before and will be honored to do so again."

This seemed to satisfy the junior officer, but his commander continued to leer at me. "*Dah*, yes, the inn will be very fine . . . but, well . . . our feelings are still hurt. You Polish Jews have been so ungrateful after all that Mother Russia has done for you. So, we also demand some women to warm our beds. To make us even *more* comfortable."

His eyes traveled the length of my adolescent form. Despite the deprivations of war, I had developed curves in the past year. A sharp, white wave of anger, shame, and terror washed through me. I swayed, only remaining standing due to my father's grip.

"This one here and your older daughter will do quite nicely," the officer continued. "Consider it a simple payback for the Tsar. Then we'll leave you and that silly boy alone. Otherwise, I'm afraid things will go very badly for you. And for the rest of your *lovely* children and grandchildren."

His voice lightened, teased, as he enjoyed our alarm at his hideous demand and his equally hideous threat.

"Yes, yes . . . we've collected information on you. Your neighbors were most cooperative. You live near the tenement house, not far from here. Your eldest son, Yakob, is married, living with his wife and young children one street away. You have three other children, including the eldest daughter who's honored your household by marrying a scholar who spends his days studying at the synagogue. That, too, is useful for us to know. We'll come to your home in a few minutes while you prepare to make us comfortable. Then you'll take us to the inn, so we can enjoy your . . . *hospitality*." The commander gestured to his junior officer that it was time to go. "We shall see you . . . later." His smile gleamed with power and lust.

But as they approached the door, I was surprised to hear the younger soldier hesitate. "Sir. I thought we were going to demand just a night at the inn. One of those *women* is really just a girl."

The older officer cuffed his subordinate on the shoulder. "Shut up, Sergeant. This is war. And they're only Jews."

The door banged behind them.

MY FATHER DREW me toward him in a quick, tight embrace. "*Maideleh*. My little girl."

The white terror that had begun with the officer's horrifying hint of interest now turned into a blaze, burning my face, my heart, my throat . . . with his dreadful demand. I looked at my papa, who understood my desperate question: What was his plan?

"The merchandise they can have. But not you and your sister. So now we run. Then you hide again. He locked the main door. "These Russians love their vodka, like little children with sweets . . ." He fumbled with the keys, his fingers shaking. "So, we'll offer them an endless supply of their favorite treat. We'll get them so drunk, they'll forget what they came for, and we can escape."

Given the vile threat facing me and my sister Celina, his plan seemed shockingly feeble. Was this the best he could do? I'd grown up comfortably believing that my mother's frightening childhood was hers, not mine. Not ours.

"Papa, why can't we just go home and get Celina, and run very, very fast and—"

"We don't have time to gather the entire family," he said. "And we can't leave them behind. The consequences would be grave."

He was right. If Celina and I stole away, the Russians would harm the rest of them. My father's strategy was the thinnest of threads, upon which everything was hanging, but we had no other choice. We had to hope it would work.

We dashed out the back. Hand in hand, we raced home, through twisting alleys so we wouldn't be seen. Our breathless arrival upset a pleasant domestic scene. Celina was stirring some soup on the wood-burning stove, while Zofja sewed an apron and my older brother, Yosef, read by kerosene lamplight.

"Girls! In the cellar. Now . . . *Hide!*" my father shouted.

Zofja dropped her sewing; our gentle papa never shouted. I yanked her to the cellar door while Celina grabbed some quilts. We stumbled down the ladder, the cuts on my leg still bleeding from earlier. Despite our blankets, the damp cellar air folded itself around me, and for the second time that day, I breathed the odor of earth long hidden away. From up above came the scrape and screech of moving furniture, as my father and Yosef rushed about, rearranging the room while Papa hurled more orders.

"Yosef. Move this table in front of the cellar door, put Zofja's mending away, hide the dinner preparations. Then run to Yakob's and tell him to lock their doors. After that, go to the synagogue and tell your brother-in-law to stay there . . ."

Of all the types of anger you can experience, anger at yourself is the blackest. If I hadn't acted so impulsively, leaping out to protect my cousin one day, and then peeking through the trap door to make sure my father was all right the next, the Russians might not have targeted us, and we wouldn't be in this predicament. I had drawn their interest beyond just ordinary Jews they could rob, and in doing so—had completely failed my family. I would have groaned out loud with the dreadful weight of it, but I had to keep quiet. At that moment, I missed my mother so much that my chest felt like a piece of cloth ripping, unevenly but steadily in two.

Focus on what you can do, and do it.

That's what she always said, and that's what she would have said now.

But, Mama, I don't know what to do. My tears became more insistent and my ribs, chest, and heart pounded with an uneven whomping sound, all the way up to my ears. Then another sound intruded—little Zofja's quiet weeping was evolving into full-scale sobbing.

My sisters.

I pulled Zofja close and stroked her hair.

"Shush, shush, I'm here . . ." I put my other arm around Celina. "We'll be fine."

I decided not to reveal the intent of the soon-to-be-arriving Russian soldiers. Celina might scream and Zofja did not need to know. Up above, my father gave Yosef one last order.

"Then race to Piotr's. Tell him to come as fast as he can, with his largest bottle of vodka." The town's blacksmith was Papa's close friend, even though Piotr was Catholic. Yosef's light steps tapped out of the house, and minutes later came the thud of Piotr's oversized feet.

"I ran as quickly as I could. I'm sorry I'm still sweating. It's the big man's curse. I'm trying to look casual, is it working?" Piotr asked, in between gulps of air.

"You got here at lightning speed, my friend," my father said. "As for looking casual, they'll be so focused on your vodka, they won't notice."

Piotr's arrival comforted me, although I had always found him intimidating: his unusual height, his massive chest and neck, his growling-bear voice, and a face that seemed enormous, even given his size. Plus, he was Catholic, with all the religious and cultural differences, and the dark history between our peoples in Poland. But he was a longtime friend of my father's and here he was now, putting his own safety at risk

Insistent pounding sounded at the door.

"I'll get it," Piotr said. "Sit down, Berek."

DOWN BELOW, IN the increasingly frigid cellar, my sisters and I pressed our bodies together for warmth and comfort, while up above the vodka flowed and so did the Russians' war stories, exaggerated tales of bravery in battle, which, under other circumstances, I would have found funny.

"You, my man, were a coward. At the Battle of Tannenberg, you were a slug, a snail. Yes. A creeping snail . . . whereas I sprang forward like a stag."

The fat commander pounded the table as he spoke. But after two hours of drinking, the slender junior officer sounded as if he was not the least bit cowed by his superior. "*No one* moved quickly, not even you. And thank goodness. The Huns had set traps and spies everywhere. The blood of our men had soaked the field long before we arrived. Their bones rest in Allenstein . . ." The younger man paused, as if in remembrance of his slain comrades.

"Whereas our bones—*our* bones—should be resting right now at the Jewish inn, with some women," the older officer roared at his own wretched joke, then I heard a smashing sound, like a chair being flung aside. "Fetch them immediately, shopkeeper, or we shall be . . . *most* upset."

Celina gasped, now understanding the threat.

I elbowed her, hard. "*Quiet.* Papa will manage them."

I'd watched him do it a hundred times when customers or suppliers became difficult. I had to trust that he'd say something—or do something—to hold them off.

"My brave men, your stories have inspired us. Our time together has passed quickly. The honorable blacksmith Piotr will bring you to the inn to get comfortable. The girls are already there. We trust that you'll then keep your pledge to leave our store and our family alone," my father said in a strained tone that didn't match his convivial words.

"*Khorosho,* good, good, *da, da,*" the Russians chorused. I heard the sound of their feet shambling as they rose from the table.

"Esteemed guests. I will escort you," Piotr said.

Aha. I sensed the outline of my father's plan. They would go to the inn with Piotr, who would show them to their rooms and pretend to be surprised that Celina and I weren't there. He'd waste time, feigning confusion and offering to come back and look for us. That would buy us a few precious minutes to escape. If the Russians were completely inebriated, which they seemed to be— they might not even protest. They might grumble but agree to lie down and wait. Perhaps it would work. No, it had to. It *must* work. I squeezed Celina's hand.

"Ah . . . but no," the commanding officer said. "You are cunning, so very cunning, my Jewish friend. And you, sir blacksmith, a devious, clever Pole helping him. But I am not an officer of the Tsar for nothing. I cannot be so easily fooled, although I am impressed by the ruse you two have concocted. You see, I remember earlier today when I encountered your charming little wolf of a girl

. . . she was hiding in the cellar. I should just like to make sure that she and her sister . . . are not there now."

Protests from my father and Piotr could not dissuade him. The officer and his partner were heavily drunk but also heavily armed. His boots clunked to the cellar door. He climbed down the ladder as best as his wobbly legs could manage. He lit a match, illuminating the three of us huddled in our quilts on the floor with our arms around each other. He grinned as he recognized me.

"How lovely to see you again. And how nice to meet your sisters." He pointed his gun at us, his false cheer gone. "Get up the ladder. Now."

MY MEMORY OF that night isn't a linear story where I could describe what happened first, second, and third. Instead, it's more a collage of sounds, images, and sensations.

The slap of the brisk night air as my sister and I left our house with the Russians.

The sheen of their guns telling us we had no choice.

The sight of my father, tears marking his thin cheeks as he held Zofja tightly.

Zofja's wide green eyes, watching her little girl's world turn ugly.

Piotr, his head bleeding—punishment for his attempt to block the front door with his bulk.

The junior officer's sweaty hand holding mine as he led me to a room at our inn.

The low weeping of Celina in the next room.

The older soldier's grunting.

The crunch of the straw mattress as the younger Russian sat down next to me on the bed.

The smell of his vodka breath as he faced me. "I have two sisters around your age back home in St. Petersburg. We'll sit here till he's done, then once he's asleep, you and your sister can go home."

The shadow of his dark, long mustache twitching as he worked to control the emotions that played across his face: frustration, exhaustion, embarrassment, sadness.

"I'm sorry," he said.

WE FLED.

Celina was a pale statue of herself, but we had no time to console her. We double-wrapped her in woolen shawls and sat her by the dwindling fire while the rest of us raced about, packing as much food, blankets, and clothing as our wagon would hold. My brothers ran through Amshinov in the dark, first to the synagogue to fetch Celina's husband, Shevah, saying that the Russians had been dealt with for the moment but not telling him what had happened to his wife. That was Celina's story to share, if she chose.

They then dashed to the store to collect the merchandise packaged and ready, hidden in the cellar. Some of it would come with us to where we were headed: Vivadorv, where Shevah's family lived. But the bulk of it, we planned to hide at Piotr's to keep secure for us until after the war.

"I'll store it for you," Piotr said as he left our home, his immense shoulders sagging with the weight of what he'd witnessed and his inability to stop it. "It's the least I can do."

He placed his massive hand on my father's forearm. "You're a good man, Berek. I hope when this war is over, everything will be as before. Now go. Who knows when those bastards might come back."

My father nodded a numb thanks. He hitched our horses to the cart, then settled into the driver's seat, my brothers and brother-in-law on the bench beside him. I crammed myself in the back, wedged between various bundles and my sisters. Yakob's wife and children huddled miserably in the other corner, opposite us.

In less than twenty-four hours, I'd been hidden twice. I'd almost been raped, and Celina had been. Now, in the middle of the night, my entire family was on the run. Pinched with cold, exhausted, rattled by the jostling cart—these discomforts I could bear. What was unbearable was my guilt. *This is all my fault.* I was strangled with regret as I saw my sisters—silent Celina on one side of me and shivering Zofja on the other. For the thousandth time, I wished that our lives could shift back to the lovely *before*. When my mother was here, when we were happy and secure, when there was no war.

The wagon hit a deep hole in the road, and the sudden bang hurt my back and hips. But it also yanked me back to reality—I could wallow in remorse – or I could do something.

I dipped a mug into an earthen crock, which held the milk we often cooked in the oven overnight until it was light brown and sweet. I'd pulled it out before it was properly done, but at least it was warm.

"Celina, here—have some," I said, offering the drink to her, surprised and grateful that she took it. I turned to Zofja. "Give me your feet." I took her shoes off and put her wool-stockinged feet onto my lap under a blanket and rubbed them. Her feet were always cold. She relaxed at my touch, and soon her eyelids drooped.

"Come here, Maideleh," I said, opening my arms and inviting her to curl up with me under my blanket.

Zofja slept, comforted at least for the moment. I stroked her brown curls while turning forward for the first time. I was struck by how deeply my father's thin silhouette curved over, and how his hands barely held the horse's reins. It was fortunate the animals knew the way—I sensed that in his anguish he would have been incapable of guiding them.

The horses lumbered along the familiar road, past the shadowy outlines of the butcher shop, the fish shop, the store that sold newspapers in Hebrew, Polish, and Yiddish. We went by the tall wooden synagogue, the Jewish community gym, the library, where my father had participated in the literary club and the drama club, to great applause and cheers. Those were golden days for my parents, for all the Jews of Amshinov. But my father had not realized in time that the village's fairy tale era was over.

Still, the events that had forced us to flee in the blackness, were because of me; my brashness, my acting without thinking, my ridiculous confidence that I—a fourteen-year-old girl—could somehow protect everyone. I touched my father's shoulder, wanting to say, "I'm sorry" and "Please forgive me." But before I could choke out the words, he placed his thickly gloved hand over mine.

"It's not your fault, Sarah."

"But Papa, I—"

"No," he interrupted, his tone low and wretched. "It's mine."

We journeyed all night in the brittle spring darkness. Clouds covered the stars.

Chapter 2
VIVADORV, POLAND
WINTER 1916. ATTACK

VIVADORV SHOWED US how sheltered and privileged we'd been in Amshinov. Here, the town's Christian leaders were suspicious of Jews, limiting where we could live and what we could do for work. It was a bitter reality for all of us, but I think it must have been hardest on my father. While he often said he was grateful that "shopkeeper" was among the permitted professions for Jews in Vivadorv, his store in a corner of the town's central square was a tiny, musty, scrap of a place, compared to the large, bright, well-stocked shop we'd left behind. Still, he put on a cheerful face.

"Thanks to the war, I have few customers anyway," he'd joke.

His quip about the war was true, it was terrible for business. By 1916, the conflict that people had first assumed would be over quickly was instead widening and deepening. Everyone we knew was poor and thin. My father accepted our lot with his usual grace, reminding us that we were at least not starving, like so many others were. But I could tell it hurt his pride to accept charity, living with the family of his son-in-law Shevah. With the arrival of our clan a year ago, the house was impossibly tight. Arguments would often break out simply because we were fed up with living on top of each other. The close quarters especially intensified my long-standing dislike of Shevah.

My brother-in-law was a member of the famed Amshinov sect, founded in our former village, whose men spent their days studying the Talmud while their wives and extended families supported them. My father was proud to do so. Most people thought it was an honor to have a religious scholar in the home, and Papa had enjoyed the increased respect and esteem his own family gained in the community after Celina and Shevah had married. But I'd never viewed Shevah as a status symbol; as far as I was concerned, he was an economic drain on our family and an affront to our work ethic. My father repeatedly told me to keep my opinions in check, especially now since we were living with Shevah's family.

"We have no other options, Sarah. Be thankful for the roof they're putting over our heads."

"Yes, Papa," I'd reply, not saying what I really thought: that we might be able to afford our own house if Shevah would lift a finger.

"HURRY *UP*, YOSEF!" I yelled up the stairs. "Papa's waiting!"

My brother and I were due at the shop on a frigid winter morning. I'd already buttoned my coat, pulled on my boots, and, in addition to the kerchief that normally covered my hair, had a knitted shawl tied over my head. I was bundled up and ready to go. Waiting for Yosef, I was growing uncomfortably warm and itchy.

"Coming, coming . . ." Yosef finally thumped down the stairs. He stopped by the door to trade his usual newsboy cap for a full-fledged Russian fur hat, complete with ear flaps and a wide, fuzzy brim. It was enormous and exaggerated the sharpness of his face. He stuck his tongue out at me. "I know, I know. At least it's warm. Let's go."

We linked arms so we wouldn't slip as we walked. The streets were empty under the leaden January sky. We crossed a stone bridge over the frozen river, passing through the part of town where the butcher shops were. The neighborhood's smoke-stained, weather-beaten wooden buildings were soon replaced by more elegant concrete and brick structures as we switched to the street where the rabbi lived and where the ritual mikvah bath was located. We entered Vivadorv's central square, quiet today because it wasn't a market day. The buildings were higher here, two and even three stories, their wooden shutters closed tight against the cold. Several wagon drivers waited in their usual spots, hoping to take customers to the train. Both the men and their horses were shivering. Yosef and I were shivering too, and I tied my shawl more tightly so only a bit of my face peeked out, while Yosef pulled his ridiculous hat down over his forehead as far as he could, without completely blocking his vision.

I laughed, both at how silly we must have appeared, and because it was such a relief to be outside. With two families living together, there was always wood to chop, clothes and dishes to wash, and meals to prepare. I detested household chores to begin with, especially cooking. Back home in Amshinov, I was often relieved of these tasks. Celina ran the domestic front, while my father preferred to have me at the store. But now in Vivadorv, there was much more work needed to be done at the house than at my father's tiny shop. I bumbled through the scrubbing, cooking, and sewing as best I could, but I was thrilled to be let loose today. I didn't even mind that Yosef, as always, wanted to talk about the war.

"Poland is again a battleground, just like I said it would be . . . the three old empires which have controlled Poland for more than a century won't give her up easily. And who'll win the prize? The Russians? The Austro-Hungarians? The

Germans? And where do Poland's Jews figure into all this? Everyone wants our support . . . but we're far from a united front."

I gave Yosef an encouraging "um-hum." Although it often annoyed me when he showed off his knowledge of history and politics, today I was happy to listen.

Professor Yosef. I smiled to myself, watching my feet due to the ice. *It's a shame that universities are closed to Jews.*

I bumped into Yosef, who had come to a standstill.

"Look. *German* soldiers outside the store."

Their helmets and guns shone in the morning sun. The team of four wore immaculate, bright-buttoned uniforms and gleaming boots. We watched from afar as they approached the shop's front door. When we'd first arrived in Vivadorv last year we hadn't noticed many Germans, but lately, we'd seen more. Everyone said this must mean that the Russians were losing the battle for Poland, and losing it badly.

Yosef pulled hard at my wrist, dragging me away. "Let's run back and get help! Don't let them see us."

I was just as strong as Yosef. I tugged him in the opposite direction. "Let's look through the back window. What if Papa needs us?"

"Did you see those *guns*? Let them take what they want. Besides, we don't want them to see *you* . . . or to know Papa has daughters. You know . . ."

I did. Still, I was determined to look and knew Yosef wouldn't leave me alone. "We'll sneak around back. They won't notice. Come *on*, Yosef."

I took his arm, and we tried to stroll, to look casual—even though no one would be out strolling on such a freezing day. Luckily, the soldiers seemed focused on the shop, not us. We walked around the building, where we were able to peek through a small back window.

Yosef's wool glove stifled my scream.

Our father was crouched on the shop floor. A burly Russian soldier was beating him, ignoring his cries for mercy; while a second, scrawny soldier filled his backpack with merchandise. But the assailant wanted something else.

"Give us the propaganda, the pamphlets, the papers . . . you Jews and your blasted Committee for the East," he growled, landing another blow. "We are not fooled . . . we know all about your support for Germany."

"I already told you; I swear I am not involved. I know nothing of this committee." Papa moaned and closed his eyes. His body crumpled.

Yosef and I watched in helpless horror as the Russian prepared to strike our father again. But at that instant, the Germans entered, aiming their guns at Papa's attackers.

"*Halt! Hände hoch!*"

The Russians seemed to understand enough German to put their hands up. Using their weapons, the Germans pointed the Russians toward the door, and they fled, leaving behind the backpack full of goods. Our father lay on the floor. Yosef and I held hands so tightly that later we would notice small bruises on our fingers. I've never been religious, but I found myself aiming an almost-prayer at the German soldiers.

Please, take what you want and leave. Then we can tend to Papa, if . . . he's still alive.

But the Germans did not leave. Two guarded the door, while a third put the merchandise back on the shelves. I was astonished by this, but even more so by what the fourth German did. He leaned over Papa and inspected his wounds. He then took a handkerchief from his pocket, wet it with vodka or water, and pressed it on a gash above my papa's left eye to stem the bleeding. But after waiting several minutes, the group's commander signaled it was time to go.

"*Das ist genug.* Enough. He'll either survive or he won't. We saved his shop. His family will at least be thankful for that."

The soldier hesitated. He leaned down next to my father's ear. Papa made a tiny movement with his head. The soldier rested his hand on my father's shoulder for the lightest of moments. Then he straightened up smartly, saluted his partners, and the four of them left.

Yosef and I bolted around the building and flew through the front door to our father's side. His breathing was ragged. His left eye remained closed, too swollen from the wound. He cracked his right eye open.

"Papa . . ." I breathed. I had never seen so much blood. *Focus on what you can do.* "We're here. Yosef will go get the doctor, and I'll stay with you."

Yosef jumped up and ran out, the door slapping in the thin January air as he did.

I bent over my father. The soldier had left his handkerchief, and though already soaked through with blood, I pressed it down on Papa's head wound to control the bleeding. With my other hand, I tenderly pushed on his back, legs, and chest, to see where he might have other injuries. He groaned when I touched his back. I was just lifting his shirt to examine further when I heard the door open again.

"Yosef, I told you to *go. Now!*"

"*Es iz ikh,*" someone said. "It's me."

The German soldier who'd tended to my father stood in the doorway. With his round glasses, he looked more like a scholar than a fighter. Wisps of curly brown hair escaped from under his helmet. He gave me a friendly smile, and, under normal circumstances, I might have smiled back.

"But you're . . . you speak Yiddish," I said.

"I know, it might be surprising for you. But one hundred thousand Jews like me are serving in the German army. And, as we gain more territory, life will improve for your . . . I mean *our* people," the soldier said, with confidence and hope in his voice.

I didn't believe a word of it, despite this particular young man's remarkable behavior and the fact that he was Jewish. He came closer. I flinched and put my arm around my father. The soldier seemed to recognize my alarm and respect it. He stepped back, took off his gun and his canteen, removed his satchel and rooted around in it.

"Here are bandages, ointment, and some morphine that I 'borrowed' from our medics," he said, turning over the precious supplies.

He had stolen medication . . . to help us?

"Thank you . . . it's so unexpected, I don't know what to say, I . . . what did you say to my father as you leaned over?"

"*Kenst mikh hern.* I asked if he could hear me. When I spoke in Yiddish, I suppose he knew I wouldn't hurt him. Once he nodded, I knew he was conscious." The soldier stood, slinging his canteen, satchel, and gun back over his uniformed chest. "There's something else you need to know. As the Russians made their retreat through Vivadorv yesterday, they asked the authorities where the Jewish stores were. Town officials were eager to tell them—adding that these could be looted without trouble."

I focused back on my father. "Just like in Amshinov," I said, quietly so the soldier wouldn't hear. But he had.

"Amshinov, you say? Is that where you're from? I know it by reputation, a wonderful village—"

"Not anymore," I interrupted. "We were robbed over and over by troops passing through. They'd come to our store with empty sacks and leave with them full. Soldiers take what they want in wartime . . . and we are powerless to stop them."

The soldier made a sympathetic *mmm* as if to let me know he understood. Which he didn't, at all.

"Then you already know that this *will* occur again. And that next time, it could be worse. Listen. Here's what your family must do. Germany has controlled Warsaw for several months now and thousands of Jews are resettling there. It'll be safe, and you can all start over."

He was generous and compassionate, but I didn't want his advice or his sympathy. Soldiers, even kind ones like him, were still first and foremost combatants, and not to be trusted. I remained kneeling by my father, turning around just enough to look at the young German.

"No. Leaving now would be impossible, with Papa so badly wounded. We will stay."

I recognized his disappointment and judgment, in the tilt of his head, the tightening of his lips. I could imagine what he was thinking: He was just trying to help, he was an experienced soldier who understood politics and war, and why wasn't this little shop girl taking his excellent advice? Well, he could think however he pleased. I had more immediate concerns: the gash over my father's eye, and some newly blossoming purple bruises on his neck.

The German walked to the door, then paused. "*Varshe,*" he called over his shoulder.

Warsaw.

WE WENT TO Warsaw. Just two days after the attack on my father, every Jewish household in Vivadorv was ordered to leave town. The local police gave us forty-eight hours to gather our belongings, close our homes and businesses, and go. They claimed that there were too many troops coming and going through the village now, so they could no longer provide us protection. As if they had given us any to begin with.

As we rushed about packing, Celina broke down. She threw the socks she'd been jamming into a bag across the room, then threw the entire bag.

"Papa is in no position to travel!" Celina screamed as she wept. "He can't even walk. Don't you hear him moaning at night? We can't leave now . . . we just can't. I can't . . ."

Celina never spoke of that night when her body had been used by a fat, foul-smelling Russian officer. I guessed that our panicked preparations—to flee, once again—ignited memories she had tried to stuff away. I should have dropped everything, even for just a minute, to hold her, comfort her the way our mother would have. But it was almost midnight, the hour when the police order would expire. Our family had to move *now*, and this time, it was mostly up to me to move them. My father was in and out of consciousness from his injuries. Yakob, my stalwart, reliable older brother, was doing all he could—but he also had to focus on his own wife and young children. Meanwhile, my other brother, Yosef, and Celina's husband, Shevah, acted like they were helping, but the two of them were both intellectuals, better at talking and "explaining" than organizing an entire family to gather what it needed to survive and flee. Zofja was only seven.

Outside, I heard the wagons of other Jewish families banging along the cobblestones, their clatter mixing in with the shouts and cries of the people, all hurrying out of town. The sounds stoked my rising impatience, to get out, and quickly. I'm not proud of what I did next, but I was a sixteen-year-old girl in a dire situation.

"Celina. Now is *not* the time for hysterics. You heard the police officer say it yourself when he came to the door, that it's become too dangerous for Jews here. You'd understand if you'd been with Yosef and me at the store." I pushed aside the image of my father bleeding on the floor, stomped over to the satchel she'd just thrown, and snatched it up with far more vigor than necessary. "Just stop your pathetic crying and give me a hand."

"No!" Celina shrieked. "No, no, no! Leave me alone! Leave me alone."

"Never mind then," I shouted. "I'll do it myself. As usual. You're useless."

Celina sobbed harder, hiding her face in a now-soggy handkerchief. I ignored her, continuing to stuff socks, scarves, and shoes into the bag, looking up only when I heard an exaggerated "ahem" at the doorway. Yosef glowered at me as he sat down next to Celina on the straw bed, stripped now of all its blankets.

"Dear Celina. What Sarah is trying to say, in her rude, heartless way—"

I shot him a venomous look, which he shot right back at me.

"—is that the village police are, in this rare instance, doing us a favor. It's not safe here, we know that now. So, we'll do what that soldier told Sarah. We'll go to Warsaw."

WE LEFT RIGHT as the departure order expired at midnight. The raw winter air dug through our clothes and attached itself to our bones. The roads were now packed with other families, some like us in simple carts, pulled by a horse or two, overflowing with bedding, furniture, candlesticks, sacks of potatoes and onions, people wedged among them. Other less fortunate souls had to walk, pulling their belongings behind them in small wagons, wheelbarrows, or carrying as much as they could on their backs. People wore most of their clothes, appearing lumpy and bulky. The men wrapped long scarves around their necks and over their caps; the women pulled shawls over their heads and shoulders. Heavily bundled babies cried, while the elderly limped along, weary and resigned. I told my brothers to concoct a long sling out of blankets to transport our father to the cart, where we put him on a pile of straw and blankets. As we left, Celina embraced Shevah's family, tears freezing in the corners of her eyelashes. Her in-laws had decided against Warsaw, seeking shelter instead with relatives in a town further west.

Unlike during our last escape, Yakob drove instead of my father. Celina, Zofja, Yakob's wife Rachel, their children, and I all huddled around Papa in the back. He slept, thanks to the morphine from the German soldier.

On the way to Warsaw, we planned to stop in Amshinov to collect the many bundles of merchandise that Piotr had hidden for us in his barn that awful night we'd fled more than a year ago. Those items, along with the minuscule amount left over from the store in Vivadorv, would provide at least a small base from which we could set up shop yet again in Warsaw. In the shroud of early morning, we entered our old village. We drove past our house, its sides smeared with smoke, its wooden slats sagging.

"It's strange to keep going . . . not stopping at home," Zofja said, gazing at the house as we passed it, then twisting around for one last glimpse.

I didn't bother to move my head. "It's no longer home."

Our wagon swayed down the familiar roads until Yakob brought the horses to a halt in front of Piotr's property; his modest cottage and a sizable wooden barn-like structure behind it that served as his smithy. Yakob and I struggled to release the barn door with our frozen fingers. It groaned open, revealing a tidy interior: a well-kept forge, horseshoes carefully hung on a beam above, hammers and other assorted tools neatly arranged. Yakob lit a lamp, and we scanned the shadows for where the blacksmith might have hidden our merchandise. I spotted a set of stairs and made my way up—the patchy lamplight revealing an upper room with . . . more tools. Meanwhile, down below, Yakob slammed the doors of empty compartments in frustration.

I willed myself not to feel desperate—not yet. To pause. Think again. Look again.

From the top of the stairs, the view down into the smithy gave me a different perspective. I saw what appeared to be a closet doorknob, well-camouflaged behind some wagon wheels stacked in the corner. It was the last possible place where a large pile of items could be hidden.

"Oh! Yakob . . . try there," I said, pointing.

"Ah. Finally. That *has* to be it. You keep watch at the door, just in case, while I move all this." Yakob grunted, shoving aside the cumbersome wheels.

I positioned myself at the barn entrance, opening up to hope. We had a plan. Warsaw. It would all work out.

Yakob cursed. "There's nothing in here!"

"What? No." I whirled around to see Yakob sitting on the dirt floor beside the open door of a sizable, empty closet. In his palms, he held a half dozen of the special nails we used to sell—proof that our things *had* been kept there, but now they were gone. Yakob flung the nails across the room. Before I could absorb this impossible situation, a dark figure approached from across the yard. Piotr.

"The Russians took everything," he said, staring at the ground.

"Everything?" Yakob and I demanded together, hoping we'd heard him wrong.

"Everything," Piotr said, his words sticky with remorse.

I did a quick calculation: a dozen blankets, ten pairs of boots, two dozen hammers, hundreds of nails, six different musical instruments, about twenty bolts of fabric, five tea kettles, and an assortment of farm tools, pots and pans. In other words, almost everything we'd counted on to re-establish ourselves in Warsaw.

"Dammit!" I shouted, the curse cracking in the frigid air. I stepped toward Piotr, not caring that women were not supposed to swear, especially young women and especially to an elder. "How could this happen? Why didn't you—?"

Piotr held up his hand. "Stop. Listen. I was alone, against six armed soldiers, including the two from that night . . . when you left."

Even in the semi-darkness, I saw how his face twisted with the shameful memory. He made a limp, defeated gesture toward his workshop.

"The officer woke up a few hours after you escaped. He was incensed that you and your sister were gone. He and his men ran to your house first, and then, finding it empty, came here, suspecting I might be hiding your whole family. One held me at gunpoint, while the others wrecked my shop searching for you; my anvil toppled over, tools flung on the floor, my woodpile dismantled. That's when they found the merchandise in the compartment and guessed it must be yours. Why else, they asked, would a blacksmith have such things as musical instruments, boots, tea kettles—stored in—"

"Sarah!" Yosef called from our wagon. "We're freezing here, and Papa is starting to moan again. So, hurry up. We need to give him more of that medicine . . . and then we need to gather our things and go."

"Moaning . . . what's wrong? Where's Berek?" Piotr looked around.

With his massive legs, it took Piotr only a few steps to reach the cart where my father still slept. His mouth tightened as he viewed Papa's injuries—the bruises and unhealed wounds, his ragged, uneven breathing. Piotr crossed himself, then put his giant hand on my papa's shoulder.

"We pray to the same God, Berek . . . and I will pray every day for your recovery, my friend." His head and shoulders slumped, and he seemed spent. "I forever beg your pardon."

Piotr stalked back to his house.

"But wait," I called, wanting Piotr to explain more of what happened, how it happened—and yes, dig into him a little more for allowing it to happen.

Yakob gently touched my wrist. "Let him go, Sarah. Let him go."

Standing in the gloom, Yakob and I watched Piotr's lumbering outline disappear.

OUR CART CLANKED into Warsaw half-empty. As we entered the center of town, a weak February sun was lifting the shadows on the buildings, the bridges, the alleys leading into the squares. I had never been to Warsaw, but I'd heard it described as a beautiful, grand city—the Russian Empire's third most important, after Moscow and St. Petersburg. Now it was wrecked by war. We drove by bombed-out structures, piles of rubble in the streets, the graceful Tsar Nicolas Bridge semi-destroyed, giant fingers of twisted wrought iron hanging, beseeching.

My father continued to sleep, unaware of our new predicament. Like Warsaw, his body was wrecked: his left eye was swollen shut, his back and neck were covered with red and purple sores, and his mind was dulled by both pain and the morphine that eased it. Yakob slowed the horses as we approached Warsaw's Muranów district, the center of Jewish life where we would settle. The change in pace awakened my papa, and he grasped my arm, his one available eye showing his alarm, making his battered face even more frightening.

"We've arrived in Warsaw, Papa. We'll make a new start . . ."

"A new start," my father mumbled, closing his undamaged eye again.

"Yes." I stroked my papa's cheek, like a child. Like Mama used to do.

"Go back to sleep," I said.

WE BEGAN AGAIN. Another store, another town—although the tumult of sprawling, crowded Warsaw was unlike anything I'd ever experienced. Everything in the Jewish district was crammed together: the narrow buildings, with shops and businesses occupying the first floor and extended families stuffed into the second and third floors above; while the neighborhood's tight streets were packed with cafés, bars, and even cinemas. These created a boisterous nightlife that often kept me awake—the shouts and singing of revelers echoing up to my window. The city had a robust black market, especially for alcohol and prostitution. If I had to go somewhere alone, I walked quickly and with purpose, holding my wallet tightly.

Warsaw was also a hive of Jewish social, intellectual, religious, and political activity. The atmosphere thrilled Yosef, now a student at the University of Warsaw, which the Germans had opened to Jews, another contrast with the days of Russian control. Yosef came home every night fizzing with excitement over the conversations he'd had, the people he'd met; Socialists, Zionists, labor activists, philosophers, writers.

"There's so much change and discussion and energy in the air right now. You should come to a political meeting with me, Sarah. You know, *women* are active in some of these movements," he said one evening after dinner, leafing through a book and still glowing from his day.

"You're wasting your time," I said. I had worked an extra-long shift at the shop and ached to lie down.

Yosef made a puffing sound of contempt. "You're such a know-it-all. And you're so boring. You have no friends, no boyfriend, you don't *do* anything. Here we are in *Warsaw*—brimming with culture and new ideas . . . and all you do is tromp to the shop every morning and tromp home at night. Your life is lonely and dull but you can't admit it. Because that would crack your all-too-perfect façade, wouldn't it?" He snapped shut his book and stomped away.

I watched him huff out of the room, too tired to respond. The *you're a know-it-all* and *you think you're so perfect* comments washed over me; Yosef had flung them at me since I was ten. And my life was far from boring. But lonely? There, it was uncomfortable to admit that he was right. I had no real friends, and even though I was old enough to be engaged, I secretly hoped my father would not begin looking for a match. Getting involved in relationships, movements, causes . . . it all felt pointless. Every morning, I wondered if this would be the day when some unforeseen event would require us to throw everything back into our cart and run out of town yet again. By 1917, the war was shifting. The Americans had joined the fight that spring, just after the Russians had pulled out, in upheaval over their internal war, the Bolshevik Revolution. The earlier confidence that Warsaw would remain stable under German control was now a question mark, meaning my family's situation could change in an instant. Why my supposedly brilliant brother Yosef hadn't figured that out was beyond me. But intelligence isn't the same as intuition. In fact, sometimes it gets in the way.

On a more practical level, I didn't have a spare minute for friendships, social clubs, or political activity. My older brother Yakob and I worked twelve-hour days at our Warsaw shop, and I welcomed it. Work calmed my anxious spirit, or at least distracted it. At night, sleep eluded me as I fretted about the war, my father's lengthy recovery, my older sister's dark moods, my little sister's long hours of solitude. I re-lived our frantic escapes; I saw again the lecherous face of the Russian officer in Amshinov; my father's battered form on his shop floor in Vivadorf. As these images assaulted my mind, I would open my eyes wide and then squeeze them shut, over and over, as if that would erase them. Instead, it only made them more vivid.

But by day, I was busy and content. Yakob and I bargained with textile producers, hat makers, leather tanners, and cobblers. We made connections with other merchants and traded. Despite our wretched beginning in Warsaw, we were successful. We'd learned from our father that the best shopkeepers do far more than just buy and sell—they listen, observe, and understand people. He'd taught us that lesson long ago.

But in Warsaw, we learned that we could do it without him.

War forces new thinking. It cracks open old social codes that no longer fit, that don't make sense anymore. In Warsaw, I imagined different ways of living beyond the traditional Jewish communities I'd always inhabited. It was not that I wanted to abandon my family, but I began dreaming wider dreams. For me and for them.

Meanwhile, my father yearned to go home. A year after his attack, he still bore the scars. His eye had healed, but his back injuries prevented him from standing up straight. His spirit was altered, too: he was more cautious, less confident, his cheerful personality diminished. As soon as he heard that Amshinov had come under German control, he didn't want to stay another day in Warsaw.

"They're firm but fair," he often said of the German authorities, "but Warsaw is too big, too busy . . . too many people . . ."

I shared my father's discomfort with Warsaw, but I had no desire to go back to our village, or anywhere in this country. Poland had breathed fear on the back of my neck for too long. I wanted *out*.

It took three more years. But I got my wish.

Chapter 3
METZ, FRANCE
APRIL 1920. ARRIVAL

SPRING SOFTENED THE city's heavy contours. As I crossed the bridge over the Moselle River in Metz, a light shower had just retreated, leaving a fine silver mist as the sun reasserted itself. Tiny pink, white, and purple flowers peeking up through the grass provided paint dabs of color. Delicate new leaves on the willow trees lining the riverbank glowed, lit up by the sunshine. Even Metz's medieval garrisons, with their imposing Prussian architecture, seemed inviting.

I paused at the middle of the bridge, marveling at the vista itself but even more at the fact that I could enjoy it. I'd left Poland just weeks ago, and now here I was, in France, simply going to work on a pleasant day.

I absorbed the luxury of it and wished my father could see what I saw, feel what I felt.

The faster I can get him and the rest of them out of Poland the better.

The country was wrecked by constant upheaval. Less than a year after the Great War ended came the Polish-Bolshevik War, in which Soviet Russian forces tried to grab back the newly independent Poland. Yakob was called up for military duty first. He ripped open the package containing his papers and thrust it toward my father.

"I'm leaving," he had said, uncharacteristically bitter. "This country's given us nothing but disrespect . . . and now it wants me to defend it, to save it? For what?"

Yakob had always played his role as responsible eldest brother willingly and well; it was Yosef who was all bluster and passion and opinion.

My father gave back the draft notice to Yakob. He crossed the room and unlocked a desk drawer. He took out an envelope.

"Take it. It's enough money for four train tickets." One corner of his mouth twitched and the wrinkles around his eyes deepened. Then he became sober, placing his hands on Yakob's head in a sort of blessing. "Go, my son. Go."

In two days, Yakob was gone. He took his wife and two young children and left Poland for the province of Lorraine, in Northern France. Thousands of Jews were flocking to the region, which offered abundant jobs in factories and mines and the French government encouraging of immigration. After a year of drudgery in the potash mines, Yakob saved enough to open a clothing store in the city of Metz and wrote to my father, urging him to let me come.

With Sarah's help, we can build a business prosperous enough to write a new chapter for our entire family. Poland is our past, Papa—France is our future, Yakob wrote. I was elated when Papa agreed, although I tried to temper my excitement when I was with him. I knew he'd feel my absence, both at home and at the shop.

"Good luck, Maideleh," he said at the train station, even though I was nineteen and no longer his little girl. "Write to me when you arrive." He cleared his throat. "I don't know when we'll see each other again." I held his hands, trying to read the mix of emotions on his face. I hadn't even considered that our separation from each other could be long, even forever. I assumed he'd eventually follow Yakob and me to France.

"But, Papa, you'll come too. You've read Yakob's letters saying how much work there is in Metz. It's just a matter of time before you and the others come, isn't that right?"

"Your brother and sisters, perhaps. They're young and can start over. For me . . ."

The train arrived and a surly conductor growled at everyone to hurry on board.

My father hugged me, quickly and hard. "Goodbye, Sarah. Write to me . . . always write."

"Yes, Papa," I said, too ecstatic to be swept up in a sentimental parental farewell. On the train, I found a window seat. As my car pulled away, my father continued to stand on the platform, waiting until my train was out of sight.

The tumble of feelings I'd wrestled with before my departure settled into only one: jubilation. I was leaving. Forever. I gazed out the smudged window at a battered landscape: burnt, abandoned houses; half-frozen, unkempt fields.

How ugly it looks. I will never come back.

But I was foolish to think I could escape Poland entirely—the country still clung to my spirit; like a sticky coating I couldn't rinse off. I still often woke in the night; certain I was back in Ashminov, Vivadorv, or Warsaw. I would sit upright in bed, my nightgown damp, my mind leaping to where the next threat might be, my gut full of something misty and grey.

Then I'd remember. I was in France, comfortable and content, living with Yakob and his family, working at his shop on Jurue Street at the heart of Metz's Jewish quarter. After these nocturnal episodes, I might lay awake for hours, but I was smiling in the dark.

Yakob and I were a dynamic team. Yakob's steady, calm nature gained him respect among Metz's expanding Jewish community; while I was eager to infuse the store with new ideas. I walked the streets of Metz, both the Jewish and Gentile neighborhoods, studying what people wore. I went into other shops, scouting out what they sold, watching the interactions between merchant and customer. I scoured newspapers to examine the fashion advertising—even though I could only read the ones published in Yiddish.

Metz delighted me. The city itself and the provinces of Lorraine and neighboring Alsace had just been returned to France after the Great War, after almost fifty years of German control. Metz felt alive with promise, renewal, energy. It was enjoying an economic revival, too—a trend Yakob and I were sure was due to a post-war influx of people just like us: young, eager, industrious Eastern European Jews. Those early days were hard but sweet: Yakob and I could see the future we were building and reveled in the certainty that it would be *ours*—no more looting, pillaging, or pogroms. We'd worked for our wealth, and no one could steal it. And best of all: Our brother Yosef would be arriving in Metz soon.

"YOSEF! HERE! OVER here!"

I'm only five feet tall, so I had to jump above the crowds at the train station so Yosef could see me. When the Polish-Bolshevik war broke out in early 1919, Yosef quickly signed up to fight, stirred by glorious promises of equality and freedom for Jews and others, under a new Poland. Since then, we had had no word of him until a one-line letter arrived in Metz a week ago. In Yosef's rushed, hard-to-read cursive it simply stated, "I'm coming." Now, he was here. I tried to jump higher, waving, and shouting to him again. It was undignified but I didn't care.

Why didn't he notice me?

Yosef stood like an inconveniently placed rock on the platform, unaware of the annoyed glances of the people who had to filter around him. A small backpack was his only possession. I pushed through the clusters of travelers and flung myself at him.

"Yosef. You made it. You'll love Metz, and Yakob and Rachel have a fine apartment, with plenty of room. Oh, and you should see their children, how *big* they are, and . . ." It was like hugging a tree. I pulled back from my embrace. "Are you alright?"

Yosef was even thinner and paler than usual. He smelled rancid, as if neither he nor his clothes had been washed for a long time.

"Are you alright?" I asked again.

No response. We walked to Yakob and Rachel's apartment, the bustling sounds of the city around us amplifying our uncomfortable silence.

After a bath, with his curly hair slicked back and wearing some of Yakob's clean clothes, he appeared more like his old self on the outside. But he remained quiet. Dinner ended quickly, as attempts to make conversation faltered.

Rachel stood up. "Excuse me, but it's getting late. I'll put the children to bed."

It wasn't late at all, but the ever-thoughtful Rachel was granting us time alone. The moment she left, we bore into Yosef.

"What happened? What's wrong?"

Yosef looked at the curtains, at a spot in the wall, at his lap. Anywhere but at us. Finally, he spoke. "I deserted. I slipped out of my barracks like a rat in the night—"

We strained to hear him; his voice was so quiet and jagged.

"—and this New Poland, whose independence I *thought* I was fighting to defend . . . is nothing but a nation of anti-Semites, just like Russia. No. Worse. At least with the Russians, we knew what to expect."

I had never seen Yosef so despondent.

"The other Jewish soldiers and I were given the most dangerous assignments on the battlefield and the dirtiest assignments off," he said, his voice growing louder. "They gave us the worst places to sleep. We endured constant insults. They'd give us pork for supper and jeer when we wouldn't eat it. I was so ravenous . . . starving . . . I even considered eating it. But I knew I needed to be in solidarity with the other Jewish soldiers who were keeping Kosher. So, another soldier and I . . . we decided we had had enough. We left."

He sipped his wine.

"Samuel and I crept out in the early hours," he continued, his inflection sharper and clearer now. "We planned it well, to leave on a night when there was no moon. We didn't know exactly where we were. "But we had our compass, and Samuel was an excellent route finder. And I had my languages . . ."

I could imagine the two of them, each using their skills to evade the Polish military. I had never met this Samuel, of course, but Yosef's ear for languages was impressive. In addition to speaking Yiddish at home, we all knew enough Polish and Russian for the basics of commerce and community. But Yosef spoke both languages well, and he'd learned some English and French during our time in occupied Warsaw when the Germans had opened the university to Jews.

"I can see that working out well," I said. Perhaps I could cheer him up with a little flattery?

He gave me a morbid look. "No. It did *not* work out well. But, yes, Samuel and I were the perfect partners. He had mapped out how we'd pass through villages at night and sleep in the forest by day. If anyone stopped us, I'd concoct some kind of story. I could manage in whatever language we encountered. We made it home to Ashminov and stayed for a night. We feared that our visit might put the family in danger, but we were *so* weary. Celina cooked a huge meal, and she and her husband urged us to seek shelter with his family in Vivadorv if needed. It was a wonderful night—what great relief it was, to be together, to eat a real dinner, to sleep in a real bed . . .”

Something seemed to kick Yosef from inside. He bent over, moaned, and pulled at his hair. Yakob moved to comfort him, but I held him back. Yosef needed to spit this story out, to purge himself of it.

“Samuel and I intended to leave early the next morning while it would still be dark, but our bodies betrayed us. We were exhausted from three weeks on the run, so we didn't slip out until almost six a.m. The village was mostly empty, but not completely. We were seen. And recognized. That person informed the local military authorities. Desertion is a huge crime. Less than an hour after we left town, we heard horses behind us. We ran into the woods. I climbed a tree. Samuel tried, but he wasn't as quick as me.”

Yosef made a barking sound, a sob that he couldn't suppress.

“They shot him while I watched from above. I wanted to scream. I wanted to shoot them but there were five of them and one of me. So, I clung to my tree, shaking and silently crying like the coward I am. Samuel was a great man, a *mensch*. He dreamed of becoming a mapmaker after the war. He had a sweetheart he was going to marry, back in his village.”

Yosef sat up, and for the first time, looked at us directly. “I hate myself.”

We placed our hands on his back, his shoulders, and murmured the small phrases we knew we should: that it wasn't his fault, he did what he could, he had to save himself.

Yosef shook us off. “No, stop it. I will never forgive myself. And I will never, *ever*, forgive *her*.”

“Who, Yosef, who?” we both asked.

“Liliana Starosta. She was the one who saw us that morning. On her way to work at the distillery. She was the one who reported us.”

“*Liliana Starosta*?” I exclaimed.

I was shocked that ancient Mrs. Starosta, daffy but seemingly harmless, had acted so dramatically. As a teenager, Yosef had charmed her at the shop one day, as he did all the elderly ladies. He'd been playing the hurdy-gurdy and singing a Polish favorite called “Sto Lat,” which was a staple at weddings and other drinking celebrations. Mrs. Starosta told Yosef that his rendition of the song had drawn her back to her wedding day, to her beloved Wiktor, who had died young in an earlier uprising for Polish independence.

Then I understood. Mrs. Starosta's husband had given his life for Polish freedom. She must have thought it shameful that Yosef did not want to do the same.

Over the next few weeks, the rest of his story came out in bits, often late and involving wine. How Yosef had trudged on to Vivadorv, seeking shelter with our brother-in-law's family. Despite the severe repercussions of hiding a Polish army deserter, they had welcomed him and had given him money and food. Shevah's aunt was a talented seamstress, and she made Yosef a disguise, an outfit that would be worn by a Polish farmer. In this convincing costume, he found a ride on a merchant's wagon to Warsaw. Then he took the train to France. He threw the disguise out the window as soon as he crossed the border.

FOUR MONTHS AFTER Yosef's arrival, his mood had not lifted. He would show up for meals, pick at his food, and slump back to bed, staring at the ceiling for hours. Dozens of times a day, I wrestled with my annoyance. As our business grew, we needed him at the shop.

One fall morning, as Rachel and I stacked the breakfast dishes, I was once again running through the long list of tasks to be done at the store, and bemoaning Yosef's lack of desire to help.

"This happens to men when they're troubled," Rachel said over the clattering of plates and splashing of water. "They can't talk easily about how they feel, the way women do . . . plus, he agonizes about your father and sisters back in Poland. He's sure that he put them in danger. He said to me the other day, 'Who knows what the authorities might do to the family of a known deserter?'"

"But," I whined, "it's been four months. Four months. Enough."

Rachel put down a dirty pot and crossed her arms, her full attention away from the dishes now and straight on me. "Well. Not everyone escapes their demons as quickly as you, Sarah. You're always looking ahead, planning, moving forward. I know it's not in *your* nature, but we're not talking about *you*. We're talking about *him*. So, you need to be patient."

From someone else, this might have felt like criticism. From Rachel, it felt like understanding. Of Yosef—and me.

"I'll try," I said simply.

Rachel put one arm around my shoulder in a half-hug. "I'll finish the dishes. It's time to take the children to school."

I hung my apron up with relief. I adored Rachel and Yakob's two children, and had gladly agreed to walk my niece and nephew every day on my way to the store. I enjoyed their chatter, their questions, those simple yet profound observations children make about the world. We'd search for birds as we walked through the park, and when we'd cross the river, play our favorite game: throwing sticks off one side of the bridge and rushing to the other side to see whose stick would appear first. But today, I didn't have the heart.

"Let's take the faster way to school," I said to the children.

They pouted but each took the hand I offered them, as I chose the route they called "the boring way": no park, no river—just the side of an ordinary road.

As my niece and nephew sulked along, my conversation with Rachel pressed upon me. What she'd said about me was almost correct, except for the part about escaping demons. I hadn't escaped mine—I was just better than most people at stuffing them away.

As we neared the children's school, I realized my niece Bina was talking.

"What is it, Bina? Sorry, I wasn't listening."

"Why don't you speak French, *Tante* Sarah? It's not hard, and besides, you're a grown-up."

Her innocent question stung. After a year in Metz, I barely spoke French; not much beyond *bonjour* for *hello* and *merci* for *thank you*. I had to admit I wasn't making much of an effort. I liked to feel competent and in control, while stumbling through French felt like the opposite. *Besides*, I often told myself, *there's such a large Jewish community in Metz. I can get by fine with Yiddish.* But it was a poor excuse, and I knew it.

As we arrived at the school, I mused on these uncomfortable realities. I kissed my niece and nephew goodbye. The two raced off to meet their schoolmates, shouting, "*Bonjour, bonjour.*"

Bonjour, Yosef . . .

Yosef's talent for languages. Perhaps I could use that to draw him out of his near-catatonic state? After four months, anything was worth a try. So, starting today, I'd heap compliments on him, ask him to tutor me in French, and tell him how wonderful it would be to have his linguistic skills at the shop, how impressed everyone would be. I decided to head back to the apartment. Why wait? We needed his talents now.

Climbing the stairs to the second floor, I heard conversation in the kitchen. Yosef's habit was to eat silently and then go back to bed. *Maybe Rachel's talking with a neighbor before she heads to the market?* But no, the voices were those of Yosef and Rachel.

"Rachel, it's me," I announced, pushing open the door.

The two of them were at the table having coffee, a small envelope between them.

"It's from Papa." Yosef held out the letter.

I grabbed the precious letter and pulled it from the envelope covered with Polish stamps. I recognized my father's neat handwriting, always the merchant keeping tidy records.

My Dear Children:

The hardships continue here with the Polish-Bolshevik war. Business is slow at the store, with families only spending the minimum. But the Poles are determined to keep their new independence. I suppose I should understand. This cause has been a long, long struggle for them. Still, I am weary of war.

But forgive my sober introduction. I write, my beloveds, with much good news.

First: Yosef, you need not worry that your desertion will hurt our family. Karol Starosta paid me a visit a day after you left. His mother told him what she'd done, and he was horrified. He said he'd ensure the information Liliana shared with the local authorities wouldn't rise up to any higher levels. There will be no repercussions against us. As the owner of the town's most important distillery, Karol's a powerful man, and they will listen to him. He was angry with his mother and told her not to speak of it again. He also asked for my forgiveness!

Second: After considerable reflection, your sister Celina, her husband, and son are coming to France. It was a hard decision. They wanted to stay in our village where your brother-in-law feels most at home with his fellow Amshinov scholars. But the Polish government needs more young men to fight the Soviets, and Shevah fears they won't make an exception for him. Also, with the war, there is simply less to eat. I do my best, but it is hard to keep everyone fed. In France, we hear there is plenty.

They'll arrive in Metz in a month. I'll miss them but feel grateful knowing you'll welcome them and help them settle. Zofia will, of course, stay with me. She's too young to leave.

Lastly, I am getting married again. A widow named Aviva and I have become acquainted. It's been seven years since your mother died, and I am ready to have someone at my side. Aviva has no children: shortly after her marriage in 1919, her husband died in the flu epidemic. Aviva is an intelligent woman who I know will be a wonderful wife and business partner.

I hope this letter finds you well and at peace.

Papa

I stood, holding onto the letter and absorbing the news that my father was getting *married* again. Meanwhile, Yosef put his cup down. But he didn't shuffle back to his bedroom, as he had every day since his arrival.

"May I have some more coffee, Rachel?" he asked. "It's excellent."

Chapter 4
METZ, FRANCE
FEBRUARY 1923. LOVE

WE WERE ARGUING again, repeating the same tiresome quarrel.

Two years had passed since Celina, Shevah, and their little boy, Alon, had arrived from Poland. I was overjoyed to be reunited with Celina, but Shevah's scholarly lifestyle from the old country had no place in the new. Our business was growing and everyone needed to work. I'd *always* felt that way, but in Poland, everyone else—including my family—would shush me, reminding me what an honor it was to have a learned man in our household. Now though, in France, the old ways were shifting, and I was no longer alone. Yosef was on my side, and after an especially exhausting day at the shop, he went after Shevah.

"We could have used your help today, Shevah. We had customers all day, nonstop. You need to set those books aside and learn to work."

As gratifying as it was to hear Yosef repeat my long-held opinion, I sensed the dispute hovering above us like an aggressive raptor, ready to dive down.

"I *am* working," Shevah said, his voice warbling as it often did when someone challenged him. "Torah study communicates the word of God to us. It helps us understand our purpose: how to act, how to live, how to *be* in this new land. What could be more important than that? Tell me."

Yakob's children gaped as Shevah shouted, "Tell me what could possibly be *more important than that?* We are strangers, we are refugees. We need God's guidance more than ever!"

But Yosef could shout, too. "What could be more important? How about *food?* Food for your son and pregnant wife?"

Celina was pregnant again, and—I thought—even more emotional than usual because of it. Also, she had been more withdrawn and fragile ever since that beastly night with the Russian officer, and I worried that these repeated family conflicts unsettled her more than the rest of us. So, for her sake, I would try to diffuse this one. I wrapped my fingers around the armrests of my chair, hoping their wooden hardness would remind me to remain calm while urging Shevah to see reason.

"Shevah, we can expand our sales, bring in more merchandise from new suppliers, and attract more customers. I know we can do this; the time is right.

People have a bit more money in their pockets now, and they'll buy more if we offer more. Then we'll have enough to take care of everyone. Including your growing family"—I hoped the reference to his fatherhood would poke his sense of responsibility—"and we can do it with just a *little* more help. You wouldn't have to be at the shop *all* the time, just on busy days and when Yakob and Yosef are out meeting with suppliers. Just so I don't have to manage the store on my own. That sounds workable, doesn't it?"

My let's-find-a-compromise demeanor probably came across as forced because it was. Still, I congratulated myself for making the effort. I did my best imitation of a smile.

Shevah scowled, examined the floor, and shook his head. *No.*

I gave up my intention to appease him. "You can't do it, Shevah. You *just can't.* This is France. Not Poland."

I leaped up from the table, my chair crashing behind me. I surged with hot, angry energy, and it felt wonderful. Liberating. I was no longer a girl in a traditional Jewish village, expected to fulfill a role prescribed by someone else. I was a young woman in a new country, in a dynamic new era. I was a key part of my family's growing success. I could say how I felt.

"Go *back* if you want, but *we* are no longer working from sunrise to sundown to feed you. There's a train to Poland tomorrow."

I stood, still blazing, next to my overturned chair, feeling everyone's eyes on me. Was my family looking at me in shock? Disappointment? Or tacit support? I couldn't read their feelings; I was struggling enough to control my own, long-held frustration. Then everyone's gaze shifted, from me to Yakob. The eldest son. The head of the family. The one who'd come to France first, setting down the foundation of our new life.

"Yakob," Shevah said, switching his tone of indignation to gentle persuasion. "You especially . . . understand that study of the Talmud *is* work, that it's of *vital importance* as we make our way in this new home, this odd foreign land. Who else can guide us, but God? Without Him, we will be adrift. We will lose the ways of our ancient faith that have guided us for so long. *This* is the work I am doing, for our family and our community. For our people."

Yakob ran his fingers through his thick hair. I knew he was drained by the almost daily fights around this issue. "*Mayn Shvoger.* My brother-in-law. I love you like my own brother. But we're not rich. You must work."

I SUPPOSE I have my brother-in-law to thank for what happened next. For the encounter that changed my life.

With the glum but resigned Shevah occasionally showing up at the shop, my brothers and I increased our outreach to other merchants and suppliers, forging new connections and attracting new customers. Just a week after Shevah began working, Yakob was able to arrange a critical meeting, for which he and Yosef would be gone for much of the afternoon.

With a melancholy pride, I watched through the window as they strode down the street. My brothers were dashing, in their new suits and brown fedoras, their well-shined shoes. Their faces exuded optimism about their prospects in their new lives.

I wish Papa and Mama could see them.

As they strode out of sight, I put my attention on a display of new dresses. I'd urged my brothers to invest in the growing trend of women's ready-to-wear clothes, and was more than a little proud that it was already paying off. Our clientele was drawn to these factory-made clothes, for both their price and practicality. We focused on dresses for everyday use, but they were attractive too; featuring smooth fabrics, dropped waists, and a floating hemline below the knee. Although I'd never be a willowy model like the women in the fashion advertisements—I was too short and curvy for that—I discovered the styles that suited me best and wore them on the shop floor. I modeled them with practiced poise: shoulders down, chest up, curls placed just right, good shoes, and always red lipstick. Our female customers took note of my "confident, modern look" and requested the same clothes that would help them achieve it.

Since ready-to-wear was selling so well, I decided to move some of these outfits from the back of the store to the front. I looked about for Shevah to help, but didn't see him—and guessed that after my brothers' departure, he'd escaped into the employee back room behind the counter, separated by a curtain from the main shop floor. Still protesting his fate, he often took whatever chance he could to retreat there. It was annoying, but it wasn't worth the trouble to fetch him. I could do this task myself. If customers came in, he knew he was supposed to appear.

The doorbell jingled. Two elegant women entered in a cloud of perfume, laughing and chatting in a fast, flowing river of French.

Oh no. "*Bonjour . . .*" I faltered.

I hoped their purchases would be simple, that they'd point out exactly what they wanted, pay for it, and leave. By now, I spoke the French language well enough, though my grammar wasn't perfect and I could never get rid of my Yiddish accent. I also understood most of what French people said to me . . . if they didn't speak too quickly. But these women began posing rapid, incomprehensible questions.

"*Havezzvoozdezshemeezhes?*"

"*Daybelleshemeezhblanshes?*"

Something about shirts. Beyond that, I was mystified. I nodded as if I understood, but they must have recognized the confusion in my eyes. I kept glancing toward the back of the store. *Where was Shevah?* Despite his indifference toward our new homeland, my studious brother-in-law had already mastered French and spoke it beautifully.

The two women waited, chins lifted, holding their expensive purses and expecting answers.

"*Pardonnez-moi, mesdames,*" I said, excusing myself to go search for Shevah. But as I headed toward the back of the shop, four customers from the Jewish community came in, clients I knew well. They regaled me with greetings and questions, wanting some suits to be altered.

I replied in Yiddish to them, while pointedly not stopping as I strode to the back of the store.

 "Welcome, yes, please wait, I can't talk right now but I can help you in a moment . . ."

As I approached the back counter, the doorbell rang yet again, and the door slapped shut. The French women must have left. Meanwhile, I could tell the other customers were put off by my brusque greeting. I slid behind the counter and yanked open the curtain to the back room. As I expected, Shevah was sitting on a stool, reading. He craned his neck to glare up at me.

"What do you want? You can't tell me what to do. Yakob's not here, and he's the boss. You *act* like you are, but you're *not*." He plunged back into his book, with exaggerated interest.

 I wanted to shout at him, but with customers milling around, of course, I couldn't. "We probably just lost two customers who I'm sure were wealthy. I had to ignore four other clients. Word will get out about our poor service. People will bring their business elsewhere. Thanks to *you*."

I whirled around before he could retort. I went back to the main shop floor, trying not to stomp. Now, in addition to the four already-waiting customers, several more people had come in, wandering about and looking at me, expecting help.

I knew this would happen. He's always blamed me for the fact that he has to work and now he's trying to make me fail.

I fixed my eyes firmly on the floor to hide my face. It would not do for customers to see me flushed and angry. Head down, I walked quickly to the front to greet the newcomers. A little too quickly. I bumped into someone.

"Excuse me," I murmured, covering my linguistic bases with *pardon* in French and *antshuldikn mir* in Yiddish. I looked up at the person I'd run into.

The most beautiful man I'd ever seen.

"*Keyn zakh nit,*" he said in Yiddish, *It's nothing.*

He spoke in a melted-butter baritone, his lively dark eyes promised a sense of humor, and his curly black hair had one lock that wouldn't stay put, falling over his forehead. I briefly, crazily, considered reaching up and stroking that tantalizing curl back into place.

"I . . . ah . . . need to tend to these other people. Could . . . you wait . . . please?"

The man gave me a smile that was magnetic yet somehow unconsciously so, as if he didn't quite fully realize how alluring he was. "I'll wait."

I headed toward my customers. They had many questions, many demands. *Hurry up*, my insides fretted, while in my peripheral vision, I was hungrily searching the room for the man's well-built frame.

Luckily, he appeared in no hurry to go. He ambled about the store, examining items, humming to himself. The shop doorbell rang out again, announcing Yosef and Yakob this time. To my astonishment, Yakob addressed the handsome stranger right away.

"Melach. Nice to see you. But your cousins said not to expect you until tomorrow."

"Yes, I know our appointment isn't for another day," the young man responded in that velvet voice, which was as perfect as the rest of him, "but they sent me on another errand nearby, so I thought I'd come in and look around for a moment. Your store is impressive."

From their conversation, I gathered that Melach worked at his cousins' wholesale textile business and that they were looking to sell some of their wares at our store.

Meanwhile, Yosef sidled up to me, whispering, "Where's Shevah?"

But my eyes, my ears, even my breath were focused on the newcomer.

"Sarah. Why isn't our good-for-nothing brother-in-law out here, helping?" Yosef smirked, expecting me to appreciate the joke. He poked me in the ribs. "What's wrong with *you*?"

Then he saw where I was looking and how I must have been looking.

He chuckled, teasing into my ear. "My, my, *my*. Our tough little sister has a soft side after all. My dear Sarah. You're in love."

Chapter 5
METZ, FRANCE
FEBRUARY 1923. PASSION

ALL THAT NEXT morning, I fussed more than worked, skittering about the shop, re-arranging socks that were already in straight lines, dusting shelves that were free of dust, and straightening coats on their hangers even though they were in perfect order. Anything that would keep me near the shop's front windows, so I'd be ready when *he* arrived. When Melach Seibert finally came into view, he seemed more well-dressed than what an informal business meeting might require: a chocolate-colored suit, white dress shirt, and tan felt fedora. Still, I didn't dare hope that he'd put on this stylish outfit for me. *Stop it, Sarah. He probably has other, more important business later today.*

I darted away from the window, hoping not to seem as if I were waiting for him—although my infatuation must have been obvious already. Yosef had teased me nonstop the night before, about my "prince" who would be revisiting our store today. I ducked into the back room, behind the curtain, relieved that no one else was there.

The doorbell clinked. I began to sweat.

"Ah! Welcome, Melach. Nice to see you again," Yakob said.

"Yes, you too, Yakob," he replied with that smooth resonance I remembered from the day before—a sound that made me feel soothed and eager at the same time.

"Let me show you around," Yakob said. "Now here, on these empty shelves by the cash register, I thought we'd display your heavier textiles with the lighter-weight materials over there. How do you think your cousins will feel about that placement?"

"Oh, I'm certain they'll agree," Melach said, although he didn't sound as if he'd given it any thought at all.

"Excellent," Yakob said, who then launched into a series of explanations about suppliers, costs, and a thousand details of our business. ". . . and out in front, we've put the ready-to-wear dresses for the ladies. That's a newer trend in women's clothing that we adopted early, and is doing quite well—in fact, it's our biggest money-maker. Of course, it's thanks to my sister, Sarah. It was all her idea." Yakob chuckled. "She always seems to see what's coming before anyone else. It's a bit mysterious, but we've learned in our family not to question it."

My brother's talking to him. About me. Now he knows my name.

Quivering behind the curtain, my lower half ached with what I would only later understand as desire. I'd come of age without a mother, in a war, an experience that molded my self-image as capable, adaptable, resilient. But I was embarrassingly naïve when it came to men. Celina never discussed matters of romance with me. My teenage friendships were scattered and shallow, given the chaos of our lives. I had nothing to guide me, to help me recognize what I was feeling or what it could lead to. All I knew was that I needed to be near this man.

Melach continued talking, his every word brushing my ears. I imagined him kissing them and felt the tips grow hot.

"Yes. That is impressive. About the ready-to-wear. Good for you . . . I mean, good for *her* . . . I mean . . ." Melach faltered. "May I, uh . . . ask her about it?"

"Yes, of course," Yakob said.

Yakob took a few steps and pulled the curtain. He absorbed my anxious crouch, my pink face, but didn't look surprised. He'd heard all of Yosef's taunting last night, about my new "boyfriend."

"Sarah," he said, in a professional manner that made me all the more grateful for him. Yakob, at least, would not humiliate me. "There's someone here who wants to talk to you about the ready-to-wear line. Are you busy?" It was obvious I wasn't busy at all—unless you count spying behind a curtain as busy.

I smoothed my curls and emerged from the back. Yakob made the introductions and stepped away, saying he needed to "check on something."

Melach and I stood in an awkward but delicious pause, thick with attraction. He waited until Yakob was out of earshot, then dropped his pretext of discussing women's clothing.

"Would you join me for a walk sometime?" he asked.

AS SPRING EMERGED, Melach and I walked almost every day. We explored our new hometown together; the canal, the Moselle River, the parks, and the city center. Sunday was our only full day off, and we made the most of it, often having a picnic by the riverside.

"Someday, I'll be able to take you to a restaurant," Melach would say. "The best. Fancy waiters in white shirts . . ."

"I don't care," I'd respond, daring to stroke his hand, but wanting to kiss every finger.

"When we're rich, we'll go out to a nightclub," Melach would vow, to which I'd say, "You're my nightclub."

And he was. He adored music, and he'd sing me the old songs in Yiddish and new songs in French. He recited his favorite stories from Jewish comedians using different voices for each character and squeezing the drama out of each punchline. He concocted hilarious tales about the grumpy customers who interacted with his equally grumpy cousins at work. He lightened me, he made me laugh. I was drunk with wanting him.

One Sunday, we were strolling as usual by the river. It started to rain, giant drops that pelted us so hard it hurt.

Melach grabbed my hand. "My apartment is closer, let's go there. You can meet my cousins . . . not that you *want* to meet them." He grinned.

We ran, our vision blurred by the rain, arriving breathless and soaked.

"Hello . . ." Melach called up the stairs. "Anyone here?"

Silence.

"That's unusual," he said. "With eight of us, someone's always home."

We stumbled up the narrow first flight of steps to the kitchen, our wet shoes squeaking and our hair still dripping water into our eyes. Melach pulled a dish towel from a drawer and swiped his face.

"Here you go," he said, about to pass the towel to me. But mid-gesture, he stopped. I saw his eyes appreciate how my drenched clothing accentuated the ampleness of my breasts, the round shape of my thighs, and the suggestion of what was between them. A whisper from my Polish village upbringing tut-tutted me, warning me that I should not be so eager to present every curve I had to this man whom I'd only met a few months ago. Yet I had never felt so bold and so certain. I put my arms around his waist.

"Melach . . ."

He kissed me, and our weeks of constant but controlled desire for each other exploded. I was no longer the Sarah everyone knew—that young woman of sound judgment and sharp mind. I was a female body. I wanted—no, needed—him to take me, right there, dripping wet on the kitchen floor. But Melach pulled out of the kiss. While his entire being radiated lust, I also knew at that pause, at that moment weighted with promise, that he loved me. Respected me. And wanted to be sure I was ready.

He picked up the dishtowel. With the gentleness of a butterfly, he wiped one of my cheeks and kissed it. Then he dried the other cheek, landing his lips upon it. Next came my eyelids, which I closed, woozily accepting his kiss on the left eyelid first, then the right.

He toweled my forehead and pressed his warm, full lips there. He dried each ear and kissed the left one, then nibbled the right. I heard someone moan and realized it was me. Still, Melach continued his controlled pace. From my right ear, he moved down my neck, languidly rubbing each side dry with the towel and then kissing it. His lips moved in tiny increments down my chest toward my breasts, asking a delicious question that I needed to answer. Shaking, I undid the top buttons of my dress with clumsy fingers.

Now, he could be sure.

In one graceful, powerful move, Melach bent over and placed one arm behind the middle of my back and the other behind my knees. I put my arms around his neck, molding myself into his chest. He carried me easily up the four flights of stairs to his bedroom; both of us consumed by one goal: *Hurry*—so that we could kiss each other everywhere, everywhere, everywhere.

Chapter 6
SEDAN, FRANCE
JANUARY 1924. DECEPTION

A THIN, SHRILL scream poked through my sleeping brain. Two-month-old Jacques lay in his cradle, shrieking only as newborns could. The sound dragged me up and through the black sludge of sudden middle-of-the-night waking. I heaved myself out of bed, staggered over to his cradle, and pulled him to my breast as I settled us both into a rocking chair. The chair squeaked rhythmically as I sat, rocking and nursing in a darkness so thick and full, I felt I could reach out and grab it by handfuls. Now I was awake enough to feel the cold of our apartment and to resent Melach, still cozy under the covers.

We'd married less than a year after we met. We had to.

Our first love-making session on that rainy day in Melach's bedroom was followed by a blur of many others. We'd create excuses to run errands to each other's workplaces, exchanging propositions when we thought no one was watching.

"Yakob and his family will be out tomorrow night," I'd whisper into Melach's ear, while purportedly picking up "something" at his cousins' store where he worked.

"My cousins are all going to the synagogue tonight. I've told them I'm unwell," Melach would scrawl in a note, slipping it into my hand when he stopped by our shop, under the pretext of "needing" to talk to my brothers.

Then on a June day as we walked in the park bursting with flowers, I said, "I'm pregnant."

I knew how he'd react.

"My darling. My Sarah," he said, and he kissed me hard, despite the stares of people walking by. He talked excitedly, spinning out plans. " . . . and we'll go to Poland, to get our parents' blessings before the wedding. You'll meet my family in Lodz, and I'll meet your father in Amshinov. Oh, Sarah. A family. *Our* family."

It was exactly what I knew he'd say. He was such a tender, good-hearted, sweet man. His complete devotion to me was clear to everyone. What was unclear were my own feelings.

Of course, I was attracted to him—the vitality and strength of his body, his luxurious black hair, and his easy smile. The physical chemistry between us was so powerful, that sometimes during our illicit moments in bed, I couldn't even kiss him, I was panting too hard. That loss of control might have terrified me with someone else; but with Melach I knew I was safe. Also, he loved children as much as I did. He was playful, funny, and big-hearted. He would be an incredible father. Still, was *I* ready for marriage and motherhood? There was only one acceptable answer. Yes.

SEVERAL WEEKS AFTER I told Melach I was expecting, we took the train to Poland. The trip was long, with many stops and switching of trains. The seats were hard and uncomfortable, all the worse because I was in my first trimester and spent much of the journey alternating between nausea and hunger. When I wasn't trying to figure out whether I could eat or should eat, I attempted to sleep. Melach folded his coat as a pillow so I could put my head on his lap. The train rocked and swayed, as my husband-to-be stroked my hair and hummed old lullabies, smiling and peering out the window.

MY FATHER MET us at the station in Amshinov, and he didn't have to guess why I'd endured a grueling, expensive journey with the polite, eager young man who towered over him. On the second night of our short visit, Melach made his formal request for my hand in marriage, earnestly assuring my father, "I'll take care of her and love her for all my days."

He sounded as if he'd rehearsed it because he had, dozens of times, on the trip. My papa listened gravely, as the occasion merited. Then he started to laugh. Melach and I exchanged an anxious look.

"My son," my father said, chortling as he had to reach up to place his arm around Melach's shoulders, "you have my blessing, of course—and I'm certain that you will love her, for all your days. But, you do know her by now? *She* will be the one taking care of *you*."

NOW, MONTHS LATER as I rocked Jacques back to sleep, I reflected on how accurate my father's comment was. Melach did take care of my emotions, and my spirit: he listened to my complaints and fears. He made me laugh, he adored me and respected me, and—unlike any other man I knew, he did the dishes every single night. But when it came to decisions around how we'd structure our lives—where we'd live, how we'd organize our household, our work, our finances—he deferred to me.

"You're just better at it than me," he'd say, kissing the top of my head or playing with one of my curls. "Why would I argue with perfection." And at first, this arrangement, these roles we'd carved out worked. But they weren't working now. We were almost broke.

WE'D MOVED TO the city of Sedan, where my sister Celina and her family were living, a few months after Jacques was born. From the start, the city felt wrong, there was something foreboding about it . . . the people, the buildings. A huge medieval fortress called the Chateau Fort loomed over the landscape. Shortly after our move, I'd asked a customer about it, who told me that the fort had been a German prison during the Great War. "French and Belgian Resistance members had been worked to death there," the woman had said quietly, leaning over the counter. "There are still bad feelings between some folks in town over who supported France or Germany."

Learning this grim history only added to my unease, but when I mentioned it to Melach, he wouldn't hear it.

"There's so much to like about this city. Why, haven't you noticed the way the Meuse River curves right through the town, the willow trees dripping toward the water? In that sense, it's like Metz. Remember our walks by the river there, when we first fell in love?" He stroked my back. "I think the pregnancy is exhausting you, darkening your view of everything."

"Mmmm," I said. The pregnancy was sapping my usual vigor, Melach was right about that. I'd barely been able to cook dinner that night and the result was not my usual mediocre-but-edible, it was downright dismal. I pushed aside my plate of undercooked potatoes and overcooked eggs. Melach soldiered on, although taking smaller bites than usual. He never complained about my lack of skill in the kitchen, one more reason I loved him.

Our poor excuse for a meal over, Melach stood and as usual, began to do the dishes.

"I have an idea, that I've been thinking about for a while," he said, over the banging of pots. "Once the baby comes, let's hire someone to work with me at the store."

My only focus at that moment was on how desperately I wanted to be lying down.

"All right," I mumbled. "Good idea."

It was not.

IN MID-NOVEMBER, near the end of my pregnancy, we hired a young man named David. Melach had met him at the synagogue and invited him to come to the store on a Monday to discuss employment.

"Monsieur and Madame Seibert, I'm honored." David beamed and shook our hands vigorously. Then he became somber. "You see, I'm so grateful for the chance to work, after what happened to my family."

"Do you mind telling us?" I asked. Deep down, I was cool to the idea of working with someone who wasn't family. But with the baby coming, it seemed the right choice.

David ducked his head, a nervous little gesture. "I am . . . was . . . the youngest of three sons. Both my older brothers were killed in the war. They were fighting for the German side, since—as you know—the province of Lorraine had been German since the Franco-Prussian war."

"Yes, we know," I said. I knew the history and found myself annoyed that he was telling me. "It was the same in Metz, where we came from."

"Right . . ." David looked over my shoulder, instead of at me.

Was reliving this difficult history upsetting him, or was he lying?

"Then, after the war came the Spanish flu epidemic. My mother's health was already weak, she was emotionally wrecked from losing two of her sons. She died soon after becoming infected. My father . . . he was with the French Resistance during the war, one of those Lorrainians who worked inside the province for a French victory. He died as a prisoner at the Chateau Fort." David twirled a loose thread on the sleeve of his jacket. "I'm alone."

Melach put his hand on David's shoulder. "I'm very sorry," he said, ever sympathetic and compassionate.

I thought David's story fit just a little too neatly into all the categories of woes that were possible in those post-war times. But I was too fatigued to ask more questions, to gather more information about him, like I normally would have.

Jacques was born on November 23rd, and David began working for us the next day. He was helpful, friendly, and the customers liked him. Still, after several weeks, I began to suspect he was cheating us. More than once, I had examined the account books and found the numbers didn't *quite* add up. But in the fog of new motherhood, my focus was off.

By early January, however, it was clear. We were losing money, and there was no other plausible reason why.

I NURSED JACQUES until he was limp, asleep; his tiny face blissful—a dramatic change from the screeching infant who'd woken me an hour ago. It was early morning but still dark. I was tempted to go back to bed myself, but now I was worrying. And wide awake.

Melach's too easygoing. And I've let things slide.

I decided I would settle the matter with David myself. I dressed, made coffee, and ate a few bites of bread, shivering in the dim kitchen, feeling brittle from both lack of sleep and anxiety over the upcoming confrontation. I scrawled a note to Melach—*Gone to the store.*

Just as I was putting the note on the table, he came into the room, humming as usual.

"*Bonjour, Gut morgn,*" he greeted me with a kiss on the cheek. He liked to practice his French before he reverted to Yiddish.

"There's nothing good about it," I groused. "I barely slept, and we must—*must*—confront David today."

"But I haven't had time to go through the records and draw up proof." I heard the nervousness in his voice. "I don't doubt you, but I haven't been able to document exactly how he might be skimming money off for himself."

I knew Melach had been conflicted about what to do. His fundamental nature was to trust, to believe the best of people. Also, Melach *had* been working incredibly hard these last few months, while I'd given birth, and was focused on our baby.

"I'll confront him and see how he reacts," I said, trying to sound encouraging, instead of how I really felt: exhausted, aggravated, and upset.

"I'm going with you. We can leave the baby at your sister's."

We woke Jacques, bundled him up, and left him at Celina's. As we arrived at the shop, Melach reached into his pocket for the key. He always opened up first, with David coming in later in the morning. But the door was already unlocked.

"David must have come to work early," Melach said over his shoulder as he entered.

I followed behind as he stepped inside.

Everything was gone.

I scanned the vacant shelves, seeing but not believing. In Poland, my family's businesses had been robbed many times, but always by outsiders; Russians and Poles. To be betrayed by a fellow Jew was unthinkable. I grasped the wooden counter where the cash register had stood, afraid I might fall over if I didn't.

"It's my fault," I said.

Melach put his arm around me. "How is that possible? No."

I shook him off and pulled away. I didn't want contact with him right now. "It is. I *knew* he was not to be trusted. But I was too busy with the baby, and you . . . you can't do this alone."

My remark cut him. His whole posture slumped.

"You're right. And I'm sorry," he mumbled.

He stepped outside to sit on the frigid front steps, elbows on his knees, head in his hands, his breath vaporizing in the January air.

I'm not sure how long I remained alone in the empty room that had just yesterday been our shop. Fragments of images from Poland swirled through my mind: the repeated lootings, the midnight escapes, and the many losses—like that frigid, terrible night when we fled for Warsaw, only to discover that the merchandise Piotr had hidden for us was gone. The room grew colder, with the door open and Melach still sitting on the outside steps. Even though his back was to me, I felt how morose he was, how miserable, how guilty.

We survived before. We'll survive again.

I joined Melach outside. "Come. Let's get our son."

We walked back to Celina's home.

"Why . . . are you here so soon?" Celina asked, looking back and forth at my husband and me. "What happened?"

"David. He took it all. There's nothing left," Melach said.

"But . . . what? How? Melach, why didn't you . . . ? How could he . . . ?"

"Celina, stop. David had a sad story. The same tale you hear from so many in this town. The war. The prison. The flu. Melach felt badly for him, and my head was too muddled with the baby to pay closer attention."

I shoved my freezing hands into my coat pockets. I hated to ask her this, given my history with her husband, Shevah. But he was well-connected at the synagogue of Sedan.

"I swear I will not ask this again. Celina, I swear it," I said. "But you must tell Shevah to help us."

Chapter 7
COLMAR, FRANCE
JANUARY 1924. WELCOME

"SO, MELACH, SARAH," the rabbi said, in his lion-purr of a voice, "how do you find our fair city?"

He tugged his long, black wool coat tighter as the January wind whirled dead leaves around the tall, rose-and-cream-hued synagogue of Colmar. Melach had attended his first worship service in our new city, and I'd met him outside the synagogue with Jacques afterward—our newborn baby offering me an excuse to not attend myself.

"Colmar is a dream come true," Melach answered. "Thank you, Rabbi Weber, for welcoming us so graciously."

After the fiasco in Sedan, Shevah had written to his friend, Rabbi Ernst Weber of Colmar. A picture-perfect, small city in central Alsace, Shevah assured us that Colmar had a solid economy, a robust Jewish community, and a rabbi eager to help newcomers establish themselves.

"Well, well, well," Rabbi Weber said with enthusiasm despite the cold that was making his eyes water. "We're glad to have your family here, and as I'm sure you've surmised, there are many in Colmar like you, who've also just arrived. I give thanks every day for the privilege of leadership in this very promising time."

Melach and I stood there, dumbly shivering, knowing we should say something but not sure what that should be; we were both so taken by this man's eloquence, elegance, and yet friendly demeanor.

"Ahem," the rabbi said, and then he stopped to cough, making me wonder if we should simply thank him and go home. The bitter wind scoured the street outside the synagogue, and I worried about the cold, for the sake of both tiny Jacques in his pram and Rabbi Weber, who was not a young man. "Yes, well." He regained control over his cough. "I'd be delighted to help you settle in and become part of our thriving community. I invite you to my home on Monday afternoon, and we can talk at length then. Does that suit you?"

"Of course, Rabbi. We'll see you then," Melach said.

Despite Rabbi Weber's open arms, however, we soon learned that some in Colmar's congregation were not as enthusiastic about immigrants as their rabbi. More than once, we overheard comments from French-born synagogue members while attending social events at the nearby Jewish Community Center.

" . . . make us look bad, speaking French so poorly. Why the other day, at René's bakery . . ."

" . . . must they dress like that? This is France, not the shtetl . . ."

" . . . nervous about the Russian ones, they might be Communists . . ."

Rabbi Weber was conscious of the cultural divides among his people, and I appreciated how he worked to bridge them. Melach told me that in his *d'var Torah*, or sermon, the rabbi would often expound upon passages that emphasized welcoming foreigners.

The stranger who resides with you shall be to you as the native among you, and you shall love him as yourself, for you were aliens in the land of Egypt.

I was grateful for Rabbi Weber's efforts and his kindness toward us. But I wasn't interested in his house of worship.

"I'll come with you to synagogue from time to time," I'd said to Melach when we first arrived in Colmar. "But I'm through with bowing, praying, pretending I believe in something that I don't . . ."

"I know," he said, gently.

My husband. As much as he frustrated me sometimes, with his carefree nature and his lack of concern about life's practical matters, he cheerfully accepted me as I was. He was perfectly fine attending synagogue without me, and he went often—although for Melach, it was just as much, if not more, for the socializing as the religion.

THAT MONDAY AFTERNOON, the three of us sat down in the rabbi's living room. It was small but well-appointed, with a stiff formal couch, an assortment of tasteful wooden tables with carved legs, and two intimidating, barely padded chairs. The walls were taken up by bookshelves stuffed with books. Out the window, a diminishing January afternoon sun glinted off the waters of Colmar's canal. Melach and I settled as best we could on the uncomfortable couch, while the rabbi's wife served coffee and offered to look after Jacques so the three of us could talk.

Rabbi Weber took a genteel sip from his delicately painted porcelain cup.

"Ahh. A favorite post-war indulgence, having sugar again in coffee. Now then, Melach and Sarah. You came here from the neighboring province of Lorraine, so you already know about all the . . . let us say . . . *interesting* changes this region has been through. I myself have lived them . . . I was French as a little boy, but grew up as a German. I actually did my rabbinical studies in Berlin. Quite interesting, and I made many friends on the other side of the Rhine. However, Alsace has always been home, and I have been happily French again for the past six years, since the peace of 1918." He took another appreciative taste of his coffee then put the cup down. "But, pardon me, I mustn't bore you with my personal history. Surely you have many questions. What can I answer for you, or help you with?"

I said nothing, which probably surprised Melach. But I was still gauging Rabbi Weber's attitude toward women, so I nudged Melach a little with my knee—a signal that I wanted him to take the lead. He took it, asking about the local economy, the city's cultural side, and the other new Jewish families from Eastern Europe, especially Poland. The rabbi gave long, thoughtful answers, and the afternoon stretched on, growing dark early as it does in January. I heard Jacques fussing for his next feeding. The rabbi's wife brought him to me, an apologetic look on her face.

"I think he needs you," she said.

"Yes, excuse us, you've both been so generous. But I think Jacques is telling us that we should go," I said.

Melach and I stood and put our coats on.

"Rabbi Weber," Melach said as he buttoned up. "What about the Christians in this town? How does everyone . . . get along?"

"Excellent question, and I understand it, given that you are opening a shop, and you'll need to draw from a wide customer base. Rest assured. Religious tolerance is almost . . . a sacred principle in Alsace."

He paused.

"Almost."

"SARAH! I'M LEAVING, I'll be home before lunch," Melach called to me as I stood at the stove stirring oatmeal. I heard the door open then close and assumed he'd left, but he must have tiptoed back. I yelped as two long arms closed around my waist and a pair of lips nuzzled my neck.

"I'll see you later," he hummed into my ear, a buzzing suggestion.

The Saturday after our Monday meeting with the rabbi, Melach was heading out for morning services at the synagogue; while I'd chosen to stay home.

"All right," I replied, trying to stay in practical mode, although my body responded to his touch. "If anyone asks why I'm not there, tell them the baby was up half the night and now we're both sound asleep."

The story was partially true. Jacques had wailed for much of the night, in between short blocks of sleep. Now he slumbered again, but I was wide awake and restless. The bright winter morning beckoned, tempting me to explore. Although I knew it was always a terrible idea to wake a sleeping baby, I did it anyway. I bundled Jacques into his pram, pulled my coat on, and walked the few minutes into the center of town.

ALONG MAIN STREET, I pushed the pram leisurely, peering into windows. I passed sumptuous displays of different types of cheeses: Munster, Bargkass, and many others with long, complicated names that I couldn't pronounce. Charcuterie was popular too, based on the incredible array of choices, made from all kinds of meats—wild boar, pheasant, and deer. And the wine. Colmar was the heart of the Alsatian wine country, and I'd already acquired a taste for the region's Pinot Gris, Reisling, and Sylvaner. Store after store advertised these, along with liqueurs made from local fruits: currents, blueberries, pears. After passing several shops showing off these tempting products, I walked by a clothing shop called *The Alsacienne*, which appeared dark inside. That was strange on a Saturday morning . . . why would the owners close at the very time when most people were out running errands? I tucked the question away and continued enjoying my exploration of our new city. Then, just as my fingers were starting to hurt from the cold, I saw it:

Pain Pour Tous, the sign on the bakery-café said. *Bread For All*.

I glanced down at Jacques, who'd fallen asleep again. I pushed the door open with my back and pulled the pram inside . . . into a postcard.

It was the coziest, most quintessentially French café I'd ever seen. The place smelled like coffee and yeast and sugar. It was warm, even steamy in contrast to the sharp winter air outside. Customers sat at a dozen small, white marble tables, filling the room with the low, pleasant sound of easy Saturday conversation. Mid-morning sunlight shone through the front windows and illuminated the cylindrical espresso machines at the back. The entire place seemed to glow.

I ordered a coffee and a croissant at the counter and made my way to a nearby table, relieved that Jacques still slept. I took my coat off and exhaled—comfortable, content, and thankful. Poland had, at least, given me that: frequent flashes of gratitude that I was *here* . . . and not *there*.

I absorbed the café's welcoming ambiance while appreciating the way the coffee bit my tongue, just the right contrast to the croissant's buttery layers. I noticed a tall, middle-aged woman enter the café, a wriggling toddler on her hip. She wore an ordinary green dress and no jewelry except a silver crucifix necklace.

Her hair was pulled back in a simple twist and she wore no makeup, which I couldn't help but notice because I always wore lipstick and made sure my outfit was perfect before I left the house. When you're selling clothing, like I did, you're also selling style. Still, I was impressed by how this woman carried herself with an unadorned elegance. I had learned early on how to read people and could see that she who knew she was. She passed by my table.

"Baby! Baby!" the little boy in her arms shrieked, pointing at Jacques. He tried to twist out of the woman's hold, reaching toward my sleeping infant. "Baby!" he screamed again.

The noise woke Jacques, and he cried out.

"Oh, my goodness, I am so sorry," the woman said.

While Jacques' crying intensified, the toddler's attention moved from him to an attractive young man cleaning cups and glasses behind the counter.

"Papa!" the little boy shouted so loudly that Jacques howled.

"Excuse me," the woman said, her face now pink and the composure I'd just admired cracking as she rushed to the counter.

"It's fine," I said, as I tried to soothe Jacques, whose high-pitched wailing was now annoying other customers. I stood, took one last, hasty bite of croissant, my enjoyable morning out already over. As I struggled to both button my coat and soothe my baby, the woman in the green dress walked back toward me—this time, with no toddler. She carried a small box.

"Please, forgive me. My grandson . . . Frédéric . . . he loves babies. Then, when he sees his father"—she pointed to the young man behind the counter—"he just *has* to go to him. I'm so sorry for disturbing you. Please, take these. With my compliments and apologies."

I was taken aback by the friendly gesture. Meanwhile, Jacques continued to screech piteously, as if someone were poking him with pins.

The woman pushed the box into my hands. "The croissants are my husband's specialty. Enjoy them."

I hesitated to speak. Although I'd lived in France for several years, I was new in this town and wasn't sure how the locals would react to my Yiddish accent and my still less-than-perfect French. But I couldn't stand there like an idiot.

"It's so generous of you, but not necessary," I said. "I understand how children can be."

"You're new here. Welcome. I'm Adele Chastain. I own this place with my husband and son. Please come back . . . and we'll try not to wake your baby next time." She held out her hand to shake mine. "What's your name?" she almost shouted over the noise of my son's crying.

"Sarah. Sarah Seibert. In fact, we're about to buy the empty storefront across from you, to open a clothing shop. So, we'll be neighbors, of a sort, and . . . excuse me . . . I think I should go. My baby . . ."

"I understand completely. Please come again another time, then, Sarah. We should get to know each other since we'll be just across the street. For now, best wishes settling in."

JACQUES QUIETED AS soon as we left the café, soothed by the movement of his pram. I was quiet too, thinking about the woman I'd just met. Adele Chastain and I seemed to have little in common. She was older than me, about my father's age. And she must be Catholic, I guessed, based on the cross necklace she wore. By the way I spoke, she knew I was a foreigner. Yet she'd been warm and inviting.

Melach came home from the synagogue around lunchtime, as promised. "How was your morning?"

"Jacques and I went out," I said. "And . . . I might have made a new friend."

"How nice!"

"Yes." I mused over the possibility of friendship outside the Jewish community. Like my mother, I didn't trust Christians, despite my father's inter-religious friendships in Amshinov. And after what I'd experienced in Poland during the Great War, sticking with my own kind seemed the safest way.

But something about that whole morning prodded me to open up. Perhaps, I had only escaped Poland physically. Perhaps, emotionally, I was still there. And perhaps it was time I left it behind forever.

I decided right at that moment to take a chance. To change. I was a new mother, in a new city, opening a new business. I would have a new friend.

It started with a small box of croissants. It would end with Adele helping us survive.

Chapter 8
COLMAR, FRANCE
JUNE 1929. UNCERTAINTY

I DREAMED OF Poland, a confusing pastiche of Russian soldiers playing the hurdy-gurdy, my sisters dancing with Piotr in Amshinov's village square, and my mother waving to me from the Tsar Nicholas Bridge in Warsaw. It was tame as far as my dreams went, but it disturbed me, waking me early.

I'm right here. It's 1929. Colmar . . .

I felt Melach's solid form beside me in bed. Even asleep, he seemed cheerful.

He's probably humming in his sleep. No odd dreams for him.

But since our second child André was born in late1925, my nights had become more agitated. I told myself this was normal, that any mother of two young children would not rest especially well. Still, sleeping poorly was one thing; my dreams were another. Soldiers were chasing me, I was trying to run away, but the snow was too deep, or I had no shoes, or I had to find my family first.

I'd awaken with my pulse rapid and uneven, and the room spinning. But I wouldn't seek comfort from Melach, because I knew what he'd say: that I shouldn't worry, that our struggles were behind us and that it was, after all, "just a dream." Poland was the past, he would say, and I should let it stay there. We'd lived in France for almost ten years, and Melach loved it. Unconditionally.

"Welcome to Liberty, Equality, and Brotherhood," he'd cheer, reciting the French revolutionary creed to any newly arrived Polish relative.

"As free and rich as America, but with better food and wine," Melach would joke to his men friends at the synagogue.

He'd often point out how we were thriving in Alsace, and he was right. Our shop catered to customers of all backgrounds, while our children had friends of all faiths.

Still, this morning's dream stuck with me, like a pebble that you just can't shake out of your shoe. I eased out of bed and padded in bare feet to the kitchen. I lit the gas stovetop, ground some coffee, and measured it into the percolator pot. The dusky odor of the grounds, the gentle bubbling of the brewing coffee were reassuring evidence of a normal morning ritual. Melach was probably right. Poland was just scratching my worry again because my father was still there.

I wrote to him regularly, entreating him to come. And as the years passed, his absence grew even more painful, because everyone else from the Old Country was here. Melach and I helped settle dozens of relatives from both Amshinov and his hometown of Lodz: long-lost aunts, unknown uncles, anyone's in-laws . . . everyone was welcome. They'd stay at our apartment for weeks or months—one cousin stayed for two years. We found them work and housing, we showed them how to navigate the school system and city hall. Our home was a busy, noisy place, with people just arriving or just leaving, offering to cook, asking for advice, or sitting at the table needing help with their French lessons. And these scenes, I was sure, were occurring in other households as well—the Jewish community in Alsace was growing all around us. In fact, by 1928, Melach's father was working with Rabbi Weber, helping to resettle Eastern European Jewish immigrants.

But I couldn't convince my own father to come. He was the last holdout. I sat down to write him a letter. To try, once again.

> *Dear Papa:*
>
> *I miss you and hope you are well. I think of you every day and wish you were here.*
>
> *The store is prospering because I learned from you. In fact, we've expanded! We moved from a tiny place on Main Street to a bigger space on an extension of that street called Rue Vauban. It's still in the central city, so we have lots of customers.*
>
> *How are Aviva and your children? They would love it here . . .*

I put my pen down. Years after my father had remarried, I was still uncomfortable with the idea that he had a new family. It was more than the fact that Aviva was not much older than me, although I had to admit that was part of it. But I also believed my young stepmother was why my father resisted leaving Poland. I had no proof, but what else could it be?

I resumed writing.

> *. . . with the Vosges Mountains nearby. We often take the boys there, to run about. They're ages 5 and 3 now, but Jacques says when he's older, he wants to join one of the many scouting groups here, where children explore the Vosges and learn about camping, fishing, orienteering with maps, and the like. These are skills I lack! But I have a sense they are useful.*
>
> *Tell Aviva that you also wouldn't have to worry about a language barrier here. The local language, Alsatian, feels quite similar to Yiddish.*

> *I've never had an ear for languages, as you know. But I've learned Alsatian easily. My French is acceptable now too, although I still have an accent. But people from outside Alsace don't know whether my accent is Alsatian or Yiddish!*

That had been another pleasant surprise of our move to the province: with non-Alsatians—French people from "the interior of France" as the locals called them—Melach and I could pass as native Alsatians because of our *Yiddish* accents. I concluded my letter:

> *France is welcoming immigrants. Please come, Papa, if only for a visit.*
> *Sarah*

I folded the letter with some guilt over my cheerful report. Yes, Alsace was wonderful in all the ways I'd described it, and Colmar especially so. But sometimes, I still questioned how much "Liberty, Equality, and Brotherhood" really applied to new citizens like us. Most of the time, in those early years in Colmar, it was, in all ways, wonderful. But there were days—like today—when I sensed a force, dormant and waiting, below the clean, fresh waters of post-war France. A feeling that older, more putrid waters still flowed just underneath that sleek, modern river.

I sealed the letter. The friendly burble of the percolator and the almost-burnt smell of the coffee pulled me out of the dream's lingering unease and into my life now. The promised warmth of a June day. The tasks that awaited me on the first floor, in our shop. My husband and sons, still asleep down the hall. The fulfillment and satisfaction of work, family, and community. I placed the letter on the kitchen table to be mailed later, hearing as I did the light slapping sound of small slippered feet.

"*Bonjour,* Maman." Jacques skipped into the kitchen. My eldest, like most children, picked up languages easily. At not quite six years old, he already spoke French and Alsatian perfectly, understanding some Yiddish as well.

"*Gut morgn,*" I replied in Yiddish. Jacques was in first grade and already loved school, books, learning—all of it. I hadn't attended much school in Poland. It wasn't considered important for girls, and after my mother died, I was needed at the shop. Then came the war.

I vowed my own children would receive the very best education, including university.

Jacques sat at the table, his skinny legs dangling from the chair, not yet long enough to reach the floor. He wiggled in his seat. "I'm hungry but I don't have much time, Maman."

"Oh! Well, my goodness. Let's get you some food, and you can tell me why."

I cut him a thick slice of bread from yesterday's purchase from Pain Pour Tous and spread it with butter. The bread was no longer soft after sitting overnight on the counter, but Jacques preferred it that way. It held together better, as he dunked it into his morning drink: a bowl of heated milk with a little coffee and sugar mixed in. I'd buy bread from nowhere else but Pain Pour Tous after Adele and I became friends. Despite our differences in age, religion, and culture, we had a connection I couldn't explain: solid, trusting, understanding. Maybe I was a daughter figure to her, since she had only one son and her own daughter-in-law had died giving birth to her younger grandson. Perhaps Adele was a mother figure to me since I'd lost my own mother so young. Or maybe I saw Adele as a tougher, more confident big sister than my actual older sister Celina. Or perhaps—because she wasn't family—with Adele I didn't have to be Sarah-with-all-the answers, Sarah-who-takes-charge. With her, I could be confused, doubtful, afraid, and it was a relief. Lastly, it delighted both of us that Jacques was close with Adele's younger grandson, Frédéric, the same little boy whose excited cries led me to meet Adele at the café years ago, when Frédéric was still a toddler and Jacques was a baby.

And Frédéric was the reason Jacques was so hurried this morning, chewing his bread vigorously, splashing his milk-coffee drink, and talking with his mouth full.

"I need to go now, early, *before* school. Frédéric and I are going to look for hiding places near St. Martin's Church and then on Sunday, he can hide there instead of going to Mass. Maybe I'll hide with him, that would be so funny." He chewed some more and paused. "Frédéric is really, really good at hiding. Maybe he can teach me."

He handed me his bowl and plate, wiped his mouth, grabbed his school bag, and shouted an *au revoir* as he left. Watching from the window, I felt that delightful ache of pure mother-love, as my adorable eldest child trotted down the sidewalk. But the moment his figure disappeared, my earlier gloom returned. I hated St. Martin's.

Like all cathedrals, the Catholic church in the center of Colmar was inscribed with many religiously themed carvings and statues. But St. Martin's exterior included two statues known as *Judensau*. Of all the ugly portrayals of Jews on cathedrals—and there were many—I found the *Judensau* the most offensive: it showed a man in a classic Jewish hat in obscene contact with a female pig. I'd encountered an example of this for the first time in Metz, whose cathedral had one *Judensau*. But Saint-Martin's Cathedral had double images of this insult, which was unusual. Every time I had to walk past, I averted my eyes, as the hideous carvings stirred my anxiety that an older France was simmering just beneath the new.

I had discovered the *Judensau* of St. Martin's several years after we arrived in Colmar, as Melach and I stopped to study the cathedral one day, on our way to the park with our children.

"These people who pretend to be modern now, coming into our shop, smiling and saying *bonjour* and *merci*," I complained to Melach while the boys played. "How many of them still feel this way?"

I was almost in tears, holding back only because I didn't want my sons to see.

Melach took my hand. "I want to show you something."

He called the boys, saying it was time to go home, but he steered us back to our apartment in a direction I seldom took. He stopped on Rue des Marchands, at Colmar's brand-new museum dedicated to sculptor Auguste Bartholdi. Melach held open the door, gesturing that we should enter. Inside stood a small replica of the most recognized sculpture in the world: The Statue of Liberty. Melach made a grand gesture with his arm:

"And . . . here she stands. Lady Liberty. Conceived and created right here in Colmar by Bartholdi, our city's most famous son." He squeezed my hand. "Don't you see? Colmar itself stands for freedom."

I wanted to believe him, and wished I possessed the same easy faith.

LATER THAT SUMMER, I received the letter I'd been hoping for:

> *Dearest Sarah,* (my father wrote)
> *I'm writing with news that I'm certain you'll celebrate. I'm bringing your little sister Zofia to France, permanently. I'll accompany her but will stay just for a visit. I know you and Melach will take care of her. We arrive at the beginning of August. I won't write more now, because I will see you in a few weeks.*
> *Your loving,*
> *Papa*

"Look, Melach!" I yelped, waving the letter. "He's coming, she's coming . . . and maybe we can convince him, finally, while he's here."

"I am at your service, Madame," he said. "Just you wait."

Melach kept his word. During my father's visit, he put on a full-scale, showcase effort. He organized outings to the Vosges, to the theatre, and gatherings at our apartment. He hosted parties and dinners, where he would steer the conversation toward how different our lives were here, compared to the Old Country. Our guests would eagerly weigh in.

"Another Jew was elected mayor last week, in a little city in northern Alsace. *That* wouldn't happen in Poland . . ."

"And yet the younger generation thinks it's all perfectly normal. Why, look at Jacques. He has friends who are Jewish, Catholic, Protestant. He can recite the Catechism *and* his Hebrew prayers, and thinks nothing of it. Can you imagine that in Poland . . . can you *imagine?*"

And everyone would shake their heads in contented disbelief.

". . . an ideal place . . ."

" . . . so wonderful for the children . . ."

My father politely acknowledged these comments without adding his own. Always a man who loved a lively conversation, a robust back-and-forth among friends—on this visit he spoke little. I knew he was taking it all in: the open political culture, the easing of social norms, the trappings of expanding Western European wealth, including in his own daughter's home. The phonograph. The refrigerator. The wine, the food. Our huge, brand-new apartment, which must have seemed like a mansion to him. My father accepted our hospitality with quiet grace but muted enthusiasm.

He's not comfortable. It's too busy, too modern . . . too much.

Zofja, on the other hand, sparkled. The timid little girl I remembered from Poland had become an exuberant young woman who was dazzled by everything. Including Melach's younger brother.

AT A LAST party the night before my father left, Melach held court in the center of the living room. Surrounded by two dozen family members and friends, he'd been entertaining everyone with his recitation of *Tevye the Dairyman*, by his favorite comedian Sholem Aliechem. Now, at the end of his performance, he was struggling to make it to the punchline, where the beleaguered Tevye is once again berated by his wife, Golde:

"'Either you're delirious or you're temporarily deranged or else you've taken leave of your senses, or else you're totally insane. All I can say is, you're talking just like a madman, God help us . . . says my wife.'" Melach paused for dramatic effect, before delivering Tevye's conclusion. "'When it comes to her tongue, she's a pretty average Jewish housewife.'"

His audience roared, and Melach collapsed, laughing so hard he was weeping.

"Golde . . . does she *remind* you of anyone, Melach?" someone in the group teased.

"Not at all," Melach responded, wiping a tear off his cheek. "Golde could learn a thing or two about a scolding from my Sarah."

He pulled me up from where I was sitting on the sofa and kissed me, full on the mouth, in front of everyone. Including my father.

"All of you, have more wine," Melach exclaimed, still holding onto my waist. "*Vive la France*! Let's celebrate." He kissed me again. "I'll celebrate with *you* later," he crooned in my ear.

"Melach, really," I protested, but it wasn't genuine. He was a little tipsy, a lot happy, and completely irresistible. I bit my lower lip, anticipating his husky promise for later as I watched his nicely shaped backside cross the room.

He sauntered over, whistling as usual, to our new phonograph. We'd purchased it just a few weeks ago, and we both were obsessed with it: Melach, for the music it provided, and me, for the simple fact that we could afford it. Less than a decade after we'd come to this country, we were already prosperous by French standards. Compared to our lives in Poland, we were millionaires.

Melach sifted through his records, choosing which one to play next. I saw him consider "Tell Me" and "With You, I'm Happy" both songs with a lively tempo. His little brother Saul happened to be sitting beside the phonograph, so Melach bent over to ask his advice.

"Ho, Saul—these two songs, I think, will both keep the party going, but which of them do you think . . . ?"

Saul clearly didn't hear him. He sat stiffly, knees pressed together, his focus intent on something . . . or someone . . . across the room. Zofja.

Melach looked over and winked at me. We weren't the only ones with romance in mind tonight.

"All right," Melach said to no one in particular. "Never mind that energetic tempo . . ."

He lifted the needle of the record player and put on "Lovers by the Old Fountain," a languid, dreamy tune. As the violins soared, several couples danced, pressing their bodies together because both the music and the crowded living room required it.

Melach poked Saul in the shoulder. "Go on." He gestured with his head toward Zofja.

ZOFJA MOVED IN with us. Meanwhile, my father departed for Poland after just ten days in Colmar. Melach and I walked him to the train station.

"It's a long way to come for such a short time, Papa," I reproached him.

"I know, I'm truly sorry. But I must get back before the height of the harvest season. The farmers will be ready to sell and trade, and I need to be there. Aviva will need my help in the shop. And politically, well . . . Poland remains uncertain right now."

"I *know* that, Papa. That's exactly why you need to move *here*," I said. I knew I'd spoken sharply, but I was wrestling with a furious mix of love and frustration: Poland had not been kind to my family in the past, and I worried it would not be kind to him in the future.

My father didn't react. He understood my bite and the love that was behind it. The three of us shared a quick, awkward goodbye at the station.

"He'll never move here," I said to Melach, as we watched my father board the train.

"Maybe he's thinking about it. Maybe he didn't say anything, because he needs to talk to Aviva first when he gets back—"

"No, Melach, stop," I interjected. "Thank you, but . . . don't. Don't try to make me feel better."

We stood on the platform, waiting for the train to pull away.

"We'll never see him again," I said.

Melach had learned not to dismiss my premonitions. They were my gift and my burden. Still, he was thoughtful enough to know that it would hardly do to agree, to say that yes, I was probably right, we would never see my father again.

Melach linked his arm in mine. "Let's go home."

Chapter 9
COLMAR, FRANCE
OCTOBER 1929. THE WEDDING

THE WEDDING VEIL would just not cooperate, its gauzy fabric rebelling, refusing to sit properly on my sister's head. Minutes before Zofja's marriage to Saul, I grabbed a handful of hairpins and wrestled the headpiece onto her hair.

"I never should have cut it," Zofja whined.

The 1920s style of chin-length bobs had arrived in Colmar only recently, but Zofja had seized on the new trend from Paris and had done what brides are warned *not* to do: make a major hairstyle change just before their wedding day. Ever the big sister, I'd reminded her of this, multiple times, but Zofja was a font of positivity as her marriage approached. "Of course, it will look right. Besides, it'll be fun."

Now I resisted saying, *I told you so.* Instead, I kissed her on the cheek, careful not to disturb my creation of veil-plus-hairstyle.

"The new hair makes a clear statement, Zofja. You're a modern bride, in a new country, starting a new life with a new husband and a new name. It's perfect."

Zofja's name change involved not just taking her husband's last name. She'd decided to use the occasion to give herself a more French *first* name: Sophie. Of course, all the siblings had an opinion on this. The two eldest, Yakob and Celina, let "Sophie" know how much she'd insulted their heritage by changing it. My brother Yosef and I cheered her decision to assimilate.

The wedding took place on a brilliant late October Tuesday. The crowd gathered at the community center near the synagogue quieted as Rabbi Weber approached the *chuppa,* a simple cloth held up on all four sides with slender posts like a roof, representing the home that the wedding couple will build together.

The rabbi intoned some prayers, and my mind floated as it always did at religious services. From the window, I noted how the sun made the synagogue's rosy sandstone glow, and I admired the building's long, sophisticated lines. Its height reminded me of the tall wooden synagogue in Amshinov, elegant in its own way, with colorful painted carvings and intricate tapestries. But along with my memories of how beautiful the building was, I also tasted, just briefly, the old bitterness that I'd always felt there, crammed in the seats upstairs with my mother and the other women and children, watching the service from a balcony behind wooden bars, while the men and teenage boys worshipped on the main floor below. I guessed that was why my sister chose to hold her wedding at the community center instead of at the synagogue itself. Here, we women could sit where we pleased, not shuttered away behind bars or curtains. *Thank you, Sophie . . . I think Mama would be delighted.*

"*Mazel tov!*" the congregation shouted, ending the ceremony and startling me back to the present. My sister's wedding day.

Many bottles of Alsatian wine were uncorked—Riesling, Pinot Gris, Sylvaner, and Gewürztraminer provided many toasts to the newlyweds. Guests stuffed themselves on tender roast chicken, herring, fried potatoes, and an array of elaborate pastries. I pulled away from the festivities to absorb it all: how people carried themselves when dressed in their finest, a little straighter, a little prouder. How their voices were yes, a little louder—but brighter; their faces, all somehow more true and more alive, lit up from inside, a radiance admittedly helped by the wine. *We are so fortunate. And yet . . .*

"Taking it all in? Wishing you were once again a bride?" My brother Yosef sidled up next to me.

"Oh! Yosef. It's you. No, I was just thinking. Look at all this. It's incredible that we can throw such a lavish party for them. Think of how we grew up. How we started over from nothing . . . how many times?"

"Too many."

"And now we're here. We have jobs and businesses and friends. We're wealthier than we could have ever imagined . . ."

"But wealth becomes you, my dear sister," Yosef teased, pointing at my new dress.

"Thank you." I smoothed the front of my lacy, burgundy-colored outfit. It did look nice, the tone accentuating my own dark eyes and hair and the cut subtly showing my curves. I had asked one of the seamstresses we employed at our shop to make it special for the wedding. It was one of the most chic outfits I'd ever owned and another symbol of our affluence.

"And Melach is tired of me saying this, but sometimes I feel it's almost too good to be true. And I can't rid myself of the feeling . . . that it's all going to somehow just . . . vanish."

Yosef made his usual judgmental "pffft" sound, which he often did as a prelude to pointing out why I was wrong.

"My lovely, know-it-all, little Sarah. This time, but only this *one time* . . . I think you have it wrong." He pecked me on the cheek and rejoined the noisy cheer of the wedding party.

I put my wine glass down. *Enough, Sarah. He's right. For goodness' sake, enjoy it.*

So, I did. I danced till my new dress was sweaty, my fancy shoes pinched my feet, and my hairstyle melted. I had more wine, Pinot Gris, my favorite. As Melach and I walked home late that night, I giggled as I leaned on his arm for support, and I've *never* been a giggling type.

"Did you see everyone's faces when Rabbi Weber blessed these 'two families that are now joined . . . rather, are *once again* joined . . . by matrimony . . .'?"

Now I was beyond giggling, I was whooping with laughter, and Melach was too, our combined hysterics a melody for the otherwise empty streets. As soon as Sophie and Saul had become engaged, the notion of a "double marriage" between the Seibert brothers and the Elkshutz sisters was a delicious subject of community gossip. The congregation had tittered knowingly when the rabbi had to correct himself.

Melach and I were still chuckling at the memory as we approached our building. But instead of pulling out his keys, he stopped us by the door and took both my hands in his.

"During the wedding, I was thinking . . . about us," he said. "Unlike Sophie and Saul, I know we *had* to get married." He curled his thumb under my chin. "But I'm so glad we did."

Maybe it was the wine, or the sweet sincerity of his face, or a delicious, lingering glow of love from the wedding. Or maybe it was just that lock of hair that still fell over his forehead and still made him look so sexy. I led him up the stairs. We said goodnight to the teenage cousin who had agreed to leave the wedding early with our children so they could go to bed. We tumbled into our own bed, kissing, laughing, and getting tangled in our sheets.

Afterward, lying on top of him, I ran my fingers over his profile in the dark.

"What you said earlier . . . I'm so glad too. With the life we've built here. With you."

"Mmmm," he said, his eyes already closed, his breathing stretching out. "Yes . . . good night . . ."

A week later, the U.S. stock market crashed.

Chapter 10
COLMAR, FRANCE
EARLY 1930S. IT BEGINS

DID I SEE it or feel it coming? The Beginning of the End of our perfect, cozy, French life? Perhaps.

For more than a year after the U.S. stock market crash, France was weirdly unaffected. Of course, our politicians said it was all thanks to them.

June 1930: Editorial: "The Daily Record of Alsace."

The simple reason France remains unfazed by the current crisis is this: Our economic policies are simply better balanced. Consider the Americans and the British. Their big, greedy companies rely on money one can't touch— financial systems held up by giant banks and unwieldy stock markets. France, by contrast, has built its post-war economy on a much more reliable footing: small businesses and small-to-medium banks. France prefers gold. One can weigh it. One can see it. We peg our currency to it, and how can one dispute the wisdom of this?

The Anglos should follow our example.

The confident editorial reflected a smug superiority that many people felt, that somehow France had figured out the secret to economic success. It was a tempting attitude to adopt, especially as we read about economic devastation elsewhere and saw no change at all in our own little corner of the world. *Is France really all that superior . . . or are we just lucky so far?* But I didn't spend much time wondering. I had two young children, a husband, a store to manage, and a wide circle of family to enjoy. I was busy. Distracted. And after years of steady prosperity in France, I decided to simply hope it would continue.

It didn't.

By 1931, the economic downturn abroad reached Alsace. Customers either lost their jobs or worried that they might soon be unemployed. They'd come into our store and browse but ultimately decide against buying that new coat or pair of pants. "Just for now," they'd say. "You know . . ." And perhaps then they'd leave their old coat or pants to be mended.

I was confident we could stick it out. I'd helped my father run a store during a war in Poland, after all. We could handle fewer customers. But I *was* worried about something else.

Germany.

Rabbi Weber traveled there often, and his reports to Colmar's congregation were alarming. The crash was having a brutal impact in Germany, he said, unemployment was rising and so was political unrest. The Communist Party was growing, agitating, holding enormous rallies. At the same time, another party was also expanding: The Nazis. And this group, our rabbi said, didn't seem to like foreigners. Especially Jews.

Melach relayed this news to me on a Friday evening, after he attended Shabbat services. My nightmares of Poland galloped back into my sleep that night, of the soldiers, the snow, the fleeing in a horse-drawn cart. I woke up feeling I hadn't rested at all, and wishing it weren't Saturday, our busiest day at the shop. I dressed without my usual attention to my outfit, hair, and lipstick. I clattered down the stairs to the store, already late.

All day, I performed the motions—greeting customers, helping them with selections, advising them on alterations we could make—while my senses were in a heightened, tunnel-like state. I honed in on the way people spoke, their inflection and word choice, how they moved, how they looked at each other and at me. I was gathering clues, churning them over, processing them. What might that person have meant by that comment? Was that customer unusually cool to me, or was she simply having a bad day? Could those people who glanced through the shop window, but didn't come in . . . have ulterior motives? It was exhausting. Finally, I was able to lock the store and cross Rue Vauban to meet Adele for our regular late Saturday afternoon coffee and pie at Pain Pour Tous. I pushed the door open, and took a full, deep breath, for the first time that day.

These Saturday gatherings were a cherished ritual for us both. We'd close our respective shops, enjoy our dessert, and just sit talking, long after our cups and plates were empty. Sometimes, we'd discuss work or happenings in Colmar, but mostly, we caught up with each other's lives. And yes, we indulged in gossip, even though as two respected women of commerce in town, we knew we shouldn't. One frequent target of those less-than-admirable conversations was Claire Mueller, the beautiful but dour owner of Rue Vauban's *other* clothing store, The Alsacienne. Claire had not said as much as "hello" to me, since we'd moved to town more than a decade ago, and I was sure she blamed us for the dead atmosphere of her shop, compared to the bustle of ours. Meanwhile, when Claire came into Adele's bakery, Adele would transform from a convivial business owner into an irritated mother hen, surveilling the young woman as she settled herself at a corner table. Claire, Adele reported, would order a pastry and a coffee, which she would take forever to finish, as she stared longingly at Adele's son. René was a catch, to be sure—a handsome veteran, a widower, a devoted father. I often teased Adele, saying she should at least understand Claire's infatuation.

AS WE SAT down with our espresso and slices of Adele's pear fruit pie, I yearned for those earlier, easy conversations. But I could no longer shut my unease in a drawer, about the Nazis, the Communists, the overall economic and political upheaval not that far away, across the border in Germany. I needed Adele's level-headed understanding and her sympathetic ear.

I did not receive them.

"I know *all about* the problems Germany could create, Sarah. I don't need *you* to tell *me*." Adele pushed back her chair and strode to the window.

I held my fork in mid-air. She'd never spoken to me so harshly. Adele gazed out at Rue Vauban, the people passing by, juggling their shopping bags, finishing their Saturday errands.

"I was eight when they destroyed my neighborhood in the Prussian siege of Strasbourg. That's why we moved to Colmar in 1871. There was nothing left for us. Nothing but rubble." She crossed her arms and hugged herself. "We knew there was a war on, but we were just children. Our parents told us everything would be all right, that it had started as a diplomatic squabble between France and Germany, that it would all be over soon. But one summer day, they went out for a few minutes to check on an elderly neighbor. While they were away, the shelling began, out of nowhere . . . the wood and stone of our home erupted like a geyser after the first shells fell on our block."

Adele's chin dropped to her chest.

"My little sister and I were protected by a miracle—a beam that fell at an angle, preventing us from being crushed. But my older brother Felix took a direct hit on the head and never rose again." Her chest shook in uneven sobs.

I rushed to embrace her, and Adele let me, which was unusual.

"I tried to stop Felix's bleeding, realizing—but not wanting to realize—that it was too late. I held his head in my lap and pressed his wound with all my strength. With an old white kitchen towel. I can still see that towel going from white to pink to red."

I continued to hold her, stroking her back. "Adele. I'm here. And I'm so sorry about your brother. And for stirring up these memories with my own worries. I'm truly sorry. Come. Sit down."

She permitted me to lead her back to the table, scattered with our coffee cups, forks, and half-eaten pie.

"We don't have to talk about this anymore," I said.

"Yes, we do." She sniffled. "Because it could happen again . . . and you and I are among the few brave enough to admit it."

Adele was *almost* right. I hadn't been brave enough, until now. But at that moment, sitting at a café table with my wise, older friend, I let that little dark corner of my soul speak. To say out loud what I had learned as a girl: Desperate people do desperate things. If Germany's situation became more desperate . . .

Adele wiped her eyes on her sleeve. I pulled a clean handkerchief out of my purse and gave it to her. She nodded her thanks and blew her nose.

"I want to talk about it," she said. "I *need* to. After that war, France had to give Alsace to Germany. We left Strasbourg. My parents did their best to start over in Colmar. Perhaps they thought new surroundings would raise fewer memories of my brother. Colmar was an important garrison city under the German regime. Claire Mueller's family, by the way, included some high-level authorities in the occupation government at that time, because Claire's half German and half French. That's why my hackles go up when I see her gaping at my son. I don't want anything from that time touching my life now."

Adele sat back down and poked at the remains of her pie with her fork. "Still, in the first few years of occupation, even I have to admit that the authorities made a concerted effort to win Alsatians over, fixing up old buildings and constructing new ones. They made a lot of improvements."

"In the ten years I've lived in Alsace and Lorraine, I've never heard anyone say anything *positive* about those decades under Germany. I'm surprised to hear *you* say it," I said.

"I know. Once France won the provinces back after the Great War and entered a messy period of being reintegrated, no one dared acknowledge that early on, Alsace did benefit, in some ways, under Germany. But my family never forgave them for the destruction that killed my brother. Besides, the Kaiser's whole goodwill campaign came to an end with the war in 1914. Suddenly, Alsatians were suspect: Where did our sympathies *really* lie; with France or Germany? We were living in a police state, our every move scrutinized. My son was conscripted. To fight for the German side. I thank God every day he wasn't killed."

Adele took a sip of her coffee. Her back was to the window, so she didn't see what I saw: something large and white flashing by. It was a stork, swooping down before it ascended to settle its huge wings and oddly graceful body on a giant nest on a nearby rooftop.

"Look. On top of that building across the street," I said.

Adele contemplated the bird, the symbol of Alsace. A migratory bird that always came home. "Ah. The stork."

The rigidity that had overtaken her body relaxed. She was back to the old Adele, elegant and in control.

"I love seeing those birds. And you can tease me for reading too much into this, but that stork makes me think about this place, this province, the people here for whom no other place on earth could be called home. That no matter which country's been in charge, neither France nor Germany ever seemed to completely trust Alsatians. And so, we've learned to trust only each other."

We watched the stork preen its feathers. I found its presence heartening.

"It was the same for us Jews in Poland," I finally said. "No one trusted us. And we couldn't trust them either."

Russians. Poles. Town officials. Soldiers. Neighbors. I told her our whole story: the lootings, the narrow escapes, Celina's rape, my father's beating. When I'd finished, we sat in a long, comfortable silence.

"Well, Sarah . . ." she finally said, maneuvering a bit of pie on her fork. She sat up straight, with that excellent posture I so admired. She took a bite. "You haven't complimented this week's pie."

"It's delicious. I'll take some home for the boys. But I should go."

Like Adele, I'd had enough traumatic memories for one day.

"Thank you for the pie. And . . . for everything."

IN 1932, THE economic and political threats around us grew, but I paid less attention to them. In the spring, I gave birth to my third child, a plump-cheeked, curly-haired girl we named Annette. Our sons doted on their little sister. Jacques offered to push her pram and to help feed her. André entertained Annette with silly faces and funny songs. Melach would cuddle her and croon one of his old Yiddish melodies until she fell asleep, and then he'd pamper me, rubbing my feet, insisting I recover instead of working, and bringing me little treats from Pain Pour Tous. Adding to the glow that seemed to surround us that year, my sister Sophie had a baby just days before Annette was born, a boy they named Lucien. We were so content, in our growing family, our close community.

We chose not to look at what was happening across the Rhine.

BY 1933, WE had to look. The impact of Germany's politics crossed the river and came to Colmar.

That spring, thousands of German Jews sought refuge from the new Nazi regime, with many of them coming to Alsace. I recognized the hurt, confused looks on their faces. I knew how it felt to be powerless against stupidity, violence, and hatred. At the same time, I was encouraged by the French government's reaction, which went out of its way to welcome the newcomers, by easing rules around identity cards, visas, and work documents.

But this warm reception did not last.

By fall, business groups—*especially* in Alsace and Lorraine—began grumbling about an "invasion" of German Jewish competition, and warning of a "veritable plague for honest French merchants." I heard people openly express these views, right in front of me, in our store. I knew better than to argue or show my anger. And sometimes, they would recognize that they'd fumbled, talking about Jews this way, in front of a Jewish shopkeeper. "Oh, but we don't mean you, Madame Seibert . . . you're French. They're foreign. You're not one of them. It's a completely different situation . . ." But I had been "one of them" not that long ago. Still, I avoided pointing that out. I rang up their purchases and wished them a pleasant day.

Politicians, from the right and the left, increasingly sympathized with these economic complaints, and began passing laws limiting the occupations in which foreigners, mostly meaning Jews, could work. Alsatian newspapers published endless debates on whether the government should crack down on Jewish immigration. Some articles insinuated that the newly arrived Jews might be German spies, darkly reminding readers that Alsace and Lorraine had been returned to France from Germany not that long ago. In several cities, including Metz, Strasbourg, and Colmar, chambers of commerce even organized protests against refugees.

Yes, Colmar.

On the day of the demonstration, Melach and I put a sign on the door that said, "Closed for family matters. We apologize for the inconvenience."

That afternoon, Adele dashed across the street and up to our apartment as soon as the last sign-waving protester had passed. Although I could have easily watched the demonstration from our living room window, I chose to stay in the kitchen and work on our finances. I told Melach it was a waste of my valuable time to observe such idiocy. But the real reason was that watching the protest would have further fueled my already simmering anxiety.

"I *cannot* believe I'm seeing this," Adele said, breathless from running up the stairs, hairs sticking out from her normally smooth, pulled-back style. "I don't know how to help or what to do . . . they are deluded, these people. What can I do for you, Sarah?"

I only had one thought: *We might have to flee.* But the words were too ominous, I couldn't say them, they were stuck somewhere between my lungs and my mouth.

Waiting for my response, I felt Adele vibrating with anger, frustration, her intense desire to help. All right. I would say it.

"There is one thing, maybe," I began, "*if* these outbursts continue, and *if* the next one feels more dangerous than today's little demonstration, you told me once about a place. Your sister, you said, has an empty farmhouse out in the country, one she never uses. So . . . if it happens again and it seems more threatening, could we stay there for a few days? Just until it cools off?"

"Oh!" she exclaimed. "I hope it won't come to that. I do expect people will calm down and be reasonable again. But yes. Of course. If that's what you think you really might need, I will ask her."

Adele being Adele, I knew she would make the best possible case to her sister.

"Thank you," I said. "I'm so grateful."

And I was. But at the same time, the fact that I even had to ask meant that here I was, just a decade after we'd moved to Colmar, already planning our possible escape.

IN 1934 AND 1935, the French government began to expel German refugees who didn't have work papers, items that had become almost unattainable. I thrust the newspaper whose headline had announced the policy into the trash.

"Where are they supposed to go?" I yelled to Melach. "Back to Hitler?"

Melach told me not to worry, to focus on our family's good fortune. We were French citizens, he reminded me, and all our relatives in France had been naturalized before 1930.

"We'll all be fine," he said. "This will pass."

THEN IN 1936, a surprising political shift made me think Melach might be right. France elected a Jewish prime minister. Léon Blum's victory was all people could talk about at Jacques' bar mitzvah a few days later. The fact that Blum had Alsatian roots made it even more satisfying.

Optimism and relief shone in the faces of our guests, who'd gathered at our home after the ceremony. I couldn't help but be infused by their hope. Perhaps what everyone said these days was correct: the Rhine River—that winding, blue-grey border between France and Germany—would be the place where the craziness stopped. Perhaps my adopted nation would, after all, stand by those ideals Melach was always quoting. *Liberty, Equality, Brotherhood.* I decided to absorb the beauty of the moment: my son's bar mitzvah, a lovely gathering, our close friends and family around us. My eldest boy had read the Torah perfectly, and despite the sagging economy, we still could afford a bountiful celebration.

It was especially warm that June day. Even with our windows open, the temperature was rising inside, with the heat of so many people. I headed toward the wine table, in search of a cool glass of Alsatian white. I passed a cluster of men, catching bits of animated conversation.

" . . . actually have a *Jewish* prime minister. They say he's going to give people paid vacations—*paid* vacations, can you imagine? Yes, I know, the industrialists will object, but . . ."

" . . . my family back in the Old Country will never believe it. There's also talk Blum will mandate a forty-hour work week. The whole thing is incredible, really. That France has elected one of *us* to lead them."

Melach was part of the jovial group.

"It's not 'incredible' at all," he said. "Jews already serve on city and town councils in Alsace . . . several even have Jewish mayors. Why *shouldn't* France have a Jewish prime minister?"

A few men argued with him, but most clapped him on the back, saying, "That's it!" and "Yes, he's right." The feeling of promise in the room became a force of its own, expanding our ability to breathe, making us believe anything was possible. I almost floated to the wine table. I poured myself some Pinot Gris, always my favorite. I let its cool, tart dryness sit for a few seconds on my tongue. A child's whine broke into my moment of contented savoring.

"Maman, I'm hot . . . I want to *go*, I need to *go*."

My four-year-old daughter Annette tugged at my skirt. Her chubby face was flushed and her curly hair had transformed into a frizzy nest. Sophie approached with her sons—Lucien, the same age as Annette, and two-year-old Noah. Both boys were whining, and Noah was sucking his thumb.

"I'll take them back to my house," Sophie said. "The boys are getting tired, too. Noah needs a nap. Enjoy yourself. You never relax. You deserve it."

"Thank you. I'll do just that, or at least I'll try. You know me—"

"Humpf," Sophie scoffed. "I *do* know you. But you're just going to have to learn. Come on, children."

Sophie shepherded the children away, and I decided to take her advice, pouring some more wine and reflecting on the extraordinary nature of the day: My thirteen-year-old son reciting the ancient words of the bar mitzvah ceremony juxtaposed with everyone's excitement over Blum's election. I wasn't well steeped in the texts of Judaism, but I knew the basic narrative of our history: time and time again, Jews had been forced to flee when the dominant culture deemed them too numerous, or too prosperous, or simply too different. Now, with a Jewish prime minister, was it possible that a brand-new chapter would be written, right here in France?

I'm thinking like Melach again.

My brothers were making their way through the crowd to the wine table. Yosef helped himself to a Riesling.

Yakob took a Gewürztraminer. "Sister. May we offer two toasts?"

"Of course," I said.

Yakob lifted his glass. "One, to Jacques, my nephew, who performed beautifully today."

We all clinked glasses.

"And second," Yosef said. "*Vive la France* and her new prime minister."

We drank.

THE NEXT MONDAY, I went about my work with an unusual lightness, still glowing from our party and hope from Blum's election. At the end of the day, Melach and I locked the doors as usual and spent a few moments tidying up. Melach was humming, as he often did, and I actually felt like humming myself as I stood at the cash register, tallying up our sales. *Not bad . . . given the inflation and unemployment we're all worrying about these days.*

"What's this?" Melach asked, picking up a newspaper that someone had left behind on a display table. "What's *La Direction Francaise*? I've never seen this before."

I closed the cash register drawer and came over for a look. France had an abundance of newspapers, and Alsace was no different. Melach and I were devoted readers of several local papers; as businesspeople, we needed to know what was happening in Colmar and in the wider province. But this particular paper was unfamiliar. I pulled up my reading glasses hung on a gold chain around my neck.

"The Invasion of France," the headline warned.

I sat down.

> Beware, all true Frenchmen and women. The recent election of an Israelite to the post of prime minister represents a dire threat to this nation. Hordes of dangerous elements—Freemasons, Socialists, Jews, and mixed-race mongrels—are now more welcome than ever in our nation. While these newcomers have been crowding our cities and

staining our countryside for years now, make no mistake: Blum's election is an open invitation to those who want to transform France into a Bolshevik nightmare. They will collectivize agriculture. They will destroy the churches. They will commandeer private businesses. The France we love and cherish—our nation of faith, family, small farms and enterprises—will be destroyed . . .

I pulled off my reading glasses.

"What is it, my dove?" Melach asked. "What does it say?"

He took the newspaper I thrust at him, scanned it, and threw it in the trash.

"Ignore it," he said. "We've never seen this rag before. No one reads this here. Maybe it was accidentally left behind by someone passing through."

Melach returned to the tasks of our regular closing routine—shutting the shades, sweeping the floor.

"Did you count all the cash, or do you want me to do it?" he asked, wiping a spot from the front window.

"It wasn't an accident," I said.

"What? The cash?"

"No, Melach. The newspaper. Someone left it here on purpose."

Chapter 11
COLMAR, FRANCE
SPRING/SUMMER 1938. OMINOUS

ANOTHER BAR MITZVAH celebration, this time for our younger son, André. Another gathering with people packed into our apartment, music playing on the phonograph, and an abundance of food and drink. I was determined to keep the celebration focused where it should be—on André, who had read the Torah flawlessly, displaying both his innate charm and mastery of Hebrew. But our guests kept reverting to the one-and-only topic that season: the spectacular success of Germany's Anschluss with Austria. Sober clouds of conversations hung over the room, and despite my intention to ignore them, I found myself pulled into a group of whispering adults.

" . . . could make the same move in Czechoslovakia now, in that region where there's lots of ethnic Germans who *supposedly* want to join Germany too," a man said, while another asked, "Right, what's that place called?"

"The Sudetenland," someone said.

The tight little circle opened up as Rabbi Weber approached.

"And if France and Britain allow him to have it, we have much to fear."

André's laughter floated past me, along with the giggles of several girls. At age thirteen, my younger boy was already an extremely capable flirt. Rabbi Weber's words contrasted with the teenage gaiety.

"Earlier this week, I made a trip across the Rhine to visit old friends and colleagues. They are frightened. They say this new confederation, Germany-plus-Austria—whatever the Nazis wish to call it—is pushing even harder on the Nuremberg laws. Do you know what these are?"

No one did.

"It means Jewish businesses must be Aryanized. So the Jewish person who built that shop, that factory, that enterprise . . . must let a pure German buy it, at a ridiculous bargain price. Sometimes that Jew is kept on as an employee, sometimes not. But what he created is no longer his."

Many of our friends were small business owners like us, and at this news, we all stiffened. "How dare they?" "What would we do?" "My business is mine. I made it through my own sweat and sacrifice."

Rabbi Weber held up his hand, and the muttering quieted. "And that's not all. Jewish doctors can't treat non-Jewish patients. Jewish lawyers can't practice law. While in Germany, I myself witnessed Jews being forced to perform humiliating tasks in public: scrubbing sidewalks, pulling weeds from between cobblestones in the streets. And this regime is renowned for its record-keeping, so now my German friends all have been issued brand-new identity cards, with a special "J" stamp for *Juden.* All of them also have a new middle name."

He took off his glasses and wiped them, as if he needed to pause, to control his own feelings before he continued.

"Yes. For those who don't possess recognizable Jewish *first* names, the Nazis have given them *very* recognizable *middle* names. So, all my men friends now have the new middle name of *Israel.*"

It was too much to absorb. These events were happening to Jews just like us, and only miles away.

"Rabbi," I finally asked. "What new middle name have they given to Jewish women?"

Rabbi Weber put his glasses back on. He gave me a grave, almost mournful look. "*Sara.* Their new middle name is *Sara.*"

THE HEAVY, HOT weather that summer matched the political climate; a mantle of foreboding that I couldn't take off. The aggression from across the Rhine, the growing acceptance of hate, the rising threat of violence . . . my mind was churning, planning, ever-watchful. I was on alert and fatigued at the same time.

"Let's go to the Vosges, for the afternoon," I said to Sophie one especially warm July day. "I could use an escape from the heat, and business is slow."

Under the cool of fir, spruce, and pine trees, we ambled along a favorite path as our children welcomed the freshness of the woods. Jacques and André were running ahead, climbing boulders, and jumping across streams, while Annette, Lucien, and Noah, screeched with pleasure as they tried to imitate "the big boys" and keep up.

"Everything feels . . . uneasy this summer," I said to Sophie as we walked. "There's talk of war everywhere, and yet no one wants it. No one except the Germans . . ."

Jubilant shouts echoed in the forest. The children had discovered frogs in a pond, and the younger children squealed as my boys splashed about, trying to catch the creatures.

" . . . and when I see all the refugees coming to France now, from Austria and Germany, I think of us in Poland, Sophie. Fleeing in the night . . ."

Rubbing her frozen feet, bumping about in the back of our cart under a black sky. Our father pushing the horses onward to some new place. The ever-hoped-for safe place. What I thought France would be.

" . . . and then I think of our children. We lived through it, but to see *them* live through that? How will we bear it, Sophie?"

"Sophie?"

Sophie was crying, and now I'd ruined what was supposed to be an enjoyable afternoon in the woods with our children. The break, the distraction we both desperately needed.

"Shush, Sophie. Maybe it will be alright. No one in France wants war. The politicians are doing all they can to avoid it. Please don't cry, Sophie. Maybe I'm wrong."

Sophie sniffled. "No. That's the problem. You're always right."

I gave her a handkerchief with a thump of guilt. I should have kept my nightmares to myself. I should have remembered that Sophie's war years in Poland had been just as traumatic as mine, perhaps more so. I had, at least, enjoyed a carefree childhood, but Sophie had been a little girl when our mother died, and then came the war. Her adolescence had been difficult too, she'd confessed to me recently. The Polish–Bolshevik War came so soon after the Great War. All the elder siblings, including me, were in France. Our papa had remarried and seemed focused elsewhere. Much of the time, she had felt frightened and alone.

She needs me to be strong now. I pulled her closer.

"Sophie. Don't cry. I'll manage it. We'll figure it out. I promise."

Sophie leaned into my shoulder, sniffled a few more times, then collected herself as her son Lucien ran toward us with Annette. Born just days apart, the two cousins were inseparable. In their small, sweaty fists, they proudly thrust forward the flowers they'd picked in a mountain meadow.

"Look, Maman, for you. For you."

ON MONDAY, I closed our shop early again. We'd had no customers for hours, as the public embraced the new gift of summer vacations put in place by the Blum government, even though Blum himself was no longer in power.

I locked the door behind me and crossed Rue Vauban, its brown and grey cobblestones emitting heat. I entered Pain Pour Tous, not intending to stay at the bakery long. I just needed bread for dinner and to tell Adele we needed to have a serious talk. I was going to ask an enormous favor, far beyond what we'd already talked about, hiding out at her sister's farmhouse.

I wanted Adele to be our Aryan buyer.

If Jewish businesses in France were going to be confiscated, as they were in Germany, I wanted to "sell" the shop to someone I trusted, who I knew would watch over it and then return it once the madness was over, a madness I knew was coming. Despite widespread hopes for peace, I would not be blinded to the reality I was now certain we'd face.

Adele wasn't behind the bakery sales counter. Instead there was a young woman who was struggling on what appeared to be her first day on the job. A line had formed at the cash register as the new employee cautiously punched each key. Meanwhile, Adele's son René waited on a few people in the café corner. Closely attuned to what his customers might want, René had transformed the morning coffee counter into a small bar in the afternoons. Patrons, mostly men, would stop by for a glass of wine or a beer before they went home. As I stood in line, the bar conversation grew louder.

"I'll tell you; I don't like Alsace being overrun by these refugees. I'll tell you. Hitler's sending us all his Jews, and I'll tell you. We have enough of *those* already."

With a tiny, discreet turn of my head, I tried to figure out who had said this. It was a portly man, whose key feature was a tightly clipped mustache. He took a gulp of wine.

"Ha! That's for certain." One of his companions snorted—a thin younger man, stylishly dressed in a vest and pleated pants. "Why, my cousin in Paris told me you can't even get a job anymore if you work in film, theater, or radio . . . the Jews have *complete* control of those industries and most of the banks too. With more of this rabble pouring in every day, who knows what they'll take over next."

I inched forward in the cashier line. Why was the young woman taking so long? Suddenly, the air in Pain Pour Tous felt too warm and the bakery's normally soothing smells of yeast and coffee were nauseating.

"Worse than that," a small man of indeterminate age intoned, "they're pushing us to *war*. I won't send my sons to fight a war that only Jews and Communists want. No Jewish war, that's what I say."

They drank, grunting and harrumphing their agreement. The fat mustached man then spoke to René, who had been quietly cleaning his countertops and arranging his glassware.

"What say you, René?"

René kept his back to them, stuffing the cork back into a bottle of raspberry liqueur. It seemed to me he was taking a long time to complete the simple act of closing the slim bottle and putting it back in its proper slot on the shelf above. Then he faced them, hands pressed on the bar, appraising the men. As if he were deciding whether it was worth his time to speak at all.

"*I* say that I served in the Great War with many Alsatian Jews who fought bravely. A war that *you*, Antoine," he said to the third, small man, "mostly managed to avoid. *La bonne blessure*, was it? What a shame."

It was a bold insult. I'd lived in France long enough to know that *la bonne blessure*, or "the good wound" was what many a soldier hoped for: to be hurt in battle but not terribly, just enough to be sent home. But I'd also gleaned from customer gossip that some of these wartime injuries were questionable, that they were either faked or self-inflicted. It was widely believed in Colmar that Antoine's occasional limp was in the latter category.

René leaned toward them, his barman's towel on his shoulder, his eyes inviting a challenge. "I *also* say . . . that it's time for this café to close and for the three of you to leave."

With that, he put his full attention back into wiping down his beloved espresso machine with forceful swipes. I finally reached the front of the line. The young cashier rang up my purchases. Did she notice that my hands trembled as I gave her the coins to pay?

NO ONE WAS home when I arrived at our apartment. I staggered up the stairs and threw myself onto the bed. The flowers on the wallpaper wiggled and waved at me.

I closed my eyes to block them out, but I couldn't shut off the tirade from those awful men at René's bar: *More of this rabble pouring in . . . Hitler's sending us all his Jews . . . We have enough of those already . . . No Jewish war, that's what I say!*

I opened my eyes. The room swirled. The wallpaper flowers were no longer waving, they were now leering at me, their centers becoming Cyclops' eyes.

No Jewish war. No Jewish war.

I slid off the bed and stumbled down the hall to the bathroom, certain I was going to be sick. I lay on the floor, waiting to vomit. In a small corner of my mind, I was grateful that Melach and the children weren't home to see me like this. Out of control. Afraid.

The bathroom floor tiles were cool, in contrast to the warm, humid air. The difference helped. I focused on how the floor felt: fresh, reassuring, solid. When I dared to open my eyes, I was thankful to see that the sink and toilet remained fixed in place, instead of spinning like the wallpaper had in our bedroom. Holding onto the sink for support, I rose to my feet. I splashed cold water on my face and caught my image in the mirror; my wrecked hair, my blotchy skin, and the muddy circles below my eyes.

The madness isn't coming. It's already here.

Chapter 12
COLMAR AND FAVERNEY, FRANCE
SEPTEMBER 1938. HIDE

LIKE AN IMPATIENT toddler, I squirmed in my chair, not absorbing any of the wisdom Rabbi Weber was trying to impart to his audience. I was attending Friday night worship only out of guilt: My father-in-law had not-so-subtly noted recently that he couldn't remember the last time he'd seen me at the synagogue.

As the rhythmic stream of chanted prayers went on and on, drowsiness replaced my restlessness. Women and children had to sit in the building's upper balcony, and the September sun had made the air warm and stuffy. Now, miniature bricks seemed glued to my eyelids, so heavy I couldn't possibly keep them open. My chin dropped to my chest, the movement jerking me awake. I peeped at those around me, hoping no one had seen me fall asleep. Luckily, it appeared my embarrassing little nap had gone unnoticed, and better yet, the service was over. But why was Rabbi Weber hesitating?

"There is something this congregation needs to know," he announced.

The rustling noises that had started as people stood up and prepared to leave stopped.

"On the wireless this afternoon there was news of concern. Our own Prime Minister Daladier and British Prime Minister Chamberlain have signed an agreement in Munich with Hitler, to give him a free hand in Czechoslovakia. Monsieur Daladier is uncomfortable with these 'Munich Accords' but Monsieur Chamberlain says they mean 'Peace with honor' and 'Peace in our Time.'"

Rabbi Weber's angular face mirrored the anxiety of the faces before him. "I fear Monsieur Chamberlain is wrong."

THE NEXT DAY, Saturday, I headed straight for Pain Pour Tous after I closed up shop. I was drained, both emotionally and physically. Saturday was always my busiest day at work. Most of our Jewish employees would take the day off for Shabbat, so I was often on my own on the shop floor. But among our non-Jewish customers, Saturday was devoted to errands and shopping, and I wasn't about to be closed for business when Rue Vabuan was bustling with potential shoppers. Adele held the bakery door open, encouraging her remaining few customers to straggle out. After a cheerful *Au Revoir!* to the last person, she ushered me in and locked the door.

"Oh my. It's nice to call it a day and to see you. So . . . coffee? Tarte?"

"No, thank you, Adele. I just . . ."

She probably thought that I wanted to discuss, once again, the use of her sister's farmhouse as a refuge—I was planning to ask for a lot more than that. I hesitated, and Adele right away caught my discomfort.

"Hold on. I think you need more than just coffee," she said.

Adele went behind the bar. She pulled out two glasses and poured pear liqueur into each.

I relished the liquid's sweet burn. She sat across the table, waiting. *Here goes.*

"First, the farmhouse. I'm so grateful. And yes, I think we'll need it, at some point, maybe soon—"

"The farmhouse is fine," Adele interrupted, which she never did. I think we were all on edge that day, with the Munich accords and the increasingly dubious promises that each Hitler land-grab would be the last. "It's all set. I've checked with my sister. You're welcome to use it. She's a city girl, she never goes to the country, and the house is enormous. There should be plenty of space for you and your extended family—which is to say, a lot of people," she teased, then turned more serious, twirling the base of her liqueur glass. "My sister did ask that if you *were* to hide there and someone *did* discover you . . . that you should claim you are squatting there. That the owner of the home had no idea. Just so . . . you know."

I knew. Adele's sister didn't want to be responsible for sheltering a substantial group of Jews. I recognized the potential risk, even though everyone around me said repeatedly, *France is not Germany.* That here, we were all "equal" and "brothers," according to our revolutionary creed.

Perhaps. But with the rise in antisemitic language and behavior I'd seen in Colmar over the past year, I was no longer sure. Adele seemed relieved that I understood the terms. She continued talking, rapidly—almost babbling. She must have sensed somehow that I was there to discuss something bigger than the farmhouse. Much bigger.

"The barn even has a secret cellar, large enough to use as a hiding space for a short time in an absolute crisis. But I still don't think you'll need them. The house or the hiding space."

"Why not?" I asked, emboldened by the alcohol. "You grew up in German-controlled Alsace. You told me once, quite harshly as I remember, not to lecture you about Germany and what it might do. Why are you so confident that they won't come marching across the Rhine tomorrow?"

Adele continued to roll the stem of her now-empty glass between her fingers. "Because France will do almost anything to avoid war." She sounded as if she had rehearsed the phrase to ease her own escalating fears. "The last war ended just *twenty* years ago. Almost a million and a half Frenchmen died. Think of all those young lives cut short. We're the most depopulated country in Europe." Her voice wavered. "So, a boy born near the end of the *last* war, like my grandsons, would be old enough now to fight the next. I think that's why Prime Minister Daladier and the rest of them will do whatever it takes to keep the peace."

Her grandsons. She'd raised them since they were babies. That's why she was clinging to every promise of peace, however thin and shredded it might be. She *had* to believe.

"I hope you're right. More than anything, I hope you are," I said. "Thank you for the farmhouse. But there's something else I have to ask. A plan for the longer term. You may need more liqueur."

She sat up even straighter than usual at that, beyond her already perfect posture. She uncorked the bottle and poured us a thumb's length more.

"I want to sell you our store," I said. "I want you to be our Aryan buyer, to protect it, in case we have to leave."

I had wondered whether saying these words out loud might intensify the scrabbling claws of anxiety inside me. Instead, voicing the plan calmed me. I focused on what I needed to do, and I was ready to do it. Now, I just needed to convince Adele.

"What? I've never heard of such a thing. What's an Aryan buyer? What are you *talking* about?" she asked.

"It's happened already, in Germany and Austria. Rabbi Weber told us about it. When the Nazis take over, they make Jews sell their businesses. To non-Jews, at an absurdly low price. Or they simply confiscate it. So, before any of that happens, *if* it happens . . . we can draw up paperwork stating that we legitimately sold our store to the proprietors of Pain Pour Tous. You're right across the street, so it makes sense that you might want to buy a neighboring business. Then after the war, we'll take it back."

It was an enormous request. And given her initial reaction, I thought she might need some time to consider it, to discuss it with her husband Claude and son René. Instead, she finished her liqueur and plunked her glass down.

"Done," she said. "But must I keep reminding you? There's no war yet. And I'm still optimistic . . ."

"I know, I know," I said. "Everyone in France wants to avoid war. I've heard it a hundred times."

"Right," Adele said, and I saw that she needed this discussion to be over. She stood and gave me a rare hug. "I have to go. We can figure out the sale paperwork later. I'll talk to Claude and René, but I know they'll agree. And of course, you can borrow the farmhouse." She fingered the silver cross around her neck. "I will pray every single day that you won't have to use it."

IN EARLY NOVEMBER, I felt it: that familiar sickening fog, beginning in my mid-section and settling down in my chest. Melach and I were alone in the kitchen. It was a Saturday night. The boys were out with friends, while six-year-old Annette was already asleep. The dinner dishes were done. As usual, Melach had washed them.

He made nervous small talk, as he always did when he hoped to avoid a difficult conversation that he knew was coming. "I had a nice walk with my brother this afternoon, in the Vosges. Beautiful. It's hard to believe it's early November. But winter will be here soon, and—"

"And after winter's over, we'll be at war," I broke in. "Look at what's happening right over the river. Only a dozen miles from here. *Look.*"

"But . . ."

I knew what he would say, and he said it. "I respect your intuition, my dove, really . . . I do. But—"

"And when war *does* come, I've found us a place to hide," I continued. "At least for a time."

"To hide! What? Where?"

"Faverney. In Lorraine. Farther from the border, so we can re-group when the Germans cross the Rhine. It's a large, old farmhouse that belongs to Adele's sister. She never uses it."

"Who do you want to hide there, besides us?"

"All of us. Your parents. Our brothers and sisters. Their children. If . . . *when* the Germans invade, at least we can make a plan together. There's even a secret compartment in the barn."

"That's *a lot* of people," Melach said.

"We won't be there forever. Just to buy a little extra time."

I felt him relenting, preparing to accept my idea. "Maybe we won't need it," he said, a final, faltering hope.

"We will."

JUST DAYS LATER, on November 12th, we left Colmar for the farmhouse in Faverney. As we waited for the train, Annette tugged on our coat sleeves, whining and unhappy. She and her schoolmates had made plans for the day and now she'd be left out of the fun.

"But why, Maman? I wanted to go to school today, to see my friends. It's a school day, not a holiday. I don't want to leave. I don't like farms. I don't like farmhouses."

Jacques and André were quiet. The news had filtered quickly to Alsace: how on November 9th and 10th, a wave of anti-Semitic violence had exploded in cities across Germany, Austria, and Czechoslovakia. The windows of Jewish-owned businesses were smashed and the buildings were ransacked. Synagogues were blown up and burned. More than thirty thousand Jewish males were arrested. Anti-Jewish laws were tightened. The papers called it *Kristallnacht*. The night of broken glass. Nazi officials described the attacks as "spontaneous," but no one in the Alsatian Jewish community believed it.

"It's time," I told my extended family on November 11th, and no one argued with me after Kristallnacht. Within days, we all had arrived at the farmhouse; my two brothers and two sisters, Melach's parents and his four siblings, and everyone's spouses and children. The house, although sizable, felt crowded. The children ran around outside, and I worried about the noise attracting attention. So, they ran around inside, and I worried they'd break something. I would yell at them to stop, then felt guilty and would try to invent games to keep them occupied but quiet. They were just children, after all—their routines had been interrupted, and they must have sensed the tension of their elders. Meanwhile, the other women resented preparing daily giant meals for our crowd, while the men didn't have enough to do. Melach fretted about our store back in Colmar, which we'd closed down, putting a "gone on vacation" placard on the door.

"Mid-November is an odd time to take a vacation," he had groused, as he put up the sign. My brother Yakob was also unhappy about leaving his shop in Metz. Meanwhile, my brother-in-law Shevah grumbled endlessly. One night at dinner, he confronted me.

"So *now* what?" he asked. "How long do we sit here? Where are the Nazis, Sarah? I haven't heard any German boots marching outside, has anyone else?"

His words unleashed the others, a chorus of everyone speaking at once, complaining about the impact of our ill-timed escape on their businesses, their children's schooling, and the uselessness of being cooped up together for days. *For nothing,* they scolded. Only Melach and Sophie kept their thoughts to themselves. That night in bed, Melach did exactly what I needed him to do: He simply listened, as I lay, agonized.

"I was so certain after Kristallnacht that Alsace was next . . . that they'd come charging across the river the next day. Smashing our store, arresting you and the boys. And that some in Colmar would welcome them. Blaming us for pulling them into war. I've had nightmares about people like that Claire Mueller saying, 'Welcome, Germans. Let me show you where the Jews are.'"

Melach made comforting, shushing noises until I fell asleep.

Exhausted from the whole ordeal, I woke late the next morning. Melach was gone, but he'd left a note on his pillow.

> *My Dove:*
> *I'll be back soon. I've gone into town on a rickety old bicycle I found in the barn. We've been isolated from what's happening out here in the country, so I thought it might help us decide our next steps if I went to buy a newspaper in the village.*
> *Love,*
> *Melach*

From the kitchen downstairs came the clatter of dishes, chairs scraping, and people talking. I was hungry, but I wasn't ready to face my family's wrath again. Eventually, though, the smell of toast and coffee won out. I pulled my robe around me and crept into the kitchen, hoping no one would notice me. They didn't . . . in fact, what was this? My whole clan was crowded around the table, and they seemed cheerful, even laughing. I peered around someone's shoulder. There was the newspaper Melach had bought.

A headline in massive letters read:

FRANCO-GERMAN NON-AGGRESSION PACT SIGNED YESTERDAY. WAR AVERTED.

Chapter 13
COLMAR, FRANCE
FEBRUARY 1939. DECISION

THE MEN CROWDED into our living room, their body heat making the air warm even though it was a fiercely cold winter night. Melach had agreed to host a meeting of several dozen members of the synagogue with Rabbi Weber after Hitler's recent speech made a terrifying promise:

The war that comes will bring the destruction of the Jewish race in Europe.

I was the only woman there. The other wives were not invited, but this was my home, after all. I wasn't going to cower in the kitchen like some servant girl. As a compromise, I pulled up a chair at the edge of the room. This time, I would not offer my opinion, although I knew Melach would have welcomed it. But I needed time to absorb. To think. To plan.

I'd never seen Rabbi Weber so uneasy. "I am not a politician," he told the assembled men repeatedly, his usual graciousness fraying. But they persisted, arguing he'd lived through two wars involving Germany—and he'd been a German citizen himself when France lost Alsace in 1871. Plus, he was their spiritual leader, and they wanted his guidance.

"What do you make of it, Rabbi? My wife hasn't stopped crying."

"What should we do, Rabbi? You understand these Germans, you've lived among them."

"If there is war, what about our sons?"

Jacques. The notion that my husband and brothers might have to sign up for military duty was frightening enough, but my son was another story.

You can't have him. Not my child.

"Hold on, everyone," my brother Yosef shouted, cutting through the hubbub. "Just *hold on.* War could still be avoided. We've all been watching the politics. The diplomacy. And if the worst does happen, it will be short, and France will win."

He leaned over to Melach, and his tone softened. "It would be over well before Jacques is old enough."

But many of the men present were less optimistic. They hurled their concerns, their questions at Rabbi Weber.

"What about America?"

"Is there still safe passage to Switzerland?"

"Shanghai is a place where you can land without papers."

"Yes, Rabbi—maybe we should leave for China before it's too late. What do you think?"

Then to my surprise, Melach spoke up, loud enough to dominate the room full of rumbling men. "*No.* We're not leaving France, the first country ever to give Jews full rights. Liberty, *Equality*, and Brotherhood—remember? Think of how you live now, compared to whatever Old Country you might have come from. We're not marginalized in Jewish ghettos; we make our homes among everyone else. We're rich here beyond our wildest imaginations. We've raised our children here, and they speak French like natives. They have friends who are Catholic, Protestant. Can you imagine this happening anywhere else? *Anywhere?*"

For the first time, the room was quiet.

I guessed what they were thinking: Melach Seibert, the synagogue's most relaxed, jovial member, was taking a firm stand.

"The Seibert family stays. We're *French*. We stay in France," he concluded.

Some men grumbled in disagreement. Others seemed fortified by Melach's speech, saying, "Hear, hear!"

"What do you think, Rabbi?" someone asked.

Rabbi Weber knitted his long fingers together and regarded the faces of the men before him. I noted how his eyes rested for just a moment on each of them. His community. His people.

"I have tried to express this before, but you do not seem to understand. I can teach you the meaning of the Torah and guide you spiritually. But I cannot—and *will not*—say whether you should stay or go."

Disappointment settled on the group, a heavy quiet. This was not what they came for.

"Do you at least have a prayer for us, Rabbi?" someone finally asked.

Rabbi Weber hesitated, but not for long. "I pray for abundant peace. And if war comes, I pray our country will be strong and protect her people." He paused. "*All* of them."

OUR APARTMENT ON Rue Vauban was extra-crowded that spring and summer of 1939. Someone from Poland was always seeking shelter. They brought alarming news of a country now squeezed between two giants, with rumors that Germany and Russia were colluding to invade Poland together and then split it, each gaining their old Polish territories back.

One rainy July morning, we were awakened early by bumping and movement in the kitchen. A family from Melach's hometown of Lodz, Poland, had arrived the night before. Melach had known Aaron Levy since childhood, and our two families had enjoyed a long, late night of eating, drinking, swapping stories, and reminiscing.

"They must be helping themselves to food, but they're awfully noisy about it," I groaned, rolling back into my pillows.

"I'll go give them a hand," Melach said.

The kitchen was next to our bedroom, so I heard him say, "But . . . Aaron. You just arrived yesterday. Why are you getting ready to leave? Is something wrong? You're welcome to stay. Let me find you some breakfast, some coffee."

"You've been so hospitable. We'll never forget it. But we need to go," Aaron said.

The couple's two young children picked up on the word *breakfast*.

"Papa, we're hungry. Please, Papa, can we have some breakfast . . ."

"It'll just take a minute," Melach said as I heard cabinet doors open and close. "Let me at least get you some bread—"

"No, thank you. We really must be off,"

"Papa, Maman . . . breakfast . . ."

Now the noise from the kitchen was a small commotion. *Ugh. I'm awake . . .*

I shuffled into the room, a bathrobe pulled about me, briefly remembering what my hair must look like. I always needed a few minutes to get my curls under control, which they never were, first thing in the morning.

"What's going on? Who wants breakfast?" I asked. I saw their suitcases by the front door. "Why are you leaving so soon?"

I went to the stove and began making coffee.

"No, don't bother with coffee, Sarah," Aaron's wife Rebecca said. "We're so grateful, really. But we must go. Our boat leaves Marseille for Canada in a week, and we *cannot* miss it. Come, children. We'll find something to eat at the train station."

Melach pressed some French francs into Aaron's hand. "Good luck."

The Levys left in a rush of apologies and thanks. It was not even six in the morning. I tucked a wayward strand of frizzy hair behind my ear, watching out the window as the family hustled down the street. Long after they were out of sight, I remained.

"People never stay long anymore," I reflected. "Remember how they used to live with us for months, while they established themselves, found jobs, while waiting for their citizenship? Now, most of them are passing through France for somewhere else. Somewhere"—I kept my back to him—"somewhere safer."

He came up behind me and kissed my neck. "It's different for them. They're not French. We *are*." He put his arm around my waist while the neck kisses became more insistent. "And . . . *you* are beautiful in the early morning, still all scruffy and barely dressed."

He picked me up easily, like he had that very first time, twenty years ago. He carried me back to bed.

THREE WEEKS LATER, he was gone.

"I'll be fine," he said, perspiring as he rushed about the apartment in the August heat, packing a few last items. He stopped to contemplate a framed photograph of me and the children. He wrapped it carefully in a handkerchief and put it in his knapsack. "Remember, it's just a *partial* military mobilization. The government's only trying to send a message that France is ready. Just in case."

"You didn't have to sign up right away," I said. "You could have waited—"

"My brother signed up early too. And many other men from the synagogue. You know."

I did. Melach and the others who joined quickly were trying to prove that Jews were patriotic French citizens, just like during the Great War. I slogged into our bedroom and lay down. The sheets smelled like Melach; male and musky. His pajamas were folded neatly on his pillow. I was overcome, but not with weeping. Instead, I was weighted by a feeling more powerful than simple sadness: doom. Melach continued bustling about. Then the shuffling, scraping, opening, and closing noises of his preparations stopped. He came into the bedroom, where I remained curled up in the fetal position.

"Sarah? What are you doing?"

"I feel it," I said. "It's that cloudy *something*. It's about you being mobilized, but it's more than that. Something heavier—darker—although I can't name it."

The nauseating fog had been building up in my chest and stomach all day, more intense than ever. Now, cool goosebumps formed on my back, despite the summer warmth.

"My Sarah," he said, dropping his pack and lying down next to me, wrapping my body completely with his. He murmured into my hair in that rich, sweet voice of his. "If this *does* lead to war, everyone says it'll be over soon, and we can get back to our lives."

I turned and muffled my face into his chest. "*Everyone* . . . is often wrong."

Chapter 14
COLMAR, FRANCE
SEPTEMBER 1939. IT'S WAR

THE NEXT DAY, I worked at the shop without Melach for the first time in almost twenty years. I kept forgetting he wasn't there. Dozens of times, I started to say over my shoulder: *Melach, could you help this customer? Do you remember where we put the men's undershirts? Should we close up now, for lunch?*

Without his cheerful presence, I was flat inside. I put on a friendly mask for my customers and somehow ground through the day.

That evening, I locked the store and climbed the stairs to our apartment, my face and body drooping from the effort of pretending all day: *I'm fine, Madame, how are you? Yes, Monsieur, I'd be happy to help you with that. Yes, Melach left yesterday, thank you for asking.*

As I approached our apartment, I put the mask back on, to reassure my children. Their father and uncles had departed for a *possible* war, in a *partial* mobilization, I had told them repeatedly. I'm sure sixteen-year-old Jacques recognized the stiff smile on my face and heard the falseness in my tone. I also think he *chose* to believe my promises, because if the war wasn't short—as everyone swore it would be—he would have to fight.

I paused at the entrance, pulled my shoulders back and my chest up. Ready . . . but what was this? I opened the door to laughter and music from inside. There, standing on a kitchen chair, was André bellowing out a song that played endlessly on the radio called "We Know That We Will Win It." A stirring piece of government propaganda, the song vowed that the Germans would be quickly defeated "like dogs," it said. André perfectly impersonated the man who sang it, puffing out his chest and shouting the lyrics in the man's overly vigorous, ultra-masculine delivery. I joined in the laughter at his rendition, and while I was not at all sure that "we would win it," as the song said, I appreciated its help in easing their anxiety . . . and my own.

The next morning, Jacques offered to quit school to work at the store.

"No, Jacques, your education is your future. I can manage," I said.

But without Melach, I soon relented. My husband was a hard worker, and his absence was felt. Jacques came to work with me. André was jealous. "No more sitting in class. Lucky," he'd grouse as he prepared to leave for school in the mornings.

Jacques would pretend to enjoy the joke, but I knew he would have preferred to stay in school. He was a quiet intellectual, who loved studying history, politics, and science. Unlike some boys, Jacques had never been drawn to tales that glorified war. He'd grown up hearing my own stories about wartime Poland and had absorbed my opinion, that glory was a gloss used to paint over horror, so that young men would sign up to fight.

My darling Jacques. While I continued to project my usual steadiness and confidence for the sake of my younger children, my oldest knew me better. He sensed the effort it took to keep up that facade. And so, in addition to helping at the store, he tried to take his father's place at home.

"Annette, let's go. I'll walk you to your friend's house."

"Leave those dishes, Maman, I'll wash them. Just like Papa always did, right?"

"I'll be back down to the shop in a few minutes, promise. I'm just chopping these vegetables for dinner."

Yes, he even began cooking. Everyone welcomed Jacques' efforts in the kitchen, his meals were already far more palatable than mine.

"This is wonderful, where did you learn to do this?" I had to ask one night, after a particularly delicious quiche he'd made. He glowed at the praise.

"Guess."

"I can't . . . oh. Adele."

"Yup. She's been teaching me while we're closed for lunch, and when you're down in the cellar . . . working . . ."

Jacques knew he was not to tell his brother and sister what I was doing down there: making bundles of non-perishable food and merchandise if we had to flee.

Just like in Poland.

I got up from the table, to kiss him on the cheek. "I'm so proud of you. For this meal and . . . everything."

I began leaving him in charge of our business almost daily. If customers wanted to talk with me, he'd say that I was out "making deliveries." But really, I was patrolling Colmar's shops. I was buying things we didn't sell, like dried and canned food, small tools, and emergency essentials such as gauze pads and matches. From our own inventory, I was setting aside practical clothes, warm outwear, and shoes. I scoured flea markets for old sheets and blankets to assemble items together for easy transport. Each package must contain a bit of everything; food we could eat, goods we could either sell for cash or trade for food. Once I'd selected what I felt was the right mix, I'd tie everything up.

As I worked in the cellar, its smell brought me back to Poland; the odor of root vegetables, of damp tools, of earth that never saw the sun. I'd often been afraid down there—a motherless girl, shivering in the dank darkness, hiding from robbers or soldiers. Now, twenty years later, I wondered whether doing the same preparations for the same reasons would haunt me. It didn't. Watching my pile of packages in the musty cellar grow larger, I felt powerful. Ready.

ON THE FIRST day of September, I was down in the cellar, putting together a special packet of more luxurious items; watches, high quality fabrics, women's silk stockings. These I regarded as rainy-day insurance: If we were unable to work for a long time, I could sell these fancier goods at a high price. While war means struggle and deprivation for most people, a few always profited from it, and I'd be ready if they longed for satin and lace. Meanwhile, Jacques was upstairs at the shop's back counter by the cash register, whistling the way Melach often did.

The doorbell's normal chime was cut short when someone opened the door quickly and slammed it shut. The person ran to the back counter.

"Jacques. Where's your mother? I need to see her immediately."

"Madame Chastain, she's not here. She's out on business."

Adele. I charged up the stairs. Jacques stared as I came out of the cellar, and I read the question in his eyes: Should Madame Chastain know about our secret project? I hadn't told him yet that Adele was already well informed. As our store's Aryan buyer, she would be protecting whatever bundles I didn't take with me, when and if we had to escape.

"It's all right, Jacques. And as you can see, I'm right here, Adele. What is it? My goodness, you're out of breath."

"Germany has invaded Poland. It's war."

Poland. My father. Papa.

Meanwhile, tears pooled in Adele's eyes, then fell down her face in fat, uncontrollable drops.

Jacques handed her a handkerchief. "Madame Chastain . . . if Hitler wants to take Poland, maybe . . . that's not so surprising . . . and . . . at least he's not invading France—?"

"France and Britain gave a protection guarantee to Poland this spring. If violated, they promised to go to war. The entire city of Strasbourg is being evacuated now, along with other communities who are right on the border."

"Oh."

Adele continued to weep as I stood in horror-struck silence. My father. Amshinov. His family. Could I go to him? No. Impossible. I had my own family. Besides, what could I do, against the world's mightiest military machine?

"You're not quite sixteen, Jacques," Adele said, between sobs. "But my grandsons . . . Frédéric is eighteen, and Henri is twenty-two. Do you understand?"

Jacques nodded. "Yes. The age of conscription is twenty. So, Henri will have to . . . but maybe it won't last long, Madame Chastain. Everyone says it will be short."

Adele looked doubtful, but she was too polite to contradict him. She blew her nose, collected herself, and turned toward me.

"Oh, Sarah. Poland. Your father. I'm so sorry, I have been so distraught over my boys, I didn't even think about that. I'm so, so sorry." She pulled me into a hug.

I couldn't return her embrace.

SOMEHOW, LATER, I managed to push my terror over my father's fate into a small side corner of my being. I would panic later. I heard my mother's words: *Focus on what you can do, and do it.*

I would reassure and protect my children as best I could.

I stayed upstairs with Jacques for the rest of the day. I didn't want him to be alone. Both of us heard non-stop talk from customers about the evacuation of Strasbourg, along with all the little towns right next to the Rhine River. People described fields full of crops that would be left untended during harvest season . . . farm animals and pets who would have to fend for themselves . . . and businesses, factories, and shops simply abandoned. Colmar was a bit too far from the border to be included in the evacuation, but more than three hundred thousand of our fellow Alsatians had two days to pack up and go. One customer showed us a copy of the map the government had put out, detailing an intricate evacuation strategy, in which each border town was matched with a host community in southern France. There were designated meeting places, transportation plans, and welcome centers for the evacuees along the way. The entire city of Strasbourg, for example, would go to the southwestern city of Périgueux, while the prestigious University of Strasbourg—professors, students, books and all—would find a temporary home in Clermont-Ferrand.

"Hearing about all these plans makes me feel a *little* better, Maman," Jacques said later in the day. "I mean, yes, it's a massive disruption, but at least the French government seems to be really looking out for Alsatians."

I told Jacques what I knew he wanted to hear. Yes, the evacuation outline was impressive, it did look like the government was doing its best for the citizens of its easternmost provinces, and I was glad he found some solace in those plans.

"We'll have to find a way to explain everything to Annette," I added.

She would hear about it soon enough, and it would be better if she heard it from us. But how do you tell a seven-year-old girl, whose beloved Papa was already mobilized, that the long-feared war was now here?

"MAIDELEH . . ." I STARTED, using my father's old term of affection, as we sat down to eat. "The war that we hoped wouldn't come . . . is coming." I leaned over and stroked her curly auburn hair.

Annette looked alarmed but not terrified. So far, so good. "Will we be all right? What about Papa? Will Germans shoot at him? Will scary soldiers come to Colmar?"

I hesitated, wanting to choose my language carefully. But in those few empty seconds, Jacques jumped in.

"Annette. Let me explain. The French government has put out a great thing called an evacuation plan," Jacques said. "That means the government is doing its *very* best to take care of Alsatians *especially*. It's sending them to special safe places. Like our Aunt Pauline, in Strasbourg, Papa's sister. They're sending her to a southern city called Périgueux with all her neighbors. And a few mayors and other trustworthy people will stay behind to make sure important buildings in Strasbourg and other towns are protected and to prevent looting."

"What's looting?"

"It's when bad people break into your store and take what they want," he said.

Annette stopped eating. "Will people break into *our* store? I don't want bad people to break into our store. Can you stop them? Will *we* have to evacuate? I don't want to leave Colmar."

Instead of comforting her, we had done the opposite, and now Annette was sitting up straight, tears forming in her eyes, clearly starting to panic. Jacques and I shared a look of dismay, recognizing our mistake but too consumed by our own fears to fix it.

But before Annette could completely dissolve, André put his fork down, leaned back in his chair, and folded his hands behind his head. "My dear little mademoiselle. Don't worry! Colmar will be fine. We're staying right here; we don't even need to evacuate. Besides, we have brave, tough soldiers like Papa and Uncle Yosef and Uncle Saul, who will punch those Germans right in the nose."

I had long admired André's smooth ability to sweet-talk anyone. Classmates, teachers, police officers . . . and now, his frightened little sister.

Annette sniffled. "But . . . but . . . what if some of them sneak past Papa and the uncles and come to our store? Then what? André, *then* what?"

"Why, *then*"—André dramatically glanced around—"then the German soldiers would have to deal with *Maman*."

We all laughed, even me.

On September 3, France and Britain officially declared war on Germany.

Chapter 15
COLMAR, FRANCE
NOVEMBER 1939. THE LETTER

Dear Sarah,

I am writing with terrible news: Your father and his entire family have been killed.

Not long after Hitler declared war on Poland on September 1st, his tanks rolled into Amshinov. Our village and our country didn't have a prayer. This new Germany is a mechanized monster. Nothing can stop them.

Right away, they let us know who was in charge, that our leaders would no longer be leading us. They held a mass execution that included the mayor, the village doctor and two priests.

Then, tragedy upon tragedy.

On Yom Kippur, in late September, your father, his wife, and their three children went to the synagogue. The Nazis waited until it was full of worshippers. Then they burnt it to the ground. There were no survivors.

I'm fortunate to have called your father a friend. He was kind, generous, and did his best to be cheerful right up until the end.

I send you my deepest regrets.

Piotr

Chapter 16
COLMAR, FRANCE
LATE MAY 1940. DEPARTURE

DIRTY PLATES, POTS, and silverware created a sloppy pile in my kitchen sink, a mess due to the fact that nine of us were now crowded into our apartment on Rue Vauban. Celina and her family had fled Sedon for Colmar in early May, as Nazi forces shocked the world, smashing through Holland and Belgium, then simply going around the fortresses and bunkers of France's Maginot Line, mocking their promise of protection. Celina plunged her hands into the soapy water, while I sat at the kitchen table. I had not yet truly mourned our father's death. And now I was saying good-bye to my children.

"I'll wash them, Sarah. I know with Melach away, you've had to learn how to do it again," she teased.

I appreciated her attempt to be lighthearted. But I couldn't respond. My entire being was focused on the question that scraped at me: *Who leaves their children in the middle of a war?*

Not Celina, that was certain. She would never consider doing so, and yet I was determined to leave, tomorrow. I had arranged with some friends who had a truck to go south to the city of Vichy, where Melach and I had business contacts. I'd bring with me most of the bundles I'd been accumulating in the cellar for months. The dried and canned food we would keep for ourselves; the clothes, shoes, and other items we would use to set up a small shop. And the time to move was *now* before France capitulated. The bulky packages were our key to survival. I had to get them to Vichy quickly. Once the Nazis came, it would be too late. Soldiers took what they wanted in wartime, I'd learned that in Poland. If my plan worked, it would keep our family from becoming destitute. If it didn't . . .

I pushed that possibility away. Doubt was a luxury of peacetime. My plan would work. And I would be back in just a few days. That was the story I told myself, over and over. But the question never left. It was always there, singing in the background, cruel and taunting:

Who leaves their children in the middle of a war? Only the worst kind of mother . . .

Me.

THE MORNING OF my departure, my body steered me toward the kitchen to make coffee, my mind already reviewing the details of my plan. The truck. Our friends. The trip. Vichy. I barely registered the shush of someone's soft footsteps.

"It's barely light outside," Celina admonished in her gentle way.

"I know. I couldn't sleep."

"I understand. You must be anxious."

I continued to face the stove. I couldn't look at her. Or anyone.

"Do you want some coffee?" I asked, flatly.

"You don't have to do this," she said. "We can stay together, then leave together . . . *if* it even comes to that."

"Don't be ridiculous, Celina, of course it's going to come to that. You were in Sedan yourself, you saw France folding with your own eyes. And someone has to keep this family fed. Someone has to make a plan, to keep us from starving. That someone obviously is not going to be you . . . or your *husband*."

I regretted the remark as soon as it left my mouth. I kept my back to her, ashamed. Celina's warm hands landed on my shoulders, and she turned me around. I saw in her face that I was forgiven. She hugged me.

"We'll take care of your children. You'll be back from Vichy soon. You know it's the right thing to do. You *know*."

A truck pulled up outside with my travel companions and dear friends Raphael and Micheline Goldstein. They were a fun-loving older couple who ran a butcher shop on Rue de l'Ours, right next to Rue Vauban. Raphael and Micheline were frequent guests at the many parties held at our home, and they were often the last to leave. I leaned out the window.

"*Bonjour* Sarah," Micheline called up to me, quietly because it was still early. "It's time."

"I won't be a minute. I just want to say goodbye."

Jacques and André's shared bedroom smelled of teenage-boy hormones and less-than-clean socks. The room seemed enveloped in a sacred, innocent hush, the only sound the deep, steady breathing of profound adolescent sleep. I wanted to fling myself at my sons, embrace them, and swear that I would do anything for them, including leaving them right now. Instead, I grazed their cheeks with a kiss, waking them just enough to whisper promises I would be back soon. I then slid down the hall in my stocking feet to Annette's door. I didn't dare touch her. She would wake and cling to me, begging me not to go. I stood by her room's entrance, memorizing how her curls spilled across her pillow and the curve of her plump cheeks. Back in the kitchen, I hugged Celina one last time.

The Goldsteins waited for me on Rue Vauban in their butcher truck. They were leaving Alsace to stay with their son in Vichy.

Raphael started the engine, while Micheline took in my pinched, sleep-deprived face.

"Don't look back," she said. "It's hard enough."

Chapter 17
FRANCE, THE OPEN ROAD
JUNE 1940. THE EXODUS

BY EARLY JUNE, the country was crumbling. Refugees from Belgium, Luxembourg, and northern France streamed southward. There were rumors that the government might flee Paris—or perhaps, that it had done so already. On my way to Vichy with the Goldsteins, we'd seen groups of French soldiers marching, but were they retreating? Heading to battle? No one seemed to know. I was astonished that amid this chaos the trains were still running, but that could change at any moment. So, less than a week after I'd dropped my bundles of merchandise in Vichy, I was on a train back to Alsace. Every seat was taken with passengers wearing the same forlorn expression, all with the same question: Will we make it home?

I had been awake all the night before, worrying about that myself. Fatigue finally won, somewhere along the way, and I fell into a hard, long sleep. When the train's lurching jerked me awake, it was already dusk. We had stopped. Outside, there was just enough light so I could read the platform sign: Besancon. I exhaled, for what felt like the first time since I'd left Vichy.

Just thirty-five miles to Colmar. Almost home.

But why wasn't the train moving? Passengers looked about. Some cried out in panic, sure that Germans must have stopped the train, that they were going to come on board and kill us all. One woman went into hysterics, causing several young children to cry. People shifted about, uncertain as to whether they should dash off right then, or hope it was just a mechanical problem, that the train would soon move.

A frazzled conductor stomped through the car, shouting, "Everyone off! The train stops here. The rails north are bombed out."

He stalked away before the distraught travelers could accost him. I was jostled and pushed in the crowd shoving its way off the rail car. People shouted and debated how they should proceed. Should they take to the highways and walk north, toward home? Should they go back to where they just came from, back south? What about their families, still in Alsace?

What about my family. Where are they, right now?

I tried to picture them, alive and well, waiting for me in our apartment on Rue Vauban. Meanwhile, other people were leaving the station, choosing to walk—either northward or southward, I couldn't tell. My brain felt sluggish and stupid. I stood on the platform, incapable of making a decision. Eventually, I was alone.

After the chaos on the train, the night was weirdly still. As my eyes adjusted to the dark, I noted that the Besancon station had multiple tracks. I dully considered the possibility that although no more trains were heading north, some might still be going south. Sure enough, a few minutes later from the far end of the rail yard, a groaning, squeaking cattle train came to a stop on the southern-destination side of the platform. Its noisy arrival infused me with sudden clarity:

I'll head back to Vichy. They know to meet me there, at the Goldsteins'.

I sprinted for the train. The cars were already choked with people, but I'm small, so I elbowed my way into a space, inhaling the sourness of human body odor and the acrid scent of human fear. The train car had no seats since it was intended for animals. Everyone stood so tightly together I could feel the people around me breathing.

I was pressed up against the wall next to a young officer. He gave me a courteous nod, then looked away. In his dirty but elegant uniform, he smoked cigarette after cigarette, staring out the window at the velvet June night. His posture made it clear that he didn't want to talk, and I sympathized. But I needed information.

"Excuse me," I said. "Do you know where this train is going?"

His handsome face sagged with exhaustion and defeat. "South. That's all I know." He took another pull on his cigarette and added faintly, "I'm sorry."

Was it a simple apology for his lack of information? Or a wider admission, that the French army had been incapable of defending our country against the Germans?

"Young man," I said. "It is not your fault."

THE TRAIN STAGGERED onward. Within a few hours, my feet ached from standing, but there was nowhere except the floor to sit down. After another hour of shuddering, jolting travel, my feet felt like numb lumps attached to the ends of my legs, upon which I was somehow supposed to keep myself upright. I told myself sternly to stop thinking about it and focus on my next move.

I'm on a train. I can make it to Vichy.

Then my legs gave out.

I sat on the dirty floor, which was smeared with mud and who knows what else from the train's previous passengers, the cows. It was wonderful. I fell asleep.

A firm hand shook me. I opened my eyes, annoyed that someone was waking me. Touching my shoulder was a dark-haired young man.

"Jacques . . . ?" I mumbled.

"Madame?" the young officer said. "Pardon me. This train is forbidden to continue. I must ask you to leave."

"But . . ."

"I'm sorry, madame. Everyone must get off."

I STUMBLED OUT of the train with hundreds of other bewildered passengers. I had just woken up, the sky was black, and I had no idea where I was. I approached a woman about my age.

"Excuse me," I said. "Where are we?"

She pointed to a sign that I hadn't noticed before. Lyon. We'd gone only seventy miles, just halfway to Vichy. I would have to walk. I tried to focus on that sobering fact alone, and not on my wider circumstances: I couldn't go home to Colmar, I had no idea where my husband and children were, it was the middle of the night, and my country was about to be overtaken by a more powerful, ruthless force than anyone had ever seen.

I picked up my small suitcase and took the road that headed west, toward Vichy. As my vision adjusted to the darkness, I understood for the first time what was happening.

It was an exodus of biblical proportions.

I JOINED THOUSANDS of others, all of us travelers on a highway of death. German Stuka bomber planes must have strafed the crowds earlier. The bodies of their victims lay by the side of the road. The outlines of dead horses and abandoned cars cast terrifying shadows. I clutched my suitcase. I forced myself to look ahead, so as not to see the horror at the sides of the road. The beginnings of hunger and thirst tugged at me, warning they would soon become sharper, more urgent. The food and water I had brought for the return trip to Colmar was gone. I had been so intent on my long-term survival plan for my family that I had overlooked the simple requirement to bring enough food and drink to sustain me for a journey that I should have known might take longer than usual. But I didn't bother rebuking myself for traveling light, or for my assumption that I'd be home in a matter of days. The entire world was astonished by the speed and success of the German advance, from top military leaders to ordinary shopkeepers like me.

AFTER MANY HOURS on the road, primal, physical needs became my obsession. My feet, sluggish and complaining. My scraping thirst. My ears, alert for the screech of a Stuka. My eyes, watchful and wary of the tide of humanity around me. Desperate people do desperate things. I dragged my body until it refused to be dragged any farther.

In the thin, emerging light before dawn, I made out the forms of dozens of people sleeping in a hayfield. I stepped among them, noticing a family lying together, the parents protectively curled around their two children. They seemed like safe temporary companions, so I pulled a shawl from my suitcase to lie upon and settled nearby.

The mother lifted her head. "If he sees you, the farmer will charge you one or two francs to stay here," she rasped. "It's shameful. We paid him last night for this spot on his field, then asked him for food and water. He refused. Said he was not a charity. Yesterday, we paid a franc each to someone else selling water along the way. These people . . . profiting from our desperation. They'll go straight to hell." She put her head down. "If the farmer comes back, I'll say you're my sister and insist that our family has already paid."

WHEN I WOKE a few hours later, the family was gone. I ached from sleeping on the ground. I was dizzy from the lack of food. But thirst overpowered all other discomforts. I knew I wouldn't make it to Vichy without something to drink. I remembered what the woman had said about paying for water. I would have gladly paid.

I tried to stand up, but the world spun around me. I crumpled back down to the ground. *Think, Sarah. Focus.* I pressed my fingers into the warm earth. But I couldn't focus while my head was spinning. It didn't help that the morning sun was already high and bright.

Lying on the ground, I woozily pondered how sunshine could be your friend or your enemy, depending on your circumstances. On an afternoon walk in the Vosges Mountains back home, I would have welcomed this full mid-morning June light. But here, the sun was malevolent—its harsh rays laughing at my predicament, as they glinted off the yellow hay that the farmer had put out for his animals next to their watering trough.

A watering trough.

The woman last night had said the farmer wouldn't share his water, so I decided to steal it. I crawled through the grass. My suitcase made it difficult, but there was no way I was going to leave it behind. The few articles of clothing and money it contained were all I had.

Crawl and drag. Stop and look. Crawl and drag. Stop and look. That's how I moved, like a drunken fox, holding onto my valise and occasionally halting my progress to peek above the grass to make sure the farmer wasn't there. My knees and palms grew scraped and raw from the effort. I would only notice this later. Right now, the trough of water—beautiful, glistening in the sunlight—was the center of my world.

A horse was drinking from the trough, dipping his tongue in rhythmically, pulling the water into his mouth in fulsome, noisy laps. Suddenly clearheaded, with my goal in sight, I weighed the pros and cons of this animal's presence. I had never lived in the country, but I was used to horses. Everyone had them back in Poland to pull their wagons. So, I knew that if this particular horse were skittish, I might spook him and attract the attention of the farmer—who was nowhere to be seen but could be as close as the barn next to the trough. At best, the farmer would chase me off; at worst, he might shoot me. But if the horse were calm, his substantial torso would block my smaller one from view. I made one final motion of crawl and drag.

"Hello, horse," I said softly.

I dunked my whole face into the trough.

MY THIRST QUENCHED, I felt renewed. Hopeful, even. I would make it to Vichy.

My feet had other ideas. After a few miles, the blisters that I had tried to ignore screamed at me to do something, anything. I took my shoes off and walked barefoot. I envied those on bicycles, in wagons, in cars. I would have begged for a ride, but every single vehicle that passed was impossibly stuffed with people and possessions.

Tiny pebbles impaled the soles of my feet. I put my shoes back on and staggered along. *Ignore the pain. Vichy. Melach, Jacques, André, Annette.*

The growl of hefty tires on the road rose from behind me. I stiffened, stopped, and turned around, as did everyone walking near me. Was it the enemy? We knew the Germans were already attacking civilians from the skies. Now, were they coming after us in vehicles on the road?

No. It was a French military convoy, a dozen large trucks with open beds in the back. The other travelers and I swarmed them, clamoring for a ride. But like every vehicle that had passed us earlier, every truck was already crammed with civilians. The soldiers' faces were tight with anguish, as they had to reject the outstretched hands, the pleadings for help. The last vehicle lumbered by me so closely I could feel its engine's heat. Then it reduced its already slow pace, enough so that several soldiers could hop off.

"We'll walk," they said to me and a few others nearby. "Get on."

THE TRUCKS MADE laborious progress, weaving among the masses of people. My face stung from sunburn and my eyes, from road dust. But I was no longer walking and my feet rejoiced.

The soldiers knew the area well and diverged us onto a smaller, winding country road that was quieter, and safer from bombardment. There was companionship, with people sharing whatever bread, dried sausage, and cheese they had. But no one had much, and after many more hours of traveling, everyone was famished. Then, we went around another corner, and I was not the only one who took a breath.

The farm before us was a picture of the way life used to be. The barn glowed pink and yellow in a wide, stretching, lazy sunset. A few fat chickens chuckled in the side yard, where a lush vegetable garden grew. Cows lowed for their evening milking. The soldiers stopped the truck. One of them climbed out, straightened his cap, and brushed the dirt off his shirt.

"I'll see if they can spare some food and let us sleep in the barn." He rapped on the door.

A middle-aged man answered. His mouth twisted when he saw the young man in uniform and he called over his shoulder to someone inside the house. "*Eh voilà*, Jeanette. Look who's come to our door. It's a truckload of France's finest, our *Militaires.*"

He faced the soldier. All of us waiting in the truck bed had heard the sarcasm and hostility in the man's response and knew that our request was doomed. The man gestured wildly with his thick arms at the soldier.

"What have you done for us lately, eh? You ought to be ashamed. Handing over our country so quickly to the Germans—*Les Boches*. When I fought in the Great War, we didn't give up so easily as softies like you. Little boys, you all are, playing at war."

"Please, monsieur. My comrades and I are so hungry, and we have civilians whom we picked up along the way. They have not eaten either. Please."

"Be gone! And shame on you." The man slammed the door.

The soldier stood still on the steps for several seconds. He walked back to the group. "We'll have to continue."

The truck's worn engine revved, and we departed, jostling about as our rescuers drove down the worn country road. At some point, the soldiers pulled over and we strangers slept, like family, huddled together.

THE NEXT MORNING, the soldiers had good news for some, but bad news for me.

"We're heading due south today," they said, and many passengers cheered. Most people thought the further south you were, the safer you were. That might have been true, but I needed to continue more westward, to Vichy.

"But . . . where are we? How will I get to Vichy?" I asked them, as they bustled about, preparing to leave.

The group's commander, who looked not that much older than Jacques, focused on me kindly, despite the rush to go. "We're outside the little city of Roanne right now. Vichy is about thirty miles from here."

"But . . . I . . . Vichy . . . my children . . ."

"I'm sorry, madame," he said. "Truly I am. But orders are orders, and we are, for now anyway, still at war."

What happened next had never happened to me before.

I crumpled to the grass, screaming and crying.

I was unaware of when the truck departed, how many civilians remained on board, and how many had stepped off with me. I knew that others in our little traveling party had also hoped for a ride all the way to Vichy, and I suppose we could have walked together. But by the time I finished moaning and sobbing, I was alone.

EVENTUALLY—I'M NOT sure how long—I raised myself from the ground, wiped the dirt off my face, and brushed the grass from my dress.

Sarah Seibert is not a woman who just falls to pieces. That's the first and last time that happens.

It wasn't.

I walked, alone in the country. The quiet was unsettling. With the heat of high noon, even the bugs and birds withheld their usual summer clicking and droning.

Where is everyone?

It was eerie, to be so removed from humanity. I walked for several miles without seeing a single person. The sounds of war were absent, which was also disconcerting. I imagined that at any moment, a bomb would crash beside me or that I'd hear the staccato of machine-gun fire.

My pace dragged by late afternoon; my blisters had reignited themselves, and I was lightheaded from hunger. I had already passed several farmhouses, tapping on the door first, before opening to the stuffy emptiness that develops when a home has been shut for some time and the occupants are gone. I searched for food in every vacant kitchen, finding nothing except a forgotten can of condensed milk tucked away in a back cupboard corner. I bashed it open with a knife and drank it. It was delicious.

As evening approached, I assumed I would spend the night in an empty house or barn, a prospect that didn't please me at all. But I reminded myself that it would be an improvement on my first night on the road: sleeping in a field that could be bombed; or my second night, in a military truck packed in with a dozen other traumatized people.

Then, in the approaching darkness, a little further down the road, lights shone from windows. *People. Food. Rest.*

The house didn't seem to get closer quickly, probably because at that point I was hobbling rather than walking due to the pain in my feet. My heels and toes no longer felt separate from each other; they had transformed into one enormous, screaming blister on each foot. Just as it began to rain, I arrived at the house.

At first, no one answered my knock, which I understood, given fears that the Germans were coming. But when I called out "Hello, helloooo," a thin woman who appeared a bit older than me opened the door just enough so she could peek out. She eyed me, judging my dirty, rumpled appearance.

"What do you want?" she asked.

"Please, madame," I said, somehow finding the energy to give her my most gracious smile. "I'm alone. I'm a mother from Colmar. I was on my way home to my family when I became separated from them. I've been on the road for three days with almost nothing to eat or drink. If you could spare a tiny scrap of food and permit me to sleep in your barn, I'd be deeply appreciative."

She opened the door a little wider, raising my hopes. But it was just so she could scan me more fully and taunt me more completely.

"*Colmar*, you say? *Alsatians.* Why, you probably welcomed them crossing the Rhine, didn't you? Happy to be German again, aren't you. Yes, it'll be fun times again for you in Alsace. You'll be back with your own kind . . . the barbarian Germans . . . you're probably a spy, aren't you? Aren't you, Madame *Alsace.*"

Now she was ranting, and I knew there was no hope. I considered collapsing in a heap, right there on the doorstep. But no. No more breakdowns. Instead, I composed my face, stood up straight, and drew upon the last ounce of shopkeeper manners I had left.

"I'm so terribly sorry, madame. I don't mean to trouble you. Please, could you tell me . . . might there be another farm nearby?"

She waved her hand in a vague direction. "Pah! The Charpentier's farm is a mile down the road. Now be gone, *Alsatian.*"

She slammed the door. The rain fell harder.

How was it possible that a pair of feet could hurt so badly and yet still be required to perform, to move? Meanwhile, my clothes were soaked in the rain, chilling me, even though the night itself was warm. I staggered rather than walked. In my delirious state, I remembered the freezing, middle-of-the-night escapes my family had made during the Great War in Poland, and how I had thought then that nothing could be worse. But at least in Poland, I had my entire family beside me. I had food and drink. I had a cart to ride in and two horses to pull it. Now, I was alone, and I had nothing but pain, thirst, and starvation.

The rain came down heavier and harder, making the road muddy and even more difficult to navigate. The one mile to the next farm became an endless, blurry tunnel. More than once, I thought how wonderful it would feel to lie down by the side of the road and rest. But I felt I might die there. I saw a light in the distance and then the outlines of the Charpentier farmhouse. The last few steps were the worst. I rapped on the door twice, swaying as I waited for a response.

Angels opened the door.

THE SUN WAS already high when I woke. I lingered in bed for just a few moments, relishing how it felt to be fed and rested. I tried to piece together what had happened last night, but all I could conjure was a haze of white: from the halo-like fuzzy hair of the elderly couple who let me in, to the bread and milk they gave me to eat, to the whiteness of the smooth, clean sheets on the bed.

I realized I was wearing a cotton nightgown, also white, that they'd given me last night while they washed my clothes. My dress hung in the closet, my battered shoes beneath. On a chair was a fresh pair of stockings. I remembered how the woman had tried to wash the blood out of those I'd been wearing, but then decided they were too full of holes to be worn again.

I splashed my face with water in the basin they'd left me, rubbing hard to remove the grime from the road. I still had lipstick and a hairbrush in my bag, and these I used, a link to my past life. I put my clean clothes on, still damp but they would do. Dressed and refreshed, I went downstairs.

"*Bonjour*, Sarah. You slept a long time. You were exhausted, poor dear. I wish we had coffee, but you know. The war." Madame Charpentier handed me a tray with more milk and bread.

"It's wonderful. Please, let me pay you," I said, reaching for my wallet.

"No, absolutely not. Put it away. You might need it; you still have some miles to go before Vichy. Monsieur Charpentier is hitching up the wagon right now. He'll drive you to the post office. You can continue from there with the mailman on his route. He'll take you a good way, but not all the way. After that, you'll figure it out. You don't seem like the helpless type."

I sat in the cozy kitchen, chewing and marveling that the hateful woman who'd sent me away last night had delivered me to these generous, good-hearted people. Monsieur Charpentier peered through the doorway, streaks of sun darting in over his head, adding to his saintly aspect.

He smiled, creating more creases in his lined face. "Ready, my dear?"

THE MAILMAN BROUGHT me to the end of his route.

"I'm sorry I can't take you further," he said. "But it's just a few hours more on foot."

He tipped his hat. "Good luck. God be with you."

I thanked him, reflecting on his comment. I'd long doubted the existence of God, but I now believed in angels, because I'd just been rescued by an elderly pair of them.

I set out on the last leg of my journey, restored, and walked the last few miles to Vichy. My blisters still stung, and my calves and knees ached, but the anticipation of reuniting with Melach and my children overrode any pain; in fact, I no longer felt anything but a wide, stretching, full-bodied joy. I reached Vichy and the Goldsteins' apartment building and knocked on their door so hard it hurt my knuckles.

Raphael opened the door. "Sarah! You're here. We were so worried." He kissed my cheeks, then shouted up the stairs, "Melach. Children. Sarah's here!"

Melach appeared in the stairwell, Annette and André behind him.

"Where's Jacques?" I asked, hoping for a simple answer—*he went to the store, he's in the lavatory, he's not feeling well.* Anything. Please, anything at all.

"Melach, what's happened?"

He could not meet my eyes. "We lost him near Besancon."

I wanted to fly at him, beat his chest, and slap his face.

Instead, I shrieked, "My son! My child!" before I fainted. I think Raphael caught me on the way down.

Chapter 18
VICHY, FRANCE
JULY 1940. SEEKING

I DIDN'T SPEAK to Melach for a week.

I put all my energy into finding Jacques, and I soon learned I wasn't the only one searching for a lost child. Tens of thousands had become separated from their families in the chaos. Newspapers were full of column after column listing the names of missing persons. All over the city of Vichy, desperate family members posted flyers in public squares, on buildings, even handing them out in the streets, a scene that must have been repeated across France.

"Her name is Lilise. Five years old. Last seen outside of Paris, wearing a blue dress . . ."

"Thomas Dunfort. Age twelve. Tall, sandy hair. Lost near Mulhouse. Please contact . . ."

We created dozens of handmade notices about Jacques. Every day, I wandered for miles along Vichy's hot, crowded streets with hundreds of other frantic people. I checked on the signs I'd already put up, and if they'd come down, I replaced them. I made the rounds of the rescue organizations, primarily the Red Cross, which was working mightily to reunite families. I scanned the lists they posted, badgered their frazzled employees for information, asking the same questions, over and over, about a handsome, dark-haired teenager named Jacques, lost somewhere near Besancon. I repeated the same routine at City Hall, but just once, because the government was now run by people who were collaborating with Germany. I decided to stay away. I already knew how Germany felt about Jews, and I could guess how its new French friends might feel.

After a week with no success, I vowed aloud one night that I would head back out on the open road the next day and find Jacques myself.

For the first time since my arrival, Melach spoke to me. "Think of André and Annette. They need you right now."

I glared at him, knowing he was right.

"It's my fault. I'll go searching—" he said.

"No." I cut him off, still so furious that my words felt like black smoke when I said them. "They've already lost a brother. They can't lose their father, too."

MUCH LATER THAT night, I lay alone in our friends' guest bed. Melach was sleeping on the floor in the other room with our children. I didn't want to talk to him, see him, touch him. I knew him well enough to realize that his guilt was the most profound pain he'd ever felt, that he was probably ill from heartache and shame. But still. He'd lost our son.

Staring into the dark, I madly ran through my mind other approaches I could possibly take to find Jacques. What hadn't I thought of yet? Who else could I contact? Was it crazy to venture out myself, to try to find him? Or was it the only way?

A slim stream of light from the hallway fell across the bed, then widened as my two younger children crept into the room. Annette lay next to me, not too close, but put her hand on my arm, the hesitant gesture itself a question: *May we be here? Can you talk to us, Maman, please?* André sat down at the end of the bed.

"Maman," he said. "We need to tell you what happened. And you need to forgive Papa."

I sat up, finding comfort in their presence, despite my despair over Jacques. I pulled Annette into my arms and patted the bed next to me, inviting André to come closer. "Tell me."

"All right. Here goes. It started mid-June with Rabbi Weber, coming to our house to warn us that the Nazis were going to cross the Rhine the next day, and we needed to leave before dawn. 'But Sarah's not back yet,' Papa protested. 'How can we leave with her still gone?' The rabbi insisted. He said there was no other choice."

"We had no other choice, Maman," Annette repeated, wanting to be part of the story. "We didn't *want* to go without you. But we *had* to."

For the first time, I imagined what the exodus must have been like for the three of them. I'd been so focused on my anger at Melach and despondent over Jacques that I hadn't even been curious about what my other children had endured. I admit, this realization did not make me proud.

"I understand, my Maideleh," I said, kissing her hair. "Go on, André."

"After the rabbi left, Papa brought Jacques and me out into the alley behind the apartment building and showed us the car, a Citroen that he'd just bought from a neighbor. It was a beautiful, stylish, cherry-red . . . but old, like it must have been one of the first to roll off the production line twenty years ago—"

"Enough about the car," I interrupted, but gently. "The story. What happened?"

"Right. Well, Jacques and I raced around like crazy, packing everything we could think of. Papa kept telling us 'Not so much,' and 'just the minimum,' but for us, it seemed like an adventure, you know? We weren't scared, we were excited." André paused. "We had no idea . . ."

I remembered the horrors I'd seen by the side of the road—the dead bodies, the bombed-out structures, the terrified throngs. My children—my innocent babies—had experienced the same nightmare.

"I'm sure you did your best. Keep going." I struggled to keep my voice steady, but I did it. For them.

"We left before dawn, all five of us in the Citroen with just a few possessions. Mostly what we brought was food and water, which was smart on Papa's part. Aunt Celina, Uncle Shevah, and the cousins followed us in their car, even more packed than ours. If it weren't for the open windows, I don't know how they could have breathed . . . anyway, we left. I wanted to bring a bunch of extra clothes, and Jacques gathered up all his books, but Papa said no, that food was the most important. So, it was pretty tight in the car, even though we didn't have that much."

"I only had my doll. That was it," Annette added.

"You were very brave, sweetie," I told her.

"Yes, she was, our Mademoiselle Annette." André said. "And at first, we all thought we would be okay. Papa seemed to have it pretty well organized. We turned and waved good-bye to our house. But then . . . we looked ahead. I have never seen so many people all at once. All of Alsace was running south. Like a river of people. And then . . . well, it didn't feel like . . . an adventure anymore."

As André's earlier bravado faded, I saw him for what he was: a boy whose family had just run for its life. He was only fourteen, about the same age that I was, when we had to flee our village in Poland for the first time.

"Go on," I said, extra softly.

"Yeah. Well, we could barely move, even though we left early like the rabbi said. Some people were in cars like ours, farm families had their wagons, lots of people were on bicycles, but most people were walking, carrying whatever they could, in baby carriages, wheelbarrows, children's wagons—all jammed sky-high with stuff. Jacques was up front with Papa, so he had a better view. He was the first to notice that mixed in with this mass of regular people were French soldiers. 'Hey, Papa,' Jacques said. 'Look, soldiers. Why are they here with all of us? Why aren't they at the Rhine? The Germans are coming, shouldn't they be at the river, defending Alsace?' Papa cursed. It was the first time in my life that I had ever heard him say anything bad about France."

Annette snuggled closer to me, and I guessed that we were nearing the part where Jacques was lost.

"About thirty-five miles outside of Colmar, the car began to make coughing noises," André said.

"It was so stinky," Annette said. "A smelly brown cloud rose from the engine; the car made a big bang—really loud. And then it *stopped*. Right in the middle of the road."

Their shared back-and-forth over the story, their eagerness to tell it, abruptly ended. As André and Annette fell silent, the air in the dark bedroom became heavy with their questions, fears, hopes, and their trust. I was their fearless Maman. I would make it all better, like I always did. But could I?

"We can finish tomorrow, if you'd like," I said, smoothing a blonde lock behind my son's ear. "It's late, and this is a hard story to tell."

"No, I'm all right," André said. "It's just the reaction of people . . . I expected better. But no one offered to help. Instead, when the car broke down, the people streaming by scowled and swore at us. Some even pounded on the windows, yelling at us to get out of the way. Everyone was furious that a dead vehicle now blocked the road. So, Uncle Shevah pulled his car over and helped push ours off to the side. 'Now what?' he and Papa asked each other. They saw a café and decided to feed us while they still could and take a moment to strategize. We were just north of Besancon, at that point."

"Besancon. That's where I got stuck," I said. "The rails were out, and I couldn't get home to you. That's why I turned around and went back to Vichy."

"Aha," André said, and I could see him working through his understanding and regret, *If only* . . . "Anyway. The café. Two women were at the table next to ours, a mother and daughter. We could tell they were wealthy, by their jewelry, clothes, and mannerisms; and we caught them stealing glances at Papa, him being so handsome and all. You know. Jacques and I started laughing into our napkins, because, well . . . in the middle of a war, you're trying to flirt with a man in a café?

"As the café owner took our order, Papa told the man our whole story. Leaving Colmar before dawn. Buying the car that soon broke down. Trying to get to Vichy. We noticed those two women listening, with obvious interest. Then the mother leaned over. 'I think we can help you, monsieur . . . and you can help us.'

"Maman, trust me. At first, it seemed perfect. They were eager to reach safety in Spain where they had relatives. They had a reliable car, but the older woman's husband had always driven it, and he was still at war. She and her daughter had almost no experience driving and they were terrified to get behind the wheel on a road teeming with people. 'Could the charming Monsieur Seibert drive them to the Spanish border?' they asked. They would pay him, of course, to drive.

They said he could drop his children off in Vichy before continuing with them to Spain.

"We could tell Papa was really uncomfortable with that last part. Once we were reunited with you in Vichy, we knew he wouldn't want to be separated again. But, Maman . . . what choice did he have? He was doing his best. He truly, honestly was."

"I know you want me to forgive your father, André," I said. "Keep trying but don't expect miracles."

"Right," he said quietly, because we'd both noticed Annette was asleep. "Outside the café, we saw the fleeing throngs were even more massive than before. The lunch I'd just eaten became a lead ball in my stomach. Then we saw the inside of the women's car. It had barely enough room for five people.

"'*Papa?*' we all yelled. Especially Jacques.

"We heard him muttering 'no, no, no' as he came to the same conclusion that we had: There was zero space for a sixth person. The car was crammed with all manner of luxury items: linens, lamps, paintings, small statues. Also, they had clothing: piles of dresses, sweaters, shoes, hosiery, and jackets. Boxes of jewelry, fur coats . . . it was unbelievable. Jacques and I checked the trunk, hoping to move some stuff there, but it was packed with food, water, and wine.

"Of course, Papa hadn't known the car's capacity when he'd agreed to drive it. Papa tried to find a solution, talking with the two women, as they were maneuvering themselves into the front seat, the daughter settling on her mother's lap. I have to admit, it *was* already an extremely tight fit.

"'*Madame,*' Papa said to the mother. 'Might you rid yourself of a few items in the back? Otherwise, there's no room for all five of us . . . and, of course, I cannot leave anyone behind.' It seemed perfectly reasonable to us, what any human being with a heart would do. But she said no."

André imitated the woman in a high, stuck-up accent. "'Absolutely *not*, Monsieur Seibert. We need to sell these items when we get to Spain so we can survive. We have no other source of income, with my husband still out there somewhere in this hideous war. Your little girl and younger son can shove those furs in more tightly and she can sit on the boy's lap. But everything—I mean *everything*—must stay."

My rage at Melach transferred to this woman. To hold onto her every last bit of wealth, she would leave a teenage boy—my son—at the side of the road, during a war?

"Then it happened," André said, almost whispering now. "In the distance we heard the scream of a German Stuka bomber. We *had* to go . . . we didn't know what to do . . . and so Uncle Shevah stepped forward. He told Jacques to follow us on his bicycle. He unstrapped it from the roof of their car and demonstrated how Jacques could hold onto the door handle of their car, rolling alongside. That way, he said, we wouldn't get separated."

Frustration and anger traded places, roiling my insides. If I had been there, I would have found some other solution, *any* other solution besides this. Refuse to drive the rich women, unless they relented and made room for Jacques? Somehow have Shevah's still-working car tow the broken-down Citroen, with my family inside? But I wasn't there. I was lost in the exodus myself. I forced myself to listen to André.

"Papa put his arm around Jacques to encourage him, while I offered to go in his place. But Papa and Uncle Shevah said since Jacques was the oldest, he was stronger than me, and he could better manage the bike. Jacques was really courageous, Maman, even though I could see how scared he was. 'I can do it,' he kept saying. 'Don't worry, Papa. I'll be fine.'

"The two cars pulled onto the road, Papa driving with the women, me and Annette inside. Jacques followed behind, grasping the door handle of Uncle Shevah's car. I gave him a thumbs-up. 'Just hold the handle, Jacques. That's all you have to do.'

"But I guess it was much harder than any of us imagined. There were so many people on the road, he must have kept bumping into people as he passed them. And the road itself was rough, with ruts and holes that were bearable for a car, but were probably jarring on a bicycle. I guess . . . his hold must have begun to weaken and then . . . he just had to . . . let go. Annette and I had been trying to watch him, but the crowds were so thick. Sometimes we'd lose sight of him for a few seconds. Then we lost sight of him for a few *minutes*. Annette started screaming. 'He's gone! Papa! Stop, stop, He's gone!' I'm sure Jacques must have yelled to Aunt Celina and Uncle Shevah before he let go, but . . . there was so much noise . . . I guess they didn't hear him."

"André. You must tell me, and you must be honest. Why didn't Papa turn around?"

"You were out there, Maman, in those hordes of people all terrified, all running in one direction. Turning around would have been impossible, like turning back a tidal wave."

"All right, why didn't your father pull over and wait?"

"There were German bombers coming, Maman. We heard them. We had to keep going. Papa sobbed while he drove. I've never seen him like that."

The wall of fury I'd built against Melach developed a tiny crack.

André got up, carefully, so as not to wake Annette. "Will you forgive Papa now?"

I hesitated, absorbing what he'd just told me, what they'd all been through. Including Melach.

"When we find your brother, yes. Then I will forgive him. Good night, André."

"Good night."

Chapter 19
VICHY, FRANCE
JULY 1940. FOUND

WE WERE STILL living with our friends, the Goldsteins, when the telegram came. I heard Raphael emit a whoop after a messenger delivered the precious envelope.

"Sarah, Melach! Come see *this*."

It was from Melach's sister, Pauline, in Périgueux.

JACQUES FOUND PERIGUEUX STOP TRAIN TOMORROW
STOP PAULINE

Pauline had been living in Périgueux since the evacuation of Strasbourg nine months ago, in September 1939. As I read the telegram, over and over, I recalled how Jacques had been fascinated with the former French government's evacuation plan, especially the notion of sending one entire French city to another—in this instance, Strasbourg to Périgueux. Somehow, he'd made his way to his aunt. We'd hear the full story tomorrow.

Melach and I slept in the same bed that night. I wasn't ready for his full body, but I held his hand.

"I forgive you," I said. And for the first time since I'd left Colmar, I slept soundly.

"THERE HE IS!" André shouted, as he weaved us through the crowd on the train platform in Vichy. And there he was, our Jacques: thinner, browner, and shaggier than before, but holding himself, perhaps, a bit taller? André and I raced toward him, with Melach and Annette right behind, bumping shoulders with strangers and probably bashing over more than one valise.

"Jacques!" we all screamed, and when he saw us and waved, the crumbled pieces of my heart joined back together.

HE WENT TO bed early, exhausted from the journey. I peeked into the room he shared with his brother and sister several times, watching him sleep, marveling that he was here.

The Goldsteins made a festive lunch the next day, of the best they could find in wartime Vichy. Two roast chickens, bread (with increasingly hard-to-get butter) potatoes, a tomato salad, wine; a beautiful meal topped off by an authentic, classic Alsatian plum pie. Where they bought that pie was a secret they wouldn't reveal.

"This looks incredible," Jacques said to the Goldsteins. "Thank you so much. I got awfully hungry out on the roads all those weeks. I could eat one of those whole roast chickens myself."

"Eat, eat," everyone said. But then we pelted him with questions.

In between enormous mouthfuls of food, Jacques explained how he'd become detached from Shevah's car. Holding onto the door handle became excruciating. It might have worked if the road had been smooth and clear. But of course, it wasn't. Jacques had to maneuver around swarms of people. He kept getting bumped. The road was rutted. Soon, his exhausted fingers let go.

"I screamed to Uncle Shevah and Aunt Celina when it happened," he said, pausing from eating for the first time and wiping his mouth. "It was the loudest sound I have ever made, an explosion from my lungs, throat, and mouth. My throat was sore for days afterward."

"How could they *not* have heard you?" I asked, again furious that so many people had failed my sixteen-year-old son. My husband. The rich women with the car. Then, my sister and brother-in-law.

"I don't know, Maman. All I can guess is that they'd rolled the windows up because of all the dust that was being kicked up by so many people . . . plus the roads were chaotic . . . I guess they didn't hear."

The image of Jacques being abandoned, left to fend for himself, forced to travel alone with no money, food, or water, while a war was underway—I wanted to tell him to stop talking. That his words filled my veins with anguish.

But perhaps Annette's reaction was the better one. She leaped out of her chair and hugged Jacques. "I'm so glad you're here. We're all together again."

"Me too, Annette," he said, hugging her back, hard—and at that point, the adults all started crying while the children focused on the plum pie.

"Could we have some dessert, while Jacques finishes his story?" André asked.

Wiping her eyes, Micheline cut the pie up and served everyone.

"Umm. Tastes like Adele's fruit tartes, back home," Jacques said, and at the mention of Colmar and Pain Pour Tous, I thought the adults would all start crying again. "Anyway. After I became separated from everyone, I hopped back on the bike and rode for a few miles. It was way easier than holding onto a car door handle."

André and Annette laughed, but I wasn't ready to laugh about anything just yet.

"But then I hit a sharp rock and broke my wheel. Of course, I had no tools or supplies to fix it. I dragged the bike off the road and sat by a stream, to get out of the sun, to think. It was hot, so I drank from the stream. I decided I would just have to walk to Vichy. I felt a little better after my rest and climbed back up the stream bank. But then . . . I saw something I hadn't seen on my way down to the water . . . several dead bodies in some high grass by the side of the road. The Stuka bombers must have already attacked earlier groups of people, you could tell by . . . the state of the bodies. I think then I panicked. Everything around me seemed to shimmer and pulse, in and out, I . . . thought I was going to die there."

Everyone was silent. Annette leaned into Melach for comfort. *This is too much for her. She's too young* . . . But Jacques continued, before I could ask him to stop.

"But then I came out of it. I thought, I'm *sixteen* years old. I've barely *lived*, I'm not ready to die. And I'm not going to. At least I know where my family is, with the Goldsteins in Vichy. That's more information than a lot of people out here have. I asked someone how far it was to Vichy, she told me it was two hundred and fifty miles. I knew there was no way I could walk that far, not without food or water. So, I would have to find a ride."

My brave, practical, level-headed boy. My heartache at what he'd suffered turned to pure pride.

"I began chasing cars, banging on the windows, asking them—politely, Maman—if they could take me. No one could . . . or would. Several French military trucks went by, all full to cracking already with other civilians. I started to panic again. But then, another military vehicle rumbled right by me, threading through the crowds. It came so close, I had to jump to get out of the way. That's how I noticed this truck hadn't taken on any civilians, although it was plenty crowded with soldiers. Still, they seemed to have just enough room for me. I sprinted after them.

"'Wait! Please, please take me on board,' I said, running, shouting, and waving like a madman. One of the younger soldiers looked down at me from his bench on the truck bed.

"'No room, kid, no room,' he replied. 'Sorry.'

"'Please,' I begged

"The soldier turned to an older, more senior-looking member of his group, seeming to ask his advice. The older man shook his head, and I heard him say,

'No, we can't. I know, it's tough. We've seen dozens . . . maybe hundreds of these lost kids today. Still, what can we do? We can't take them all.'

"But he said it . . . in *Alsatian*.

"I chased the truck as it rolled past me. What did I have to lose? With my last ounce of energy, I yelled up to the soldiers, but in Alsatian instead of French:

"'Wait! Wait, please! I'm from Alsace, from Colmar. My parents own the clothing store on Rue Vauban. Until the war, I was a student at Bartholdi High School . . .'

"The first soldier I'd spoken to looked back at his superior, who nodded.

"'Come on up,' the younger man said—in Alsatian, of course. And he pulled me in."

MY DELIGHT OVER my reunified family co-existed with dread, in those turbulent days of summer after France fell. Vichy crackled with a sinister, new energy. The city once known for its spas and mineral water had become the capital of a re-configured France, the southern part of the country unoccupied by the Germans and called "The Free Zone."

"There's nothing free about it," I'd often mutter to Melach.

I did not share the public relief over the announcement that Philippe Pétain, France's hero from the Great War, would be head of the new Vichy government, with the new title "Chief of State." When Pétain urged the people to "follow him with their eyes shut," I told Melach we needed to keep our eyes open wider than ever. Pétain's new "security measures" made me insecure—suspending liberties, collaborating with the Nazis, and expanding internment camps to house anyone labeled "undesirable." It was shameful enough that the former French government had created these miserable spaces to hold people it didn't know what to do with: Spanish Civil War refugees, anti-Nazi Germans and Austrians, foreign Jews. What other unlucky souls would the new Vichy government now place in these camps? We'd barely arrived in this city, and I was itching to go.

But we couldn't leave just yet. My brother-in-law Saul was a prisoner of war.

From the lists of POWs printed in the newspapers, we learned that he was being held at a kind of temporary, transit camp called a *Frontstalag*. It was located near Nancy, a city in Lorraine—that part of the province which had not been annexed into Germany. But Nancy was in the zone newly occupied and administered by the Nazis.

For the first time in our marriage, Melach and I fought over what to do. He thought we should wait, that French POWs would be released soon, since the war was over, at least as far as France was concerned. That was the prevailing assumption, and the Vichy government made soothing assurances that it was true. But I wasn't convinced. Germany was still at war with Britain, and it needed manpower. POWs would provide the perfect compulsory workforce. We needed to free Saul now.

And I had one more reason to move quickly: Sophie was barely sleeping or eating. She and her two sons had made their way to Vichy to live with us while Saul was imprisoned. Sophie's bright spirit was broken; we all felt the presence of her distraught, anxious shadow. I had to rescue him. For her. No matter what Melach said.

"I'm going to Nancy with Sophie tomorrow," I announced one morning, just days after Jacques' homecoming. I continued stacking the breakfast dishes for Melach to wash. I was done quarreling with him about it. It was time.

Melach's forehead creased. His worried look. "I love my brother, you know that. But we've gone over this before. They'll let him out, likely very soon. I just read that in the paper again yesterday. In the meantime, he's probably as safe at the POW camp as anywhere else these days. And the punishment for an escape attempt could be death, if he's caught. If *you're* caught helping him—"

"He's Jewish. Have you forgotten that? He's no ordinary POW."

I had him there, and he knew it. Of course, in the summer of 1940, no one had any notion of what would transpire as the war continued—the deportations, the camps, Hitler's "final solution." But we knew enough to worry: the promises the German leader had made before the war . . . *The destruction of the Jewish race in Europe.* So, what would they do with a French Jewish POW like Saul? We shouldn't wait to find out.

"Agreed . . . you're right," Melach said. "But I don't want you to go alone. It's too dangerous. I'll go with you."

"I won't be alone. Sophie's coming with me. I *already* told you that. Half a dozen times."

Now we were facing each other across the kitchen: dishes forgotten, arms crossed, digging in. Why was he being so difficult? I had already decided what should be done and that it had to be done *now*. And yet, Melach continued to argue with me.

"The war's just barely over," he said. "There are vigilantes, fascists . . . all sorts of armed and crazy people out there. Even before you try to free him . . . which is a ridiculous risk . . . you might not even make it across the border. The country is in total and utter chaos!" His voice rose, which it seldom did.

"But, Melach," I said calmly. "Think about it: the chaos will work to our advantage. The border is still unsettled, before they can build all the checkpoints, roadblocks, and come up with all kinds of rules about who can cross and who can't. The confusion right now helps us . . . but it won't last. And among those millions of people still making their way home, I'll bet thousands of them lost their identity papers in the war and the exodus. Which is exactly what we will say. Besides, no one will suspect that two middle-aged women could be up to any mischief."

I finished my part of our kitchen cleanup ritual, putting the dirty plates and silverware on the counter and wiping the table. I took my apron off.

"Dishes?" I asked, pointing to the pile to be washed and trying to sound playful, but also indicating that this conversation was over.

He gave me a brutal look that I had never seen before. Then he did something he'd never done before.

Melach walked out on me.

"Where's Papa going?" Annette called from her room, where she'd heard the door slam. "Maman . . . ?"

FIVE MINUTES PASSED. Ten minutes. Fifteen. I started to do the dishes myself. When I heard Melach's familiar, solid gait approach the kitchen entrance, I stayed at the sink. I understood that he was upset about Saul and nervous about my departure. But he'd never just *left* while we were talking, or in this case, arguing. I was still processing what this meant, for both his imprisoned brother and for our marriage, which was still fragile after what had happened to Jacques. Even though we'd since heard that possibly as many as ninety thousand children had become separated from their families during the exodus, and I'd forgiven Melach, I still blamed him for losing our son. It was a raw spot in our relationship that had yet to heal. Now, I stood rigidly at the sink, my hands wrinkling in the cold dishwater.

His warmth and his scent enveloped me from behind. He wrapped his arms around me and leaned into my neck.

"Sarah. *Sarah*. You, Jacques, André, Annette; you're all I want. You're all I've ever wanted." He tightened his arms around me. "Until this war, I was the happiest man alive. With all we had. Our extended family, our store, our community, our beautiful little city . . . and then it all just . . . dissolved. Disappeared. Everything. In the exodus, I thought I'd lost a son *and* a wife. I cannot bear to be in that much pain again. I just can't bear it."

He released one short, choppy sob.

"Jacques . . . it was all my fault. It was madness out there. But I should have been more vigilant. I was trying, I was . . . to do my best in that awful moment, where in seconds, I had to choose among unthinkable choices. Should we accept the ride with the women and hope for the best with Jacques? Should we say 'no' to their offer and subject ourselves to the dangers on the highway? And then we lost him, and then I didn't know where you were, and I was terrified that *both* of you might be dead. When you finally arrived in Vichy, you were so furious . . . and you should have been. Any mother would have been. And, if the worst had happened, and we'd lost our son forever . . . I knew I would have lost you forever, too. You would have never forgiven me. And I would have never forgiven myself."

I took his arm, guided him to the sofa, and sat him down. I stroked his cheek while pushing back the adorable curl that always fell over his forehead. At age forty, he was still the most beautiful man I knew. I picked up his hand and held it.

Minutes passed, as we sat on the couch. As impatient as I was to leave *right now*, to release Saul, I realized I had to take this at Melach's pace. I leaned over and kissed him with more meaning than the quick pecks that had defined our marriage lately. A kiss of true understanding. Of a promise that I would take care of us.

"I love you. And I have a plan to save your brother." I whispered my plan in his ear.

"Uh-huh. Hmmm," he said, with a slight movement of his head. He was coming around. "Yes . . . all right. It just might work. I only wish I could be there to see it."

SOPHIE AND I left the next day. The crowds on the trains and the roads were massive, as people streamed north to reclaim their homes, businesses, and farms. Doubt marked their faces: what would life be like under Nazi oversight, for those heading into the new German occupied zone? But the uncertainty was even greater for Alsatians. The province had been annexed, and Alsace was considered part of The Reich.

As we traveled, the atmosphere was unsettled, the armistice was just about a month old, and security was haphazard. It was exactly as I'd hoped. As Sophie and I switched from train to train, sometimes we were asked for our tickets and identity papers and sometimes we weren't. We heard from other passengers that the demarcation line between Vichy-controlled southern France and the German-controlled north was still fluid, although no one thought it would last.

"Almost there," I said, a few miles from the new border. I patted Sophie's arm, feigning confidence. I hadn't told her yet, but my strategy to free Saul had a major hole in it. Now, we were about to see whether it was a hole we would close . . . or fall through.

The train huffed to a halt. Then came the single, sharp bark of the border commander ordering his men to jump on. Several guards entered the train, including in our car, where a middle-aged German official lumbered down the aisle. He went wearily from passenger to passenger, asking to see the *Ausweiss*—the difficult-to-obtain special pass the authorities were starting to require to enter German-occupied territory. Sophie and I didn't have one, and that was the main weakness of my plan. But getting an *Ausweiss* was an arduous, time-consuming process. You had to produce multiple sets of identity documents and receive approval from several levels of government. I had decided that it was more important to get Saul out quickly, while the new occupiers were still settling in, while new restrictions, both physical and bureaucratic, were still being put in place. But now, as the man's stocky frame clad in his grey-green uniform approached—had I made the right choice?

"Show me your *Ausweiss*," the official said, in German-accented French.

"Oh. Pardon us, sir," I replied in Alsatian. "But we don't really speak French. We've never needed it, you see, out in the countryside, where we live. French, well . . . it's for those sophisticated city-types, and my sister and I are just humble Alsatian farmwives." I beamed at him, vacantly.

"Alsatians, eh?" The official switched to German, guessing that since the two languages were so similar, I'd understand. "Well, I'm sure you're on your way back home then. With the province now back with the Fatherland where it belongs, congratulations." He didn't quite smile, but I could tell he was pleased, as in *These are exactly the type of passengers I want to see.*

"Yes, that's correct, sir," I said, sounding as bright and eager as I could. "After we enter the Occupied Zone, we'll switch in the city of Nancy for Alsace."

"Excellent. I hope to see many more of you Alsatians coming home. The *Führer* needs all of you, to win the war and build a strong, prosperous future. You ladies must rally your Alsatian compatriots to join you, and soon. The Reich won't wait forever . . ." He went on, and on. How not enough Alsatians had come back yet. How wonderful it was that the province was now in its rightful place. How France's rapid defeat proved the righteousness of Germany's cause and the brilliance of its leader.

I am not an actress, but thanks to my lifelong work as a shopkeeper, I was able to hold my face in a pleasant, neutral position while the official seemed to relish his chance to impart a river of propaganda.

Well, Mr. Nazi guard, I don't think you actually would want me *to return, because Alsace is now Judenrein. But even if it weren't declared free of Jews, home is the last place I want to be right now, and every Alsatian I know, Jewish or not, feels exactly the same way.*

That's what I thought. What I said was, "Oh, yes. You are so right."

"Very well, very well," he said, seeming to suddenly realize that he needed to move on to other passengers. "Now, where are those papers, ladies? An *Ausweiss* is soon to be mandatory for border crossing, and you really should have one now."

"Oh." I sighed, looking distressed, contrite, and helpless all at the same time. "We could not obtain one quickly enough. We were so anxious to be home. But all our identity papers were lost, sir. Lost in the exodus. With so many of our things . . ."

I pretended to be overcome with emotion, wiping my eyes, a damsel in distress.

"Yes, I can imagine," the official said with half-hearted sternness. "When your weak, pathetic country fell so quickly, it was indeed chaos. And I'm pleased that you ladies are returning to the Fatherland so quickly and with such enthusiasm. So, I will let you through, given the circumstances."

A flood of relief swept through me, so powerful I thought that water might exit my pores.

"However," he said, staring at me now with authority.

And did I see something *else* in his eyes? *Oh no. Oh please, no.* In the space of two seconds, I re-lived the night my sister was raped in Amshinov.

"You must know that the new Nazi authorities in Alsace won't be anything like the sloppy French government that preceded them. They will be very strict about proper record-keeping, and they'll issue you papers promptly. Once you have them, don't even think about traveling without them again."

I gazed up at him, simple and innocent. "Oh, no, sir, we would not. We have little intention of traveling anyway. Once we reach home, we only wish to stay on our farm and make cheese."

"All right, then," the official said. He moved to the next passengers.

Beside me, Sophie was shaking, with what I thought was fear.

"You can hardly cook, never mind make cheese," she said, in a barely controlled laugh.

I pinched her elbow, to keep her from laughing out loud. Then I pinched myself, but it wasn't to curb my own laughter. We'd just had an incredibly lucky break, entering enemy territory. But it could have turned in an instant because we were now completely at the Nazis' mercy.

IN NANCY, I found us a cheap hotel room near the prison camp.

"Come on," I said to Sophie as soon as we'd dropped our bags in our room. "Reconnaissance mission."

I wanted to go by the camp, to observe the inmates' comings and goings. I had a general idea of how we'd get Saul out, but I was still working out the details in my head. Of course, I didn't tell Sophie that. Nor did I tell her why I had brought a small, extra suitcase, filled with a set of Melach's clothes.

We walked by the camp, which was enormous. Its walls were made of heaps of hideous-looking grey slag, surrounded by barbed wire. Dozens of wooden barracks that must have been erected hastily stood in rows. Groups of thin, slouching men waited in long lines—perhaps for food or to use the toilet, I guessed. Their fatigue and illness were evident, even from the far-off spot where we watched. Sophie stopped and gaped.

I took her hand and squeezed it. "Keep going. Look casual. I'm right here with you."

I pulled her along at a purposeful step. Just two ordinary women passing by.

THE NEXT DAY, I told Sophie to stay at the hotel. Her early enthusiasm about coming to rescue Saul had changed to complete distress. She was an emotional wreck.

"It's horrible, horrible." She hurled herself down onto her hotel bed, weeping, after our walk. "Did you see how wretched those men were? What if he's sick? They won't give him medical treatment. What if he dies? They won't care." She quieted after a long cry, but in the middle of the night, I heard her crying again.

I walked by the prison for two more days alone, each morning and afternoon. I made special note of when the German guards went out to shop for supplies, bringing with them a prisoner to translate. It made sense that they would choose a prisoner from Alsace because many Alsatians understood and spoke German. Just as Saul had explained.

POWs were permitted to write and receive letters, although the system wasn't reliable. How well the mail moved depended upon the mood of each camp's overseers. We'd received only one letter from Saul since the end of the war, and he'd kept it light and cheerful: funny stories about the other prisoners, jokes about the dismal conditions, and his small pleasure at being chosen for translation duty, accompanying the guards when they left camp for the local general store.

Quite innocently, Saul had helped me craft his rescue.

THE STORE WAS easy to find. It was large and close to the camp. I visited it the day after we arrived in Nancy, buying a few small items so I would look like a legitimate customer. I approached the counter to pay, offering the elderly cashier my most friendly smile. I needed to connect with this woman but not draw suspicion.

"*Bonjour,* madame. What a nice shop you have. So well organized and well-stocked, not an easy feat these days. And my compliments are from one shopkeeper to another. Until the war, I ran a clothing store with my husband in Colmar."

"Why thank you, madame, for the praise. It's very kind of you."

"You're most welcome. And . . . again, from one shopkeeper to another, may I ask . . . how is business for you now, with the camp close by?"

I kept my tone neutral. The shop owner might be a German collaborator.

The woman's amicable demeanor darkened. "Business is good, very good. At least for my pocketbook. But . . . the *Boches.* Taking our beautiful country. It is hard, on my heart."

I knew then that she would be sympathetic.

"Ah. I understand." I leaned in. "And then, watching our own imprisoned soldiers helping them with their errands, I imagine that would be painful for you as well. Men like that tall Alsatian who often comes, with the dark eyes. I'm sure you've noticed him . . ."

The shopkeeper made an appreciative noise. "Ah, *Oui,* it's hard *not* to notice him, eh, madame? He's easy to look at, that one."

"Yes, of course. Do you see him often?"

"Why, he comes almost every day, mid-morning. The guards buy very little for the prisoners, it's mostly luxuries they get for themselves. Chocolate, coffee . . . of course, the *Boches* don't speak French, so the young man translates."

"Oh. Interesting. Lastly, do you have a lavatory? For customers, of course." I indicated my purchases.

"Yes. You'll see the door in the back by those high shelves. You're welcome to use it. It's nice to chat with another merchant. Colmar, you say? Lovely little city. I wish you the very best of luck, regaining your store someday."

MID-MORNING THE next day, I went back to the shop, this time with Sophie. My sister had transformed in the few days since our arrival. *She's ready. And she needs to be.* Because what we were about to do was beyond risky. It was deadly.

We entered the store carrying our suitcases, chatting lightly, about what we should buy to eat before we got on the train. The elderly shopkeeper held her usual place behind the counter. She gave me a pleasant nod of recognition while she tended to some other customers. The store was busy. *That will help. More people means more distractions.*

The door opened. Saul, dressed in grey prison garb, entered with a Nazi soldier. I grabbed Sophie and pulled her behind a shelf. I didn't want Saul to see us. He had no idea we were there, of course. Luckily, Sophie and I were both short, so our heads weren't visible above the shelving.

"Once they move to another part of the store, we do it. All right, Sophie?" I whispered.

She cracked open the small suitcase, checking for the hundredth time that Melach's clothes were still there. She clicked the case shut.

"Ready," she whispered.

Despite the danger of what we were about to do, I enjoyed a warm flare of pride. Sophie had put her initial terror somewhere else and locked it up. I wanted to hug her, to tell her how proud I was of her. But that could come later.

Sophie made her way toward the toilet closet, and I strode to the counter.

"Excuse me, madame," I said as loudly as I could without yelling. "My sister *Sophie* needs to use your *lavatory*. Would that be acceptable? We have a *taxi* to catch."

Several other shoppers stared at me. *Good,* that meant I was loud enough for Saul to hear. The shopkeeper replied that it was nice to see me again and that yes, my sister should feel free to access the *toilettes.*

"Thank you. *Sophie* will be so glad to have use of your *lavatory* before we *leave* in a *taxi*," I replied, again at full volume. This time, even the store owner gave me a look.

Sophie entered the toilet room and left the valise containing Melach's outfit there. Then she exited the shop where the cab I'd reserved waited outside. I left the shop as well, crossing right in front of Saul and his guard. We avoided looking at each other, but I heard Saul say exactly what I needed him to say.

"*Bitte*, please sir," he said in German to his guard. "I have to use the toilets."

"*Ja*," the guard said, distracted by a display of candies. "But be quick about it."

For one thick, painful minute, Sophie and I waited inside the taxi. In those sixty seconds, I lived and relived dozens of outcomes, all of them horrific. Saul never making it out to join us. Saul coming out of the shop in his disguise, but flanked by a furious Nazi guard. The guard appearing at the taxi door instead of Saul, handcuffing us and dragging us away. The cab driver somehow becoming involved in our detainment.

The click of a door handle. Saul squeezed in next to us, in Melach's clothing. No guard.

"Quickly, please," I said to the cab driver. "To the train station."

My nerves screamed but I forced my vocal cords to stay calm. If the driver suspected trouble, he might turn us in. And if we were caught, we would be arrested and likely shot on the spot, no questions asked. Melach would lose a wife and a brother. Sophie's children would lose both their parents. And my children . . .

I addressed the cab driver again.

"Our train leaves soon. I'll pay you double if you can get us there in five minutes."

I KNEW THAT as soon as we'd boarded the train, Sophie would want to throw herself into Saul's arms. But I was adamant that we not attract attention. "No kissing. Not here. Come."

I found us an empty four-seat compartment.

"I'll give you some time alone."

"Not needed," Saul said. "We should stick together."

But I could see the need on Sophie's face.

"I'll be back in ten minutes," I said.

When I returned, Sophie was crying, her head buried in Saul's chest.

"We got there just in time," she said, between gulps of air and bouts of weeping.

"Sit down, Sarah. We're fine now. We're fine." Saul stroked Sophie's hair. "But she's right. You *did* arrive just in time. All those assurances you probably heard about how France's POWs would be sent home soon? Lies. The camp authorities were drawing up plans to send us to work in Germany. Not all of us, just the white prisoners. The French colonial soldiers—the Senegalese, Vietnamese, Moroccans, and others from the colonies were to stay behind. As desperately as Hitler needs workers to keep his war economy going, he draws the line at non-white people. He doesn't want them on German soil. But white British and French prisoners are being transformed into an enormous involuntary labor force for the Reich. Most of the guys hoped they'd be sent to a farm, where at least there might be more food. That was our obsession. Always food . . ."

I noticed for the first time how malnourished he was—his cheekbones too prominent, his skin an unhealthy yellow-grey, the fibers of his neck visible because there was so little flesh. It hurt to see this once robust man so reduced, rasping as he told his story through dry, cracked lips.

"But not everyone wanted to wait out the remainder of the war on a German farm," Saul continued. "And there was no guarantee you would. You could be sent to a factory too, a nice target for a British bomber . . . or some treacherous underground mine. And then, for me . . . the thought of actually being inside Germany . . . as a Jew . . . it wouldn't take them long to find out."

Saul tightened his arm around Sophie.

"So, a surprising number of men I was captured with slipped away in the early days, when security was disorganized because the camps weren't fully set up yet. I considered joining them, but at first, we thought it wasn't worth the effort. Most of us just assumed the war would be over soon and then we could go home. The guards worked hard to make sure that's what we believed; some of them even denied us the postcards they were supposed to give us to write to our families. 'You don't need to bother sending them,' they said. 'You'll be home before the card gets there.' But soon, the rumors began that they had other plans. Then, when the first transport cars showed up, we knew it was all a lie to keep us docile. I didn't know what to do: Should I try to escape and risk death? Or should I go to Germany as a forced laborer and pray for the best? That I would live to see my wife and sons again?"

A long series of coughs shook Saul's body. He seemed to have expended his last ounce of energy. But rather than slump back in his seat to rest, he shakily stood up.

"Excuse me. I'm still a bit troubled by dysentery. I have to use the toilet. Again." He managed to produce a weak chuckle that sounded more like a huff. "No, *this* time I really do. And I promise not to change clothes."

I laughed, and the joke even got a smile out of Sophie.

Chapter 20
NÎMES, FRANCE
AUGUST 1940. SETTLE

MELACH MET US at the train station in Vichy. His tall form was easy to spot above the others in the crowd. We waved to him, and he sprinted to us. I thought he might embrace Saul first, and I would have understood. But he pulled me to him and gave me a prolonged kiss in front of everyone.

"You did it," he said, his voice husky. "I was frantic with worry."

Then he stepped toward his brother. "Saul."

They threw their arms around each other, and it was a long time before they let go.

SAUL STRUGGLED TO eat at first. We learned not to make meals that were too rich, even though our instinct was to fatten him up. But at the camp, he explained, there was little to eat besides weak broth and bread, often just once a day. And that was ample compared to what he'd eaten during his five-day forced march to the prison camp when the Germans gave them nothing. Saul said he and the others survived only thanks to small scraps of food that sympathetic French citizens tossed at them, as his group was marched through town after town.

"People knew they weren't supposed to give us food, the Germans ordered them not to," he told us one night when he was feeling well enough to stay up and talk. "It was a risk, but they took it. We were so grateful for anything."

Later came even more harrowing stories. How, on the march, those POWs who lagged behind due to illness or injury were poked and prodded by the butts of rifles and shot if they fell. How some men were so ravenous, they ate grass. How some colonial soldiers, including those with whom Saul's unit was captured, suffered a terrible fate.

"When we first surrendered, they separated the white soldiers from the black soldiers. Those from Senegal, Madagascar. Exceptional fighters they were, too. Well-trained. But before our march to the prison camp even began, the Germans took the black soldiers to a ravine and shot them all. Said they were not legitimate combatants and therefore weren't covered by the conventions of war." Disgust shadowed his haggard face. "Bastards. I heard one laughing when he emerged from the ravine, saying that was the proper way to deal with blacks and Jews."

SAUL RECOVERED STEADILY. After about ten days, he declared himself ready for more hearty foods. Cheese. Meat. And especially wine.

Sophie cooked a special meal, or as special as it could be, given the upheaval in the food supply. Our friends the Goldsteins were again working as butchers, as they had in Alsace. They found a roast, and Sophie prepared it just how Saul liked it, with potatoes, onions, and carrots. I traded some of the goods I'd transported from Alsace for a few bottles of excellent red wine.

As we sat down to celebrate, Melach offered the first toast. "To my brother's release. To my amazing wife. To our families, two sisters and two brothers *more closely related than most.*"

Everyone at the crowded table chortled at the old joke. What a relief it was, to laugh and drink. To be together, in this loving little circle.

Melach turned to Sophie and me with a more serious expression. "If anything had happened, I could not have lived with the guilt of letting you go alone."

"But we made it." Saul held up his glass. "Thanks to my crafty sister-in-law."

"And Sophie, too," I protested. "I couldn't have done it without her."

Saul took Sophie's hand across the table. "Yes."

He looked almost like his old self, except for the emerging fuzz on his head, which had been shaved in prison

He lifted his glass for a second time. "To Sophie. To all of us. May we not become separated again."

WE SEPARATED.

The morning after our celebratory dinner, our communal glow of reconnection was replaced by reality: we needed to leave Vichy, now that Saul seemed healthy enough. The city was crawling with French fascists, eager to create a *new* France, or what they called "The National Revolution." It sounded a lot like Nazi Germany to us, and we all wanted to escape the capital city of this weird, sinister version of our country. But we couldn't agree on where we should go. Saul thought Grenoble was the best choice, in the southeastern corner of France, near Switzerland and Italy. It would be safer there, he contended, since Grenoble was occupied by Italian troops—Nazi allies in the war, yes—but with a famously relaxed attitude about enforcing the rules.

I was tempted to go with them. But I'd already made up my mind: Clermont-Ferrand.

"Grenoble's too tucked away," I reasoned. "And there are lots of Alsatians in Clermont-Ferrand, remember? The whole University of Strasbourg was resettled there, during the evacuation late last summer."

"But we just said last night, we shouldn't be separated again," Saul retorted. Unlike Melach, he was a more ready opponent when it came to an argument.

"The Alsatian connection has been an unexpected guardian angel for us, throughout this whole ordeal. It's why those soldiers let Jacques ride with them. It's why that German border guard let Sophie and me through. It'll help us get back in business more quickly."

"Never mind the Alsatian connection, what about the *family* connection? What about Sophie and me, and the boys? We're in dark times, Sarah. You know that better than anyone. We should stick together."

Meanwhile, Melach sat at the table nursing his coffee, the curve of his mouth betraying his misery. Sophie fluttered about the kitchen, wiping countertops and washing pots, even though the room was perfectly clean. They were grieving, I realized, and at some unexamined level, so was I. But grief could come later. We needed to move. Still, I softened.

"I understand. I do. But we have family scattered across France now, and if they need us, Grenoble is just too far."

I put my arm around Sophie, so she would stop her skittish cleaning. "I love you so much, my little Zofjya," I said, using her old Polish name. "But they might need me too, just as Saul did."

Sophie leaned into me, and for a sweet moment, we savored that sister bond. The familiar warmth, that chemical, physical understanding created by shared history and shared blood.

"And if you need *us*," she said. "We'll be waiting for you."

"Thank you, Sophie," I said, although I couldn't imagine how we'd need their help.

But I was wrong.

ON OUR FAMILY'S first morning in Clermont-Ferrand, I planned to start apartment hunting right away. The five of us had spent the night in a stale-smelling hotel room, which we were lucky to find. Half the country, it seemed, was still on the move. Despite French and German authorities urging everyone to go home, countless families had no idea if they had homes left. Many Northerners weren't sure if they wanted to return to their towns and villages, located now in the German Occupied Zone. That was especially the feeling among Jews and other "undesirables," as defined by the Nazis. But for us, there was no wrenching choice between staying put or going home, since Jews were now banned from Alsace. It was our new, appalling reality, but I'd already put it aside. There was too much to do, and I refused to waste time and energy ruminating on the repulsiveness of the new regime. I was eager to settle down and was optimistic about our prospects in Clermont-Ferrand.

I sent André and Annette to the bakery just around the corner that we'd noticed the night before.

"Get something small for us to eat for breakfast. André, hold your sister's hand."

"*Oui,* Maman," they chorused and bolted, excited to see a new neighborhood.

Five minutes later they were back, pounding at the door.

"We saw Germans!" Annette yelled.

"Soldiers, a dozen of them, riding in motorcycles with sidecars," André reported.

"You should see their uniforms, so stylish. With shiny boots and leather coats," Annette continued.

I eyed Melach. He caught the look and understood it. Perfectly.

"Jacques, André, Annette. Let's go, children. We'll find breakfast elsewhere, maybe at the train station," he said, in a won't-this-be-fun manner that he used so effectively with them, much more convincingly than I did. We hadn't unpacked yet, so it was easy to pack up again. We took the next available train further south. Much further.

AS WE APPROACHED the ancient city of Nîmes, Jacques and André pressed their faces to the window, pointing out the Roman ruins they'd learned about in school. I tried to appreciate that my sons found Nîmes fascinating: the giant Roman arena, the aqueducts, and bridges where the sandaled feet of Roman soldiers trod centuries ago. But all I could see were shabby buildings and unkempt public squares.

I rented the first apartment for five I could find. The proprietor insisted it had been cleaned, though I grumbled to Melach that night that this "cleaning" had likely occurred during the Roman era.

"Ha! Well, at least we found a place" he said. "We'll manage to—"

Annette screamed. "Papa! Help. Bugs. Everywhere. Big ones and small ones and everywhere."

Then Jacques yelled, "Rats! There's a rat's nest behind my bed."

In the end, we moved four times, before we found a place that was as good as it got in Nîmes: clean, with enough room for all of us, and well-located, near the municipal theater and gardens. Melach opened a store with the merchandise I had brought to Vichy just before France fell. The shop was more like a large closet, but it would do. As Melach and I arranged the shoes, textiles, and clothing on the narrow, high shelves, I pictured myself packing up these very same items in Colmar, hoping that we wouldn't need to transport them but expecting—all right, *knowing*—that we would. I paused while folding a shirt, the scenes drifting through my mind, of all that had happened in just three months. The madness of the exodus. The stunning, rapid fall of France. The incapacitating grief when Jacques was lost and the breathtaking joy of finding him again. The daunting but necessary risk of the POW camp rescue. The exhaustion of moving, always moving: Colmar, Vichy, Clermont-Ferrand, and now, Nîmes.

Still, I felt we could begin a new, more stable chapter here. While optimism was out of character for me—I left that up to Melach—I'd been through enough to appreciate my blessings. We had food. We had a business. We enrolled our children in school. We became friends with other Jewish families in Nîmes, both long-established residents and newcomers like us. We didn't expect to find such close kinship in this scruffy, ancient city, and it was a welcome surprise that we did.

"It's not so bad here," Melach would often say. And for a brief time, I thought he might be right.

Chapter 21
NÎMES, FRANCE
SUMMER 1941. EXCLUSION

LOUD, HIGH CRYING in the hallway. Even before Annette opened the apartment door, I heard her wailing. My daughter charged in, her nine-year-old face heated with anger and smudged with tears.

"I hate them! I hate them! I want to kick them and pull their hair."

Annette buried her face in my shoulder. I held her and stroked her curls, not asking who "they" were, because I already knew: Gisele and Ginette, two classmates who had made a sport of terrorizing another student, a Jewish girl named Rose, calling her dirty, a communist, an insect. Annette often came home with tales of the constant insults Rose endured, and how the little girl cried all day in class.

"And the teacher, she does nothing . . . *nothing*. How can she do nothing, Maman?"

Back in Alsace, I would have marched down to the school myself and told that teacher a thing or two. But not now.

"You can't, sweetie. I know it's hard for you to stay quiet. But you must."

I had ordered our children to keep a low profile as we were settling in. Stay out of trouble, and if asked about their backgrounds, they were simply to say they were "from Alsace."

It was a common answer that raised no questions. Not yet.

ANNETTE CHEERED UP when André sauntered in.

"Hello, hello, everyone," he sang. He noticed Annette's tear-stained face and bent down to her level. "Why, what's this? Did Mademoiselle have a bad day at school? Yes? Well then, let's fix this. Let's go to the fountain and look at the people and make jokes about them. Then we can run in the park. It's a perfect June day, ordered up just for Mademoiselle. Maybe we'll see Jacques on his way home from school."

André dampened his handkerchief and wiped Annette's blotchy face.

"Come on. Let's go." He clapped his hands, urging Annette up out of her seat.

"Thank you, André," I said. "It has been a difficult day for our Annette."

"Of course, Maman. We always have fun, don't we?" he said to Annette.

André took Annette's hand, and as they left, he belted out a children's song often heard on Radio-Nîmes called "My Toys at Night." It was one of Annette's favorites.

"My toys at night, they argue and fight . . . they want to go out and play . . ."

As the boisterous singing faded down the hallway, I marveled: Well into their teens and at ages when most brothers would want nothing to do with a little sister, Jacques and André doted on Annette, often sweeping in with excursions, jokes, and treats when she was sad or upset.

It's due to the war. They're just trying to do their part. But then, *No. They've always been thoughtful and attentive. They're just like their father.*

Thinking of Melach reminded me that he was late coming home for lunch. It was an odd role for me, the wife-waiting-at-home-for-her-spouse. But for now, we were going along with the new "Family-Fatherland" Vichy culture, pretending to adopt the government's propaganda that women should have "no aspirations beyond hearth and home." In fact, the regime's constant promotion of female domesticity had become a family joke. Melach would return from the store and say, "How's the hearth?" "Fine," I'd reply. "And don't worry . . . no aspirations here." Then I'd grill him about that week's sales and outline exactly what he needed to do to improve them.

Our standard of living was nothing like before, but we were managing, thanks to the bundles of merchandise from Colmar and our own efforts. *We can make it,* I told myself, as I opened some canned food for a makeshift stew and dumped it into a pot. I stirred the lumpy food with gratitude . . . for it, for our health, for the new friends we'd already made in Nîmes' Jewish community. I still found the city hot and dingy, and I still yearned for cool, clean Alsace, but Melach was right. Nîmes had a certain charm and spirit; we could wait out the war here happily enough.

The apartment door groaned open and banged shut.

"I'm in the kitchen," I called out, guessing it was Melach, at last, home for lunch.

I poked at the gloppy mixture on the stove as it bubbled, expecting his usual humming entrance and his greeting with a kiss on the forehead or a squeeze around the shoulders, always with a how-was-your-morning. But Melach walked right past me, heaved his lanky body into a chair, and slumped.

I turned to him, ladle in hand. Brown stew dripped on the floor. "What's wrong? What is it, Melach?"

My gregarious husband was oddly quiet. Finally, he said, "The word out in the community is that there's another Jewish law coming, and this one includes a census," he said haltingly, as if he were still working through what to say. "Of everything and everyone . . . an accounting of Jews in each town and all that we own. By mid-summer, we have to report to City Hall, listing the names and ages of everyone in the family, as well as all our property. Homes, businesses, shops, merchandise, valuables . . . whatever we have. Jews who do not register are in for severe punishment. And you know what *that* could be."

I could guess. Foreign Jews were already being sent to so-called "internment camps," as part of the Vichy government's first Jewish Law passed last fall. That earlier statute had also excluded Jews from top positions in public service, such as the government, medicine, and the military. It dramatically reduced the number of Jews in professions that could "influence public opinion," such as the media, teaching, or theater. But at the same time, the government had vowed back then that it wouldn't touch Jewish property, that there would be no discrimination against Jews in the professions still open to them, and that its main concern was foreign, or what they called "stateless" Jews. The property of "true" French Jews, we were assured, would be protected.

Some of our friends in Nîmes had believed those pretty promises, especially those who'd lived in France for generations. But I did not, and I was not alone. Those of us who had been "foreign" not that long ago had grown up with persecution and lies. We were certain there'd be another round of Jewish Laws, and that these would be even harsher than the first round. And so, we began gathering information. Forging connections. Making plans.

Now, I put the stew ladle in the sink, sorting through my emotions; disappointment, but not surprise, that skeptics like me had been right. I poured Melach a glass of water and brought it to him, where he still sat, slouched over.

"I don't understand," he said. "We never had to do this before. Never. Not in Metz, Sedan, or Colmar. Registering people by religion just isn't French. What happened to *Égalité?*"

Melach took a long drink. "But this is the worst part. The census allows them to completely shut us out of the economy. Once they know who we are and what we have, the plan is to Aryanize everything. Just like in Germany, the Aryanization that Rabbi Weber told us about, before the war, remember? They give our property to some designated trustee, who then decides what to do with it. That person might liquidate it, sell it, or continue to run it. They give us an insulting, token amount for our business and then we're destitute."

He raised his face to me, his handsome features marked with grief and confusion: How could the country he'd always venerated turn on him with such sudden, cruel deceit?

"What should we *do*, Sarah? What *can* we do?"

I untied my apron. "No. We are *not* filling out that form and we're not giving them a damn thing. I stockpiled that merchandise for months in Colmar because I knew war was coming. I dragged it to Vichy as the country was collapsing around us. Because of those packages, I *left our children*, with you still away at war. I could have died trying to get back to Colmar, then to Vichy. I don't care if the little frightened fascist men running the French government say our business is now theirs. It's not. It's *ours*."

The frustration that had smoldered in me since Vichy's first Jewish Laws ignited into a flame. It burned my chest, my lungs, my throat . . . but I welcomed the heat. It gave me clarity. There was no way I was going to hand over to the government our only means of survival.

Melach made a grunting sound that I knew signaled doubt. "But if we don't register, we could be fined or even *arrested*. You've heard the rumors."

Yes, I'd heard them. That even some Jews who were naturalized citizens, like us, might have been sent to the internment camps as well. No one knew yet what the ultimate purpose of these centers was, whether it had changed from the previous government's goal of housing refugees, however crudely. But we heard that the camps were becoming more crowded, that conditions were deplorable, and that hundreds were dying there from disease. Still, I would not let rumors frighten me into submission. Into poverty.

"Just do what I say. Sell everything in the shop quickly, then . . ."

Young voices sang in the hallway. Melach and I plastered our everything-is-fine look on our faces, as André and Annette arrived home, bubbling about their excursion.

Annette ran into the kitchen. "Maman, it's so much fun. You'll never believe it."

"What, Maideleh? What is it?" I asked with exaggerated cheer.

André followed, bouncing on the balls of his feet. "We found out that Radio-Nîmes is inviting children from displaced families to sing at their studios. It's their way of making people who had to resettle from northern France feel welcome, I guess. They're creating a group of little kids who'll sing every Saturday afternoon, live on the radio. Lots of songs, including . . . which one, Mademoiselle Annette?"

She was bursting to speak. "'My Toys at Night!'"

They both belted out the song, as a beaming Jacques came in.

"André. There's a party tonight at the Lespaques' house," he said. "Then we're going to the theater after. I asked if I could bring you, and they said yes. That is, if it's alright with you, Maman."

My three children, who'd been through so much, were finally settling in, enjoying themselves, and making friends. A normal childhood.

"It's fine, boys. Have fun. Now, who wants some canned stew for the third time this week?"

I would break the news to them tomorrow, that we were, once again, leaving.

THAT EVENING, MELACH and I studied a long sheet of numbers. On one side of the ledger, I listed what we had left to sell at our tiny shop in Nîmes. On the other side, I wrote what merchandise remained stored in Colmar, watched over by Adele. I congratulated myself for making her our "Aryan Buyer" long ago. Altogether, it would provide enough money to live on for several months, but eventually I would have to get that last bundle from our shop at home, and I'd have to cross the demarcation line into what was now part of Germany.

I would need help, and I found it in Nîmes. The city once controlled by faraway rulers in Rome had its own spirit of disobedience. I'd met plenty of people who weren't about to roll over and obey the new authorities: Jews like me, especially those who hadn't been born in France; also, the city's many Protestants, with their own historic reasons for distrust; and a handful of international relief groups, whose *stated* mission was war refugee support, but some of whom were beginning to more broadly define the meaning of "support"—helping targeted people like us through underground means.

I asked questions. I listened. And more than once, I heard the name of a particular small city with a particularly helpful person . . .

Melach rose from the table and went to the window, taking in the view of central Nîmes: the palm trees, the fountain, the wide stone plaza, the amphitheater. "I just don't know. On paper, it all seems to add up, but—"

"There's no *but*, Melach. Of course, it adds up."

I was doing the math, the organization, and the planning, for yet another escape. And he was questioning me? I rubbed my eyes.

"We should sell our stock of shoes first; those always get a good price . . ." I looked up, expecting some response from Melach. Nothing. "But we won't sell or trade any of the canned food. I know we're all tired of it, but food is something we should never give up . . ." I glanced at Melach again. "Still, I shouldn't have to go north to Alsace just yet, to get the last of our supplies. If we sell what we have here, that should give us enough to survive reasonably well, for a while, in a new place."

Melach threw his arms up. "Where? Where is that new place? There's nothing. There's nowhere."

I ignored his despair. I had enough problems before me. "Shush. If you're not going to help me with these numbers, then be quiet and let me concentrate."

Several minutes passed. I added and subtracted.

Melach stayed at the window, tapping his fingers on the glass. "I can't believe I'm proposing this, but . . . maybe we should try to emigrate like your cousin did, to Portugal. Or we could join your aunt's family in America. I know it's near impossible to get out of France now, but we could try . . ."

I threw the account book on the floor and stood up. "*No*, Melach. Stop it! Just *stop*."

Another wife—a nicer, "better" wife—might have found some compassion for what her husband was going through. Anguish over the betrayal by his beloved France. Panic over how we would survive, without any legal means to make money. Vacillation over whether we should register our family as Jews: what would be more dire, to ignore the order or to obey it?

This other, "better" wife would have understood him, held him, and tried her best to comfort him. But I wasn't that wife.

"I've had it up to here with you!" I said, instead. "I don't need you to be desperate and floundering right now, suggesting hopeless, stupid ideas. I need you to help me *think*."

Was this the moment when Melach started to fall apart? I can't say for sure, because I was so focused on survival: Sell items. Close store. Leave Nîmes.

Melach stepped away from the window and sat down at the table. "I didn't mean it when I said let's leave France. I don't know what I'm thinking . . . or saying . . . anymore. I don't even want to leave Nîmes. I'm so tired of being on the run. How many times have we moved since we left Alsace? How many apartments? And this question of Jews registering . . . everyone else is going to do it. Why shouldn't we? The government is still run by French people, we're still French citizens. These laws will be relaxed again, eventually. Besides, the registry is a *national* mandate from the Vichy government. Even if we do go to a new place, it'll be in effect everywhere. The national authorities will still require local officials to obey it." He paused, as if something had just occurred to him. "Wait. You said 'in a new place.' What *is* the new place?"

"Just quietly sell everything and close the shop. Then we'll make our move."

Chapter 22
GANGES, FRANCE
JULY 1941. IDENTITY

HIS NAME WAS Hector De Beauville. I was told I'd find him at the front desk of City Hall, in Ganges, a modest city at the base of a region called the Cévennes. I'd never heard of either place before our time in Nîmes, but my contacts there described the region in an almost mythical way. A rugged, mysterious landscape, populated by an independent, rebellious citizenry. Apparently, the Cévennes was a Protestant stronghold, and its people had a long memory about the repression they had suffered under France's Catholic kings.

"You'll find a lot of folks in Ganges eager to help you," I heard again and again. "But Hector's your most important first stop."

RIGHT BEFORE NOON, I walked from our hotel across Ganges' stone-paved central square, grateful for the abundant shade of its knobby Sycamore trees. City Hall was on the other side of the square. It looked like an old convent, a white concrete building with a large courtyard. I pushed open the door that said, "Mayor's Office," welcoming the coolness that the thick walls offered. My clothes were already wrinkling in the heat.

A young man was combing through a file drawer. A plaque on his desk said, "Hector De Beauville. Assistant to the Mayor." He lifted his head.

"*Bonjour*, how may I help you?" he asked.

My first thought was how ordinary-looking he was. He had thick, medium brown hair that hinted it might soon be receding. He was tall, with a normal build, an unremarkable nose and mouth. It was his eyes that stood out: They were an unusually dark brown and seemed to reflect the deep, genuine goodness of this man. I have never been a trusting person by nature, but I trusted Hector De Beauville immediately.

"*Bonjour*," I said, glancing around the office. It appeared we were alone, but I wasn't sure how freely I should speak.

"Don't worry," he said. "It's been especially hot this July, and everyone else has left early for lunch. I think I know why you're here."

"Thank you. I was told you could help us with some documents. Identity papers."

"I absolutely can. But not here or now. I don't like to conduct this 'business' on city property, even though, if I had to guess, I'd say all of my colleagues here would support what I'm doing." He picked up a pen. "Ganges is not what you'd call a hotbed of support for the Vichy Regime."

He wrote down his address on a scrap of paper, gave it to me, locked his file drawers, and stood up. His handwriting was meticulous.

"Here's my home address. Bring your family on Saturday afternoon. And now if you'll excuse me, madame . . . ?"

"Seibert," I said. "Sarah Seibert."

"Madame Seibert, then. I'll be happy to see you and your family on Saturday. But I do need to close up the office now. My wife is waiting for me, to have lunch at home."

He put an especially warm emphasis on the word "wife" as he touched his gold wedding ring on his finger.

"You're newly married?" I asked.

"No," he answered, almost blushing like a teenager. "It's been six years. But . . . well, you'll meet my Jo-Jo on Saturday."

SATURDAY AFTERNOON, WE arrived at the De Beauville home, nestled among chestnut, larch, and sycamore trees in a neighborhood high above downtown Ganges. It was a warm, dry midsummer day. A sweet, light pine scent hung in the air, and the sky was an achingly perfect blue. The house had an inviting back yard, with an odd, curved brown brick structure in one corner.

"It's a mausoleum," Monsieur De Beauville explained, as he opened his back yard gate in welcome. "They're traditional for Protestants in this area, from way back when. Not being Catholic, we weren't permitted to bury our dead in public graveyards in town. So, we built our own home-based burial plots instead."

My family stared at the mausoleum. We'd never seen anything like it.

"It must seem odd, I admit," Monsieur De Beauville said. "But some mausoleums, including mine, have an added benefit. They lock from the inside, so if a family got word of an anti-Protestant raid, back in the day, these made excellent, although perhaps unnerving, hiding places."

My sons giggled at that; the spooky prospect of hiding out along with one's dead relatives. Monsieur De Beauville smiled at them. He had two sons of his own, I'd learned, although much younger than Jacques and André.

Across the yard from the mausoleum was a majestic chestnut tree by a picnic table. I hoped that we could meet there, the perfect spot on a beautiful day. But Hector, as he now insisted we call him, said it would be better to gather indoors.

"I trust my neighbors," he said. "But one can't be too cautious these days."

He brought us into his library; every wall lined with bookshelves full of books. Hector's wife, Josephine—or Jo-Jo as he called her—greeted us with cookies and herbal tea she'd made herself from her garden. She leaned over and kissed Hector on the cheek, and I saw him glow again, as he did the other day at his office, when he mentioned his wife's name.

"I'm sorry there's no coffee," she said. "Hector and I don't even bother with that coffee-chicory substitute that some people drink. We think it tastes like dirt mixed with unsweetened caramel."

"It's not important, thank you, this is lovely," I said, liking Jo-Jo De Beauville right away.

We settled into our seats, balancing our teacups and cookies, with Jo-Jo perched on the armrest of a leather chair next to her husband. She lovingly tucked a wayward strand of Hector's hair behind his ear and then rested her hand on his shoulder. Jacques was the last to sit down, taken by the tall shelves of books.

"You have so many books, right here in your own house," he said, wistfully. "It's just like the library at my school, in Colmar."

"That's true, I do have a lot," Hector said. "But it's not unusual for around here. Many Cévenol families keep personal libraries at home. It's part of our Protestant heritage; people say we chose to educate ourselves instead of simply accepting and trusting what kings or bishops told us . . ."

I was starting to get a sense of that famed, feisty Protestantism that defined the Cévennes. I would see more of it over the next few years. A lot more.

"You can borrow some books if you'd like. I'd be happy to share them with you," Hector added. "When we're done here, you can take some back to your hotel."

Jacques didn't respond, but I could tell that yes, he would like that very much.

"Right," Hector said. "Let's get started. First off, what's your goal? Is it to remain in France or to emigrate? As I'm sure you know, leaving is almost impossible now, with Vichy putting up all sorts of bureaucratic barriers and neutral countries like the U.S. offering almost no visas. But if that's what you want, I will do my utmost to help. It's still worth trying, especially if you have relatives elsewhere."

"We do have family in Portugal and America," I said. "But we are staying in France. We're French. That hasn't changed."

Jo-Jo De Beauville stood up to get her tea pot and poured us all a little more.

"Pardon me, I know we've just met, but I don't know if I could *stand* to stay, if I were you. You must feel so . . . I can't even find a way to express it. Disillusioned? That's not strong enough. Disgusted? Furious? How can you tolerate staying here, especially with your children, when the country has turned against you? When all the values this nation once stood for . . . are *gone?*"

"But, Madame De Beauville," I said quietly, "those values are not gone. Look at you and your husband, and what you're doing right now. For us."

Jo-Jo put her teapot down and hugged me. I barely knew her, and yet I didn't mind. As she returned to sit next to her husband, I felt—for just a moment—a shift in his friendly, cheerful manner. Nothing was said, but I sensed between them a mix of pride and sadness, perhaps—pride in the work he was doing and despair that he had to do it.

"All right," Hector continued, back to business. "So. You want to stay in France. I can prepare new identity papers and food ration cards. It won't be difficult. I'll change your religion to Protestant and play around with your names. If you'll give me your current documents, I'll conduct my usual magic. It'll just take a day or two."

We handed him our papers with some trepidation. It was not a time to be without them. As we stood to leave, Hector reminded Jacques to take a few books and invited Annette and André to do so as well.

"By the way, how did you learn about my husband, all the way over in Nîmes?" Jo-Jo asked me as our children browsed the many, varied titles in Hector's library. "It's at least forty miles from here."

"Oh, you know, Jo-Jo, it's just haphazard," Hector jumped in. "I know a few people from the groups over there, like the Red Cross, the Protestant youth organizations, the international YMCA . . ."

She's worried he's becoming known too widely for this work. And she might be right.

THE BOOKS WERE a welcome gift. Our children missed the friends they'd made in Nîmes, but I couldn't enroll them yet in school, without the false papers Hector was making for us. I wouldn't even let them venture out to explore our new region, which I, myself, was eager to do. The Cévennes was unlike anywhere we'd ever lived: wilder, craggier than the gentle hills and mountains of the Vosges, the long-cultivated fields and vineyards of Alsace.

But as tempting as our new surroundings were, it was just too risky for three children, new to town, to be wandering about. Even in the Cévennes, you could never assume you were completely safe. The local police still had their orders from Vichy, and we had no way of guessing which officers would turn the other way and which would be more diligent about following orders.

André suffered the most from being confined. Jacques had borrowed a tall stack of nonfiction from Hector De Beauville; on history, politics, nature, economics. Annette, too, had always been happy to spend an entire day reading; she loved stories that took her off to faraway places—China, Mexico, the United States.

But André was a more social animal, with a lively, outgoing nature that drew everyone to him. "When you're with André, you *know* you're going to have *fun*," his friends back in Colmar always said. Now, cooped up in a tiny hotel suite for several days on end, our middle child was restless and crabby.

He would pick up a book from Jacques' pile and in five minutes slam it shut. He'd leave the room, then come back. He'd release a too-loud sigh, grab another book, and begin the cycle again.

"Could you please just *stop* it?" Jacques finally said by day three. "If you don't want to read, fine. But at least let *me* enjoy it."

It *was* annoying, but still, I was taken aback. Jacques never spoke sharply to André or anyone for that matter.

André pouted and flounced on the couch. "Sorry. But . . . I'm not you. I'm not an intellectual. I need to go out. I need to be with friends, girls, *people*. Life isn't just about books. I've had it with being inside all the time!"

"Here," Jacques said, tossing a book at him. "Try this one. *The War of the Camisards*. You might like it . . . it has battles and kings and so forth."

We were all grateful and more than a little surprised when, after an hour, André had not bothered anyone at all.

"Hey, André" Jacques said, "You've been quiet for a long time. What do you think?"

André lifted his head from the book, his old sparkle returned. "Imagine this, just imagine." He flipped back a few pages. "Listen. King Louis the Fourteenth wants to consolidate his power, so he demands that *everyone* be Catholic. One King, one Church, that no one can question. He kicks all of the Protestant ministers out of France and hopes that ends Protestantism once and for all. But! Here in the Cévennes, that's not what happens. Instead! Some ministers go into hiding, and meanwhile . . . all different sorts of regular people, bakers and shepherds and shopkeepers, continue practicing their religion, no matter what lousy old King Louis says. Then! The king gets wind of it and sends in a nasty mean priest to *force* everyone to convert. But! The priest gets assassinated because everyone hates this guy. Then! His murder starts a whole series of conflicts called The War of the Camisards, which lasts two years. *Two whole years*. And these rebels, the *Camisards*, were able to hold on for so long because the local population supported them. Plus, they knew all the great places to hide. The woods, ravines, grottos, and caves around here . . . so they can stay hidden for days, weeks, months . . . and then, just at the right time, they leap out on the bad guys, who never see the attack coming." André jumped up and snapped his fingers as if he'd just been endowed with the world's best idea. "Hey. Maybe we can be *Jewish* Camisards, Jacques, huh? What do you think?"

"*No*, André," I snapped. "No rebellions. No Camisards, Jewish or otherwise. We're playing it safe, remember?"

But André didn't listen. He'd dropped right back into his book.

WE RETURNED TO the De Beauville home the next day. Hector had documents piled in five neat stacks, one for each of us. Jo-Jo was out with their sons, likely another effort to keep the boys from becoming curious about why their father was always so busy. The De Beauville boys had also been away during our first visit.

"Let's begin, shall we?" Hector said, settling in at his desk and inviting us to make ourselves comfortable in the library's various chairs and small couches. "First off, I didn't change your last name. Seibert sounds perfectly French, I think. Sometimes, I do have to alter last names; for example, last week I made the Cohen family into the Colin family. But that's only if I'm playing with a person's existing papers. Most often, I'm working from blank City Hall documents: identity papers, food ration cards, marriage licenses, birth certificates . . . so it's pretty easy. I just fill them out. I have all the tools, too: municipal stamps and official seals that I 'borrow' at the end of the day and bring back in the morning. I'm always first in the office. No one misses them."

Hector seemed almost lighthearted, explaining his work, even though according to the Vichy regime he was engaging in a serious crime.

"Monsieur De Beauville . . . Hector, that is," I said, stumbling over myself, searching for a way to express how grateful we were.

"This is *amazing*," André said. "You're really kicking those guys in the government, and all in *secret*. What do you do when you need a photo? Do you have a clandestine darkroom, too?"

"Ha. I'm afraid not," Hector replied. "Photos have to come from my mysterious partner in Montpelier—an old man with a long, Father Christmas-like white beard who I meet every few weeks. I give him blank documents and he helps me with photos. But I don't know his real name. I only know him as Monsieur E."

"Wow," André breathed. "You're part of the French *Resistance*. I thought it was all guys with guns and explosives, blowing things up, shooting at Nazis. But it's also you."

Hector looked from us to his desk, surveying the papers, seals, pens, scattered there. He picked up a municipal stamp and twirled its wooden handle. He turned back to André.

"It's funny . . . but I never thought of myself that way," he said. "I was always the obedient child, the diligent student who got top marks for penmanship. Here we are now, though, and I guess it *is* me, sitting behind my ordinary little City Hall desk. But it's also many of us in Ganges. Farmers, factory owners, merchants. My wife, Jo-Jo, too. She's anxious about my involvement, but she's involved too, making meals and delivering them to all kinds of people, sheltered in the countryside. It's kind of a shared secret among folks around here . . . hiding, housing, helping the ever-growing list of people considered *enemies of the state*. And then there are the local ministers. They don't even try to hide their contempt for what's going on."

"Wow. That's *so* brave. *Thank you*, Monsieur De Beauville," André said. Through his teenage admiration of the nascent French Resistance, he had expressed perfectly what I had been struggling to say.

"Of course. Let's get started," Hector said. He put the stamp he'd been toying with down and picked up a stack of documents. "So, Sarah. You are now"—he presented me the new identity papers he'd crafted—"*Solange*. It had a nice ring to it, I thought. Solange Seibert."

I knew right then that I would only use Solange in public. There was nothing wrong with the name, but it wasn't *me*. And it never would be.

"For your place of birth, I said you were born in France, not Poland," Hector continued. "Even though you and your husband have been citizens for years, Poland now sounds suspicious, too *foreign*. So, I put down that you were born in Guebwiller, a little village not far from Colmar."

"Guebwiller is a charming place," I said, "And Solange is a nice name, too."

I accepted the papers already feeling lighter. I was now, according to my official Ganges documents, a Protestant, and could live freely.

Hector next turned to Melach. "And Melach, you are now"—he unfolded the papers—"Max. Max Seibert."

"Max," Melach said. "I like that!"

Instantly, I knew Melach would forever be Max. It fit. In Hebrew, Melach was a weighty name, meaning king, or counselor. I suppose my husband's parents gave him the name because he was the oldest son. But I'd never thought it matched his easygoing personality. Max was perfect for him, and Max he would stay.

Hector looked as pleased as my husband. "Name changes aren't always so enthusiastically welcomed. I'm glad you like it. And you're also now officially from Guebwiller, like your wife. Do you see it, right there?"

The newly named Max examined his documents. "It's brilliant. Thank you."

Hector then showed the children their papers. He'd not changed their first names, he explained, as they were already French. But he had made one key alteration for our oldest boy.

"Monsieur De Beauville," Jacques asked, "why did you change my birth date, to make me more than a year younger than I am? According to these papers, I was born in January of 1925, so I'm just eleven months older than André."

"Important question, with a tough answer. Because right now, you're just months away from turning eighteen. Which is old enough to be called up for some type of forced labor program, if it comes to that. That's why I made you younger, to protect you for as long as possible."

Max put his arm protectively around Jacques' shoulder. I was aware of this ugly possibility, but I'd chosen not to share it with my son. Now, thanks to Hector, Jacques couldn't be shipped off to toil in some terrible place. For at least a little while longer.

Hector gazed at both my boys, a shadow passing over his dark eyes. "I know it's unusual to make Jacques and André so close in age, although it isn't physically impossible," He smiled. "But I've had to show some creativity lately, with these birth date changes. I've been doing a lot of them, for teenage boys like Jacques. Because while the Nazis haven't demanded French labor yet, they will. It's a simple manpower issue. With their attack on the Soviet Union last month, they'll need every last German male to fight on that enormous eastern front. Who's going to power their factories, farms, and mines? I expect they'll look to occupied countries for workers, including France."

Max tightened his hold on Jacques' shoulder. "But Hector. We're not in northern *occupied* France, where the Nazis are in charge. We're in *Vichy* France, which is controlled by Frenchmen."

"Yes, that's true. But these are not Frenchmen you can trust."

It was a reality we knew full well already. Still, hearing Hector speak this truth was sobering. The arrival of a slender tabby cat in the library distracted us from our gloom.

"Look, Maman, at the kitty!" Annette exclaimed.

"His name is Minou, and he loves children. Everyone, really," Hector said.

Annette petted Minou, admiring his fur's perfect grey and black patterns, pure-white chest and paws and vigorous purring. The cat jumped on her lap, demanding more affection, and enchanting my daughter.

"She's so young," Hector said, faintly. "The same age as one of my boys."

He knelt down to Annette's level. "And now, I have a question for you, mademoiselle. Your papers and your brother André's have hardly changed at all. But can you see what's different?"

"Um . . . here? At the bottom? It says I am Annette Seibert, Protestant from Alsace."

"That's right. Excellent. And that's exactly what you'll say when people ask. *I'm Annette Seibert, a Protestant from Alsace.* Can you do that?"

"Yes," she said, regarding Hector with complete trust.

"Good girl," he said, the words coming out tight and thick. He looked at Max and me. "That Protestant identity is critical. The Cévennes and Alsace are among the two most Protestant parts of France, so no one will question why you've chosen to come here. It'll make complete sense. Better yet, people will hear your accents as Alsatian, not Yiddish. Also, with these Protestant papers, Max can work. I know some managers in Ganges' silk stockings industry who are looking for help."

"Oh. That's a relief. I'd appreciate you connecting me," Max said. "You see, we had to sell off everything in Nîmes, but that money won't last forever."

"Right. It's tough and I've heard the same story from other Jewish families. You're living off funds liquidated from your last assets, after Vichy shut you out of the economy, with no legal way left to make a living. Don't worry."

With our false papers to protect us and the possibility of a job for Max, there was just one more item to address before we could truly settle in Ganges.

"If I could ask," I said. "We're still staying in that little hotel by the fountain. What about a place to live? Could you give some advice?"

"That depends on what you need. If money's a problem, there's a woman who runs a jewelry shop downtown who inherited a huge, ancient chalet from her parents. It's way out in the woods, almost inaccessible by car. She's hidden people there since the Spanish Civil War. I know for a fact that there's another Jewish family there now."

"We can pay," I insisted. "I want my children to go to school and live normally."

"Of course," Hector said. "But recognize that decent apartments are tough to find, with so many northerners choosing to stay in the south. Not that I *blame* any of them—not that your family has a *choice* to return—sorry. It's such a mess."

"It's all right," I said. "Really. And I understand. We faced the same problem in Nîmes."

Hector pulled out a sheet of paper and wrote a few addresses down. Again, I admired his impeccable handwriting. No wonder he was so adept at document forging.

"Here are a few apartment buildings I know about offhand," he said. "You can ask the hotel owner for more, if these don't work out. Oh, and the third one on this list is especially well-located, and I hear it's nice." A wry smile spread across his mouth. "But watch out for the owner. Claudine Paquette. She's an ardent fan of our Chief, Pétain—and that whole pack of wolves running the government."

He burst out laughing.

"She might not even rent to you. She doesn't like Protestants much, and only rents to them if she absolutely has to."

Chapter 23
GANGES, FRANCE
AUGUST 1941. NEW TENANTS

I KNOCKED ON the door but she didn't get up right away to answer. I saw her through the office window, sitting with perfect posture, leafing through forms, scribbling a note here and there. Her desk wasn't far from the door, she would have to be deaf not to have heard my knock.

All right, I can see that we're going to play some little games here. Fine.

I was used to difficult customers. I knocked again. Claudine Paquette unfolded her lithe figure from her chair and glided over to the door.

"Yes?" she asked, conveying impatience.

Her hair was black, with a distinctive white stripe down one side. She wore it pulled tightly back, in a sleek chignon. Her outfit was impeccable: a dress with a fitted bodice, a pleated skirt reaching mid-calf, fashionable high-heeled pumps, and a thin black leather belt that set off the whole look. As a woman of style myself, I could not fault her ensemble; in fact, I admired it. But her attitude? She was a complete snob.

"*Bonjour*, pardon me for the interruption," I said. "Do I have the pleasure of meeting Madame Claudine Paquette? I've heard you have apartments to rent, and that they are the nicest in town."

I decided to counter her own shabby manners with impeccable manners of my own. Claudine looked down at me, which was easy to do. She was tall and elegant, and made the most of our height difference, drawing herself up even taller.

"Oh, my. You're *Alsatian*. I can tell from that dreadful accent. French that sounds like *German*. Well, I suppose you can't help it. Yes, I have apartments. May I see your identity papers? We can't be too careful these days, with Communists and foreigners stirring up trouble, now, can we?"

She scanned my papers quickly.

"All right, well . . . Madame Seibert. I have an apartment I can show you. Come along."

We went up one flight of stairs. Claudine unlocked the door. I knew right away it would not do. The apartment was small and dark. It still carried the cooking smells of the previous renters, and its paint was peeling. Still, I showed polite interest and pretended to consider it, taking several minutes to inspect the cramped kitchen and the two tiny bedrooms.

Claudine sighed too loudly. "You don't miss a detail, do you, Madame Seibert?"

"I am so sorry, Madame Paquette," I said, "I do appreciate your time. But I have three children and a husband. It will not be nearly big enough."

"*Well*, Madame Seibert. As you must know, it's next to impossible to find a decent apartment in this entire region these days, with Alsatians and other northerners like you deciding to stick around. The war is over, and you *could* go home but you *choose* to remain here in southern France. Under the circumstances, I suggest you be less particular."

I could tell Claudine enjoyed reciting this little speech immensely, wondering how I would react. I continued with my display of extreme deference and civility. In fact, I was starting to enjoy it.

"Yes, Madame Paquette. Apartments are scarce, that is such an astute observation. You are so right. And it is *such* a pity this one is not quite the right size. Do you perhaps have anything else?"

"Well, why . . . yes. But I am sure it's too expensive for you."

"Could I see it please, if it's not too much trouble?"

"Madame Seibert. I am quite sure you cannot afford it. Most of the northern families re-settling here like yours have very few resources left. And yet, you must understand that I am running a business. The third floor offers my largest and finest apartment, and I cannot rent it to you at a reduced price."

"How much, Madame Paquette?"

"*Mon Dieu,* you are persistent, Madame Seibert." She named her price.

"I can pay you six months of rent up front right now. Could you show me the apartment please?"

"Hmpf. But of course."

We climbed up one more flight of stairs, and I could see the gears turning in her head: *How could this Seibert woman from Alsace have so much cash?*

"Does your husband have a job, madame?"

"Oh yes. He works at the silk stockings factory. He's very happy there."

"And what is his name?"

"Max. Max Seibert."

"And your children?"

"The children are Annette, André, and Jacques. They are aged nine, fifteen, and . . . sixteen."

Claudine didn't seem to notice my tiny hesitation when it came to Jacques' newly created age. We reached the third floor, taken up entirely by the apartment.

Claudine unlocked the door, and I saw the pleasure on her face when I said nothing right away. But I wasn't going to say out loud what we both knew: the apartment was stunning and perfect for a family of five.

It boasted an ample kitchen, four bedrooms, and was newly painted. Its best feature was the living room: a wide, inviting space with extended windows, from which you could see the rocky, dry bed of the Rieutord River and the mountains and forests beyond.

"We would take this apartment if you would be willing to rent it to us," I said.

"Well, well. Not so fast, Madame Seibert. We'll have to fill out some papers and your husband will have to sign, of course. And I still must consider the applications of many other people who are also interested. Let us return downstairs."

Back in her first-floor office, Claudine returned to her desk, without inviting me to make myself comfortable. I stood, taking in two large, prominently displayed portraits of Vichy Chief of State Pétain, and several ashtrays with his likeness on her desk and on the coffee table. On a windowsill was a framed photo showing a younger version of Claudine, arm-in-arm with a devastatingly handsome, dark-haired soldier in a uniform from the Great War. The office contained a few other pictures of the same man, always young in all of them.

He looks a little bit like Melach . . . Max . . . I corrected myself, still getting used to his new name.

Next to the Pétain ashtrays on the coffee table lay copies of the same right-wing newspaper we discovered in our shop in Colmar years ago, *La Direction Francaise*. There were stacks of them. I wasn't about to pick one up and read it. One glimpse was enough, with headlines warning of the "Judeo-Bolshevik Threat" and a "Collapse of Traditional Values," which the sub-headline claimed was responsible for the last war *and* this one.

Claudine continued to go through the motions of sorting through papers, occasionally tapping one with her pen, and saying, "hmm," or "my, my."

She's stalling. She has no other prospective tenants at this point, but she knows there will be other inquiries. On the other hand, I just offered to pay six months cash up front. She's tempted, but she's still wondering why I can offer that much. She's thinking, everyone says Jews are rich . . .

Her next question confirmed I was right.

"Madame Seibert, if I may ask, why don't you go back to Alsace? The government is certainly urging you to do so, and I'm sure you have important personal and economic ties there . . ."

Alsace had been declared *Judenrein,* or "free of Jews" for a year, and everyone knew it.

"Excellent question, Madame Paquette. As you know, the Cévennes has many Protestant families, going back centuries . . ."

"Yes, I'm quite aware of that unfortunate fact," Claudine muttered.

"And as lifelong Protestants ourselves, we also have relatives in this region who need our help right now. But, of course, we are eager to return to Alsace someday."

She took a long, exaggerated moment to examine me, her brown-gold eyes outlined with kohl and her lashes perfectly made-up, like a film star instead of a small-town landlady. I could tell she was softening but wasn't quite ready to give up the fight.

"Hmm. Well. I still have matters to manage, with the other possible renters. In the meantime, you can fill out these documents. But your husband will have to sign them, as the head of the household. It's the proper thing to do. As I am sure you know."

"Yes, of course. I told my husband to come by before his lunch break. I would never expect you to wait. I'm sure you are quite occupied with your business, but perhaps we'll be fortunate, and he will arrive soon."

Claudine finally motioned that I should sit down, gave me a pen, and pushed the papers toward me. But before I could begin, there came a knock.

"My husband, no doubt," I said.

Claudine opened the door, and her haughty demeanor melted. I saw Max as she saw him: a tall, muscular man with luxurious dark hair and a smile that made you want to smile back.

"Madame Paquette," he said, bowing playfully. "Max Seibert. I am most delighted to meet you."

"Monsieur . . . eh . . . come in, please." Claudine's face and neck flushed bright pink.

I stifled a laugh. After two decades of marriage, I was used to this reaction when women met my husband.

"Max," I said. "There are papers for you to sign, but Madame Paquette has informed me that we must wait. Others are interested in the same apartment that would suit us best."

"It's yours," Claudine said, as her movie-star eyes lingered on Max.

IN A MATTER of days, we were moved into our grand new apartment. Max seemed settled in at the silk stockings factory and the children were enrolled in school. Still trying to play the role of a dutiful, Vichy housewife, I stayed at home. Besides, we had no shop for me to run—we'd sold everything when we'd left Nîmes. All those survival packages I'd planned and put together years ago had served us well . . . *very* well. But they were gone.

Except for one.

Chapter 24
COLMAR, GERMANY
JANUARY 1942. REBELLION

WE NEEDED MONEY. Shortages, war profiteering, and an unbridled black market made food and fuel beyond expensive. Max's salary at the silk stockings factory just wasn't enough for a family of five, including two teenage boys who were growing and constantly hungry. It was time for me to make a final trip to Colmar. I would fetch that last, most-valuable stockpile of luxury goods that remained hidden in the basement of our shop, now "owned" by Adele. But crossing the border was a dangerous prospect. You couldn't just hop into Alsace for the day. You had to have specific economic reasons for entering a territory that was now part of Hitler's Reich. However, with the herculean help of Hector De Beauville and some sympathetic businesspeople in Ganges, I now had the necessary *Ausweiss*, required to cross the border. With this crucial document in hand, I thought I was prepared.

I wasn't.

As my train approached the boundary line, I was certain the temperature fell with every mile. I sat with my shoulders hunched, legs squeezed together, each finger and toe mashed next to its neighbor in hopes of finding warmth. The newspapers said France was experiencing its coldest winter in eighty years. I wore a thick coat, but this January, no coat was thick enough. Worse than the weather was my fear.

I'm Solange Seibert, Protestant of Ganges. I have my papers. I'm fine.

But would they be enough to get through what lay ahead? The sentry boxes and barriers curled with multiple layers of barbed wire. The Nazi guards with their guns and snarling dogs. That choking moment when they asked for your papers.

The border approached, a menacing marker between Alsace and the rest of France. In jarring contrast to the province's smooth, snow-covered hills and bucolic countryside, the checkpoint bristled with ferocity. The train braked in nauseating lurches. The instant it stopped, sentries scrambled on board, demanding papers. A young guard approached my seat.

"*Ausweiss*," he demanded.

I didn't immediately reach into my bag like I should have. He was so familiar.

Vivadorv. The German Jewish soldier who saved Papa after he was attacked by the Russians. Who gave us bandages and morphine and told us to go to Warsaw. He was so helpful. He spoke Yiddish. No. It couldn't be him . . . that was twenty years ago. They were different then . . .

"Madame. For the *last* time. Your *papers*. Present them immediately."

Now my hesitation had made him suspicious. "Pardon me. It's so cold. I, uh . . ."

I gave him the falsified *Ausweiss*, hoping he would think my shaking hands were due to the frigid weather. He took a long, deliberate look at my documents. I kicked myself for not responding to him right away.

"Hmmmm . . . Solange Seibert. Sei . . . bert. What *kind* of a name is that?" He studied my clothes, hair, face, then once again, my papers.

I need to recover from this.

I straightened up and with effort unclenched my shoulders. "It's Alsatian."

He was young, about the age of my sons. The comparison saddened me. "Well, I see that this is a commercial pass, for business affairs. That is good. But now I am compelled to ask you another question. If you are in fact . . . *Alsatian*, why are you continuing to live in Ganges, as it says here? Why didn't you return to Alsace, while there was still time? Because the deadline for Alsatians to come home has long passed, as I'm sure you know. So, I must ask, *Frau* Seibert . . . why do you choose to stay in lazy, disorganized, *defeated* France . . . when you could be a citizen of the Reich, the most powerful and successful nation in history?"

Chin up. Steady and confident, Solange. I had repeated my fake name to myself, over and over, during the journey.

"That is exactly why I am on this train, sir. My business partner in Colmar and I are making plans for me to close our southern France store and resettle in Alsace, just as you said. I was prevented from doing so earlier, due to a family illness. Now, I'm traveling to Alsace to request an exception to the deadline for return."

I kept my regard on him, my face and eyes inscrutable. I imagined myself as a block of wood, not a terrified human being.

He scanned me once again. He thrust my papers back. "Excellent idea. You may go."

AS THE REMAINING miles to Colmar rolled by, I reviewed the carefully planned strategy Adele and I had invented, back in the spring of 1940, when we drew up the paperwork for her ownership of our store.

Adele and I had planned to meet at the Colmar train station, greeting each other casually. We wouldn't draw attention with displays of emotion, and hugs and kisses weren't part of Adele's personality anyway. We would walk to Adele's car, which she and her husband were permitted to keep because their bakery was important to the economy. Adele would take from the trunk two shabby suitcases containing the last of what was hidden in the shop basement. We would conduct the exchange quickly, and when we were sure no one was looking. I would then board the next train headed south.

Preparing for this trip, I had taken care to make myself look unremarkable. I dressed as drably as possible, although this wounded my stylish soul. I also abandoned my usual red lipstick and covered my hair with a kerchief, even though I considered my curls one of my best features. For once in my life, I was grateful to be short. If I were tall, like Max, I would stand out.

Lastly, as much as I lamented the signs of middle age—the lines along my mouth, the crow's feet around the eyes—these too, worked in my favor. Fascist ideology assumed that women, especially older women, were less capable, less intelligent, and therefore less trouble.

If you only knew. And if a middle-aged woman was considered less suspect, then Adele, with her gray hair and wrinkles, would completely escape the Nazis' notice.

I STEPPED OFF the train, acting as if my arrival here in Colmar was nothing out of the ordinary. But I was stunned at the scene before me.

The station was covered with red Nazi flags, flapping in the January wind. Heavily armed German guards with hostile faces patrolled the area. But the change that pained me the most was the complete disappearance of the French language. Signs. Newspapers. Everything. French was outlawed, and every trace of it gone. And just in case anyone forgot, there were propaganda posters, in German, plastered everywhere:

Alsatian Men and Women! Here in German Alsace, we speak German!
The German Homeland Welcomes You!

I think it was that last sign that did it. I was in "The German Homeland." What an insane idea it was, coming here. What would happen if my identity were discovered? They would kill me, torturing me first. How would Melach and the children manage without me? They would never survive.

I considered reversing direction, right then, and getting back on the train. No Adele meeting, no suitcases, no transfer. Just return as quickly as possible to the relative safety of Ganges and my family. My family. What was I thinking? I was crazy to take this risk. With my scratchy woolen glove, I wiped away a tear that had already started to freeze. It hurt.

An ancient woman approached me, as I stood there, debating what to do.

"Sarah?" the woman asked, in a brittle voice.

"Adele?" I said, baffled that this aged, bony woman was my friend. I hadn't seen her since the spring of 1940. Adele had been in her late seventies then, but as strong and solid as ever. In just two years, she'd aged a decade.

"Follow me," she said.

We reached her car. But instead of opening the trunk as planned, Adele opened the passenger door.

"Get in," she ordered.

"But . . ."

"Just get in," she insisted. "I'll explain later."

Adele turned the ignition, with the car complaining about the frigid weather and the ersatz gasoline in its engine. Real gasoline was reserved for the war effort, so civilians made their own, mixing all manner of ingredients into whatever petrol they had, including beet juice. The car coughed and complained as she pulled away from the curb.

"Adele. What are you doing?" I exclaimed. This was *not* part of the plan. Had she gone crazy, living under Nazi rule? "We agreed we should do nothing— *nothing* out of the ordinary. Let's get these final packages out of the trunk, and I'll leave on the next train."

"There are no more trains this afternoon or tonight. The excuse they gave was that the cold made the tracks too dangerous. But I think it's a security sweep. Probably another group of young people trying to get out . . . who decided they don't want to live in a Nazi Paradise." She snorted. "But I also want to talk to you—because you're my friend and I'm old. Who knows if, or when, we might see each other again? Who knows how long this war will go on? I don't know how much longer I have on this earth . . . but I do know this. If we sit in the car conversing, they'll suspect us. And I'm not allowing you to sit in a freezing train station all night. So, you're coming home with me. The goods are in the back. I'll take you to the train tomorrow."

"Home with you to downtown *Colmar*? Adele—no. I can't. This is ridiculous. The German border guards bought my story, about our joint enterprise. You own the shop here and I own its subsidiary down south. It worked because they have no idea who I am, but everyone who lives in this town knows me, they know I'm Jewish. This province is *Judenrein,* have you forgotten? Someone will see me and report both of us. This is insane, stop. I'll spend the night at the station. It's too dangerous."

Adele focused on the frozen road. "We'll go straight home."

"Adele. *Turn around.*"

"Sarah. I know you're the queen of your family, but I can be just as bossy as you, my dear. I'm not taking you back to the station. Shall I let you out to walk back? Maybe you could hitchhike? Perhaps a nice Nazi soldier would give you a ride."

"You're impossible."

We both laughed.

ADELE SET THE table for dinner with care, but there wasn't much food on the plates and in the bowls she put out, brightly painted in the Alsatian style, with flowers, grapevines, and birds. She spooned some cooked potatoes with a bit of precious milk into the bowls and put a meager slice of bread on each plate. Then, indicating that I should sit, she committed a small act of rebellion.

"*Bon Appetite*," she said to me and her husband Claude.

Claude gasped in mock horror. "How many times did you do that today, Adele? Do I have to keep watch over you *all* of the time?"

Adele laughed; her old self more apparent now than the wizened woman who'd met me at the train station. "Just one other time, I promise. To a customer who I've known for years. He's just as bitter as I am, and we were alone at the bakery."

I hoped that she really was alone and that the customer really was trustworthy. Over the past two years, I'd met plenty of displaced Alsatians, who described how there were spies and traitors woven into everyday life in Alsace, and one easy target was the arrest of people speaking French. It was a critical part of an extensive campaign to erase all traces of French culture from the province. The first step had been to expel those judged incapable of becoming obedient German citizens: Jews, like me—but also a wide group of other "unassimilable" people: North Africans, Asians, and Alsatians deemed "Francophones or Francophiles." But even though that last category could have easily defined Adele and her husband Claude, they'd decided to return to Colmar.

"Adele, why? Why did you come back?" I had to ask as we took small bites of our food, trying to make it last. It was a painful question, given the fear and deprivation that they now lived with. But I wanted to know, and sensitive matters like these couldn't be discussed in letters.

Adele smoothed an imaginary wrinkle in the embroidered tablecloth, over and over.

"We just couldn't see starting over in southern France," Claude answered for her. "Everything we have is here. Our home. Our business. But it's the worst decision we have . . . ever made."

"Oh," I said, now ashamed that I'd been so blunt, with these selfless, loyal friends. Then I had an even worse thought. "You didn't come back, in part, because you were the new owners of our store, did you? Please, tell me you didn't . . ."

"No, no. Not at all," Adele insisted. "We barely operate your shop at all. If anyone asks, we say that war-related supply problems mean we have too little to sell. Either Claude or I open the store an hour or two a day, just to keep up appearances. So, it looks like it's still a legitimate business. Just one that's closed . . . often."

"Are you *sure*? You're not just saying that, to make me feel better?" I had to be certain.

"It absolutely was *not* your store that pulled us back; it was the bakery. Could we have started another bakery in southern France? Perhaps, but here, we own the building. The equipment. Every spoon, cup, table, and chair at Pain Pour Tous, we bought it. We didn't see how we could ever amass the money to do all that again. So, we came back. All five of us: me, Claude, René, and the boys." Her voice wavered. She fussed with the tablecloth again, looking down at it, as if it were critical that she memorize its flowered patterns.

"I'm sorry," I said. "We don't need to talk about it anymore."

"No, it's all right," she said. "It's just . . . well, we can put up with the surveillance, those obnoxious busybodies they call the *Blockleiter*, coming through the neighborhood, checking on us constantly. We'll speak German if we have to. Claude won't wear his berets in public, and I've boxed up my French literature. We can even tolerate them taking—excuse me, *requisitioning*—two-thirds of our daily bread output and all of my pies, which they seem to love."

"Adele . . . Your pies. I miss them. I have such warm memories of us, on Saturday afternoons after work. Pie and coffee and gossip. Remember?"

"Yes, and," she said, rising from her chair, "as a matter of fact . . ." She lifted the seat on her piano bench and pulled out a pie, which she triumphantly put before me. "It's blueberry. Your favorite. I hid it in a trash bin when they came by the bakery today for their 'requisitioned' bread. I told them I didn't have enough flour to make pie this week. So here. Enjoy."

We devoured the forbidden treat, partly because dessert was so rare in those days, but also because the Blockleiter could barge in at any moment. We cleared the table quickly, especially evidence of the illegal pie. Adele washed the few dishes that our skimpy meal required, dried her hands on her apron, and faced me.

"Just to finish what Claude was saying. About how this was our worst decision, to come back to Alsace. You see, the Nazis are after much more than just our pie and bread." She eyed Claude.

"Soon, they'll want our grandsons," he said. "As soldiers. Just like their father before them."

I WORE MY coat to bed. Fuel was scarce, and as night fell, Adele's house became achingly cold. But my discomfort had an upside: The weather was so unbearable, that even the Blockleiter didn't venture out. There was no one to take note of a sudden guest in Adele and Claude's home. The next morning, I was on the first train heading south, with the last of my merchandise beside me in the two suitcases. My emotions were scattered: gratitude for Adele and this unexpected visit, anguish over what might be awaiting her grandsons, and relief that my own sons, for now, were hidden behind their false papers.

As the train lurched into motion, I set each part of my face into a perfect, neutral expression. Eyes—out the window. Mouth—a straight line. Forehead—no scrunching between the eyebrows. Physical signs of feelings were a tip-off, that you might have something to hide. I put my mind on the task ahead. Return to Ganges and my family. I would not even think about the fact that I now had no reason to come back to Alsace again.

Chapter 25
GANGES AND GRENOBLE, FRANCE
SPRING 1943. SEPARATION

"MAX, WAKE UP."

I shook his shoulder again. Even as the threats gathered more tightly around us every day, Max somehow managed to shut them out at night. I elbowed him, hard.

"Get *up*," I said.

He grunted and rolled over. "Sleep."

"No, wake up. The children. We have to split them up."

He sat up. "What? No. No!"

"*Yes*," I said, trying to convince both Max and myself that this was what we must do, but feeling as if I could hardly breathe. "There were more roundups in Lyon yesterday. And all around us now—in Avignon, in Carpentras, in Nîmes. Nîmes, Max. That's practically right next door. Remember Nîmes last summer? Those children . . ."

His reply was to reach for me, his breath now as constricted as mine. People still talked about Nîmes, in haunted whispers: how dozens of children had been pushed onto trains, little children. I'd heard that the youngest had been a two-year-old boy named Henri with his two sisters, aged four and eight. The authorities' longstanding official line that Jews were being transported to "work camps" in the East remained, but the lie was now obvious to anyone who cared to look. Small children, the elderly, the sick . . . were clearly not being sent off "to work."

"Where?" Max breathed the question, letting the words hang in the air of our dark bedroom, as if speaking them clearly would make it too real.

I hesitated. It didn't help to know that other Jewish parents were struggling with the same grim calculation.

Keep the next generation alive.

I outlined my plan methodically, as if we were talking about where the children should go to school.

"Jacques can go to Issoire, near your father. I found him an apprenticeship in architecture there, which still meets the Vichy work-service requirement because it involves repairing bridges and roads. André can go to the University of

Toulouse, near your sister Freda. There's work in the mines there, and your sister loves André."

I could tell he wasn't enamored with the idea of sending our sons away. After losing both me and Jacques in the exodus, Max had become extra-sensitive toward losing anyone again. He'd panic if one of us was late coming home, peering out the window a hundred times, running his fingers through his thick hair so much that it would stick up from his head. But he grunted his approval. After all, our boys were now capable young men who'd shown themselves to be resilient, resourceful, and adaptable these past three years.

"What about Annette?" he asked, in a dead tone that I knew concealed his agony.

"I've found a place for Annette at a convent in Grenoble."

Max sagged against me. "She's only eleven . . . that's awfully far." But he already sounded defeated, which worried me. For once, I would have almost preferred that he give me an argument.

"I know it's far. But Saul and Sophie are there, and even better"—I tried to brighten my delivery—"Grenoble is in the *Italian*-controlled zone. As much as I hate to admit it, your brother was right. Everyone says the Italians are largely ignoring the Jewish laws, and demands for deportation. Someone at church said the zone's been dubbed 'The French Israelites' new Promised Land,' because so many Jews are fleeing there."

I waited for his response, not sure if I would get one. My happy-go-lucky husband had become moodier over the past year; some days he was his normal, talkative, humming, loving self. But other days, he spoke barely at all.

"Promised land, perhaps," he muttered, finally. "But Annette won't see it that way."

"NO, MAMAN, *NO*. Papa, tell Maman *No*."

The entire week before her departure, Annette screamed, cried, pleaded, and even hid in the attic for a full day. She tried to divide our united front. She tried to enlist her brothers as allies.

I held firm. Even though it shredded my insides. *Annette will be safe there*; I assured my husband and sons. They didn't question me, not out loud, anyway. But I measured the doubt in their eyes, heard it in their unnaturally quiet voices. Meanwhile, I tried to ignore my own qualms. *Other families are making the exact same choice.* But since when did I follow what other people did? That should have been my first sign.

THE TRAIN PULLED into Grenoble.

"Here we are," I said to Annette brightly, as if we'd arrived at the beach or had found a perfect picnic spot. She hadn't said a word the whole trip, and I guessed that staying mute was her final protest, her last punishment to her horrible, terrible mother.

I held out my hand to help her step off the train. Annette refused to take it. She also refused to pick up her suitcase, which I willingly carried. I knew that in her eleven-year-old mind, I was now the most evil parent a child could possibly have.

After days of begging to stay in Ganges, Annette realized we were not changing our minds, and she'd focused her ire on me. "I *hate* you, I hate you, I hate you! What kind of a mother leaves her little girl? I will never forgive you, Maman— never, ever, ever."

I understood Annette's reaction was to be expected. Still, I felt emotionally cut open and left on my own to bleed. Max, who'd always been able to soothe me, had nothing to offer. He was wrestling with his own darkness.

The convent was a short walk from the train station. The building was made of cream-colored stone and concrete, shaded heavily with trees, and covered with ivy. The building construction and the foliage made it cool inside, even though it was a warm spring day. It felt large but not enormous; I'd been told that it housed about one hundred people total, including several dozen girls who slept in dormitories.

A young, petite nun answered my knock. She greeted us with a quick bow. "Welcome. Do you have an appointment?"

"Yes. My name is Solange Seibert. From Ganges. I have communicated with the mother superior."

"Welcome, madame. I'll bring you to her. Please, come in and follow me." I was grateful for the young nun's friendly demeanor.

The mother superior was the opposite: statuesque, imposing, and direct. "Sit down, please. We will not draw this out. So. According to your letter, your little girl is here for our excellent education. You are also Protestants, according to your papers . . . you do understand that our education includes the teachings of Catholicism, the only true form of Christianity?"

"Yes. I understand," I said, distracted by the sound of Annette quietly crying and how it made my chest hurt.

"You do understand that she is expected to recite Catholic prayers, attend morning and evening mass, and learn what it means to be a good Catholic?"

"Yes. Yes, I understand."

"I have only a few more questions. Besides her immediate family, is anyone else allowed to visit your daughter?"

"Her aunt, uncle, and cousins live in Grenoble. I'll give you their names. They are permitted to visit. No one else."

"That is very important for me to know. We have had several cases of people posing as relatives and requesting visits; we must ask these questions to protect our girls."

Aha, they're watching out, that's good. "Thank you, Mother Superior."

"We take this very seriously, madame. My last question for you is this: You are Protestant. I would like to know how far back that lineage goes, and whether your family background includes any *other* religions?"

She knows, and she's asking in order to protect everyone who lives here. If the convent is questioned, she can say, without lying, that I assured her we were not Jewish.

"We come from a long line of Alsatian Protestants," I said.

"I see," the mother superior said, her eyes communicating both an understanding and a promise. She would do the best she could to keep this little Jewish girl safe. Her silent message didn't eliminate my grief and anxiety. But it helped.

The nun stood, her unusual height making her all the more regal in her floor-length robes. "And now, Mademoiselle Annette, it is time to say goodbye to your mother. No dramatics, please. This is for your own sake, and you must always do what your parents say. As the Ten Commandments tell us, 'Honor Thy Father and Thy Mother.'"

Despite the mother superior's warning against drama, I expected a scene. But Annette seemed wrung out, defeated. She gave me a limp hug.

"*Au revoir*, Maman."

Chapter 26
GANGES, FRANCE
SUMMER 1943. FAITH AND FRIENDSHIP

I STOOD AT the living room windows, staring but not seeing.

Below lay the smooth, gray, jumbled stones of the bed of the Rieutord River, which was dry most of the year. Just beyond, were clumps of forests between tidy villages with red-clay rooftops, and then the broad foothills of the Cévennes mountains. I'd often admired this vista, but now, it didn't even register. I was twitchy and restless.

With all three children gone and no store to run, I was not busy for the first time in my life. It felt fundamentally wrong—almost offensive. And now, I needed activity more than ever, to counteract the steady, thrumming worry that something terrible could be happening, *right now*, to my sons and daughter. Germany had taken control of all of France the previous fall, except for the small southwestern Italian Zone. The Vichy government was in name only, and the demarcation line between northern and southern France was gone. And now, Nazi "security" forces were aided by a homegrown paramilitary group: the *Milice*. They were just as vicious but more cunning: because they were French, they knew our ways, our hiding places, the tricks we might play. Aided by these eager recruits, roundups of Jews and other "enemies of the state" expanded. The fear that we would be denounced, revealed for who we were, buzzed just beneath my skin.

Enter Jo-Jo De Beauville.

When her husband had given us our papers identifying us as Protestants, he'd also suggested we attend church, to play the role of devout, displaced Alsatians. Max and the boys went just enough for appearances' sake, but Annette and I found we enjoyed going to Sunday services. We both made friends at the little brick church by City Hall. I often sat in a back pew with Jo-Jo, marveling at the minister's boldness. Hector had not been exaggerating when he'd described the pastors of the Cévennes. Week after week, I heard sermons condemning hatred, racism, and any person—German or French—who propagated it:

"Anti-Semitism is a sin. It is a total negation of Christianity and the value we place on the human soul. Hitler's racism is anti-Christian . . ."

The minister never failed to remind his congregants that for hundreds of years, Protestants had suffered and died because they were a religious minority. The message from the pulpit was clear. Help the Jews now.

I soon learned that's what Jo-Jo was doing, in her own quiet, unglamorous way. She and Hector were part of a much wider network in Ganges who were protecting Jews, French Resistance members, Communists, and most recently, young men seeking to avoid the despised *Service Travail Obligatoire*, or mandatory work service.

One Sunday after church, I asked Jo-Jo if I could join her. It would distract me from my worries and give me a small sense of power, that I was doing *something* to counter the evil people running the country. That my actions could maybe, just a little, weaken them, like a mosquito biting a mighty warrior. And in Ganges, there were *lots* of mosquitos.

Jo-Jo told me to come to her house the next day.

"I have a mission for you," she said, "but you'll need to wear comfortable clothes. Slacks would be best, if you have them. No dressing up," she added, teasing.

I knew that on Sunday evenings, after the traditional long French Sunday afternoon dinner was over, Jo-Jo would head back to the kitchen to make meals for those hiding in and around Ganges. Mondays were her delivery days. She'd hop on her bicycle and ride through town and then out into the countryside, with paper-wrapped sandwiches and other items that wouldn't spoil quickly, stashed in wicker baskets on the front and back of the bike. Compared to the severe food shortages in much of France, there was still enough to eat and to share in Ganges. Farmers still tended their herds of goats and sheep. Orchards were full of the apples nicknamed "little queens." Then there were the chestnut trees, lush and abundant, which had nourished the Cévennes for centuries, so fundamental to local sustenance that people called them "bread trees."

I arrived at the De Beauville home on Monday morning, dressed as plainly as I was capable; although of course I still wore lipstick. Minou the cat greeted me at the doorway, issuing a series of warbling *mrrrooows* and rubbing himself up against my ankles.

"Why, hello, Minou," I said, surprised to find myself so pleased by the slender tabby's welcome. "Jo-Jo, I'm here and ready for my mission, captain," I called down the hall.

"There in a minute," she replied, entering the kitchen from the garden out back.

She placed a basket of cucumbers, lettuce, and a variety of herbs on the counter. She peeled off her gardening gloves, humming, as she then washed the dirt off her fingers. Something had changed within her, she seemed more . . . alive, happy even? Were we still allowed to be happy, in these frightening times?

"I have news," she said, drying her hands. "I'm pregnant again."

"That's marvelous. I thought you seemed a little, well—*rounder* lately. But of course, I wasn't going to ask. Tell me more, how you're feeling, what Hector thinks, whether you've told your sons?"

"Thank you. But later. Right now, you do have a mission. And because of my new . . . situation . . . *you're* going to make the Monday deliveries instead of me." She thrust two large, bulky packages of wrapped sandwiches, apples, carrots, and bread at me. "Put the big one in the back basket and the slightly smaller one in front."

I wasn't sure I still knew how to ride a bicycle. I'd only done it several times. Cycling certainly wasn't anything we did growing up in Poland, and once I arrived in France, I was far too busy working and having a family. Max had made bicycle deliveries from the little shops we'd owned, early in our marriage. But once we had our large store in Colmar, he didn't need to do that anymore. Only our children rode bikes.

However. I was determined to be useful. I was tired of fretting, alone all day in the apartment.

"Tell me where to go," I said.

"Here you are." She handed me a sketched-out map. The lines all led into the forests and foothills, winding paths that no reasonable person could call a road. "I can still do the in-town deliveries myself." She chuckled at my obvious surprise. "I saved the fun part for you."

And so, all that summer, every Monday, I biked into the woods, bumping over roots and rocks, past clear, green-tinted rivers, massive cliffs, and dramatic ravines. I crossed fields, surprising grazing sheep and goats and hitting many piles of sheep dung. I got lost, more than once, trying to find the little stone shacks called Clèdes. A staple of the Cévenol landscape, the Clèdes were decades, even centuries old, tucked deep in the woods, blending into the surroundings. Once used for drying chestnuts, they were now a convenient hiding place for Resistance members.

Monday afternoons, after I'd return the bicycle to Jo-Jo, sweaty but energized by sunshine and exercise, she'd always invite me in for a cup of her herbal tea. We tried to keep our conversation light, given the heaviness around us. Sometimes, we succeeded. Often, we didn't.

"Tell me about my landlady," I asked Jo-Jo on one such Monday visit, when she'd insisted I stay for lunch. "What do you know about Claudine Paquette?"

I hoped this would be an easy chat. We could, perhaps, gossip about Claudine's ever-present stiletto heels, her Paris-model makeup, and her snooty ways. But Jo-Jo made a disapproving *uh-uh* sound.

"Keep an eye on her, because she's got her eye on everyone. Especially people new to town, like you. And the ministers. And anyone else she thinks might be inclined to help. Like my husband. He told me the other day that Claudine's been making an unusual number of visits to City Hall lately, to have business documents approved that don't require approval. The other day, she asked for a third copy of her husband's death certificate. It was an odd request, but Hector complied. He figures it's wise to keep her content."

The lightness I normally enjoyed after my Monday morning bicycle deliveries evaporated, imagining our snooping, fascist, landlady just one floor below.

"What happened to her husband? I've seen some pictures in her office. He was handsome man, in fact, they were both striking."

"Yes, I suppose I could dredge up a little sympathy for her there. She and Jean-Paul fell in love as teenagers and married right after high school. And like you said, they were a gorgeously matched couple: tall, slender, those luminous olive complexions, the high cheekbones. Both of them had raven-black hair too, although Claudine's always had that white stripe. *My beautiful little skunk,* Jean-Paul used to call her."

I had difficulty imagining the stiff, condescending Madame Paquette being anyone's "little skunk." But then I remembered the lascivious way she'd eyed my husband.

"Did Jean-Paul die in the Great War?"

"No," Jo-Jo said. "He came back, but like so many veterans, he was shattered. One of the thousands post-war society dubbed *Les Mutilés*. The Mutilated Ones. He could barely walk, apparently because he still had tiny shards of shrapnel in his legs. But his true damage, people said, was psychological. He served at Verdun, under Pétain. The longest and most ferocious battle of the war. Shell shock, everyone called it. I saw Jean-Paul only once after his return; it was downtown, it must have been in 1920 or '21. He seemed drunk, and it was quite early in the morning. He died in 1936. Hector filled out the death certificate back then. Claudine said that it was due to internal war injuries. But Hector was convinced it was suicide."

I thought again about the photos I'd seen in Claudine's rental office, before the Great War stole her husband, her happiness. And Jean-Paul's suffering all those years . . . it must have been immense, bottomless.

"I feel sorry for her now," I said.

"Maybe," Jo-Jo replied, unusually harsh. "Yes, it's sad, but she's not the only one who lost a husband, a brother, a father, an uncle. A million and a half men died. And most of their loved ones *haven't* reacted like Claudine, with a fixation on some perfect pre-war era that never existed, and an obsession to cleanse France of undesirables so it can return to that mythical time." Jo-Jo put down her teacup a bit too forcefully. "Her son Giles might be helping with that goal, by the way. Cleansing France. He used to be a police officer in Le Vigan, the town next door. But now, no one's sure what he's up to. There are several French paramilitary groups out there these days, like the Milice, happy to carry out the Nazis' orders."

A tiny memory flashed through my mind.

"I saw him in that uniform. Giles, I mean. In his Milice outfit. The form-fitting, blue wool jacket, his pants tucked into boots above the ankle, brown shirt, and a wide blue beret."

Jo-Jo smiled, knowingly.

"I know . . . I pay attention to clothes, so I noticed. I was coming down the stairs from the third floor as he was saying good-bye to his mother on the second. I considered scampering back upstairs, but he turned as I approached and gave me a pleasant, friendly greeting."

Jo-Jo placed her hand on the curve of her stomach. "A friendly fascist. Ha. Anyway, watch out for Giles. And his mother, too."

I remember feeling a slight chill then, thinking it was due to the late afternoon sunlight, which slid behind the foothills as Jo-Jo and I chatted. But I should have recognized it as a premonition. Jo-Jo and Hector were not in church that following Sunday. And on Monday, when I went to their house, no one answered the door.

Minou was outside, pacing and yowling. I scooped the cat up and brought him home.

ON TUESDAY MORNING, I went straight to City Hall, right when it opened. Hector was not behind his desk. An older man was there in his place. Hector's name plate was gone.

"Excuse me, monsieur," I said. "I'm looking for Hector De Beauville?"

Before the De Beauville's disappearance, I had assumed everyone at Ganges City Hall was safe, but now, I was no longer sure. Had one of Hector's co-workers denounced him?

"He's . . . gone," the man at Hector's desk said, and from the concern I heard behind his slow, careful words, I gathered he was a friend. "May I help you with something, madame?"

"No, thank you. Do you have any idea when Monsieur De Beauville might return?"

"I'm very sorry, madame. I do not know."

I understood he was playing it safe, not telling me anything more. And it was entirely possible he had nothing to tell.

"Thank you, monsieur. Good day."

I strode across the courtyard, hoping no one noticed my tears.

Chapter 27
GANGES, FRANCE
SEPTEMBER 1943. THE SHIFT

I MOVED CLOSER to the window for better lighting. Had I read the headline correctly?

Italy Signs Armistice. Germany Takes Over the Italian Zone in France

"Max?" I called, wanting to tell him and then remembering he was at work. And even if he were home, I might not have received a response. More and more, he was curled up in his emotional shell, worn out and depressed, I knew, by the unceasing war, the round-ups of Jews, the disappearance of the De Beauvilles . . . I understood my husband's despair, but I didn't have the energy to coax him out. Max's problems . . . would have to remain Max's problems right now.

I resumed reading, not at all surprised that the official press presented this obvious setback for Germany as good news for the Nazis. The article said the Italian Zone had never been well-managed and rebuked Italy's forces there for being more engaged in wine and revelry than enforcing the rules. The paper assured readers that with Germany now controlling the entire land mass of France, citizens would finally see some law and order.

I put the paper down, a new worry faintly ticking inside the back of my head. I knew that "law and order" were Nazi code for arrest and deportation, and the Grenoble convent housing our daughter was in the now-*former* Italian Zone. But after years of living on edge, my instincts were fraying. I was struggling to discern what the dangers were, when every day seemed to bring new, unimaginable perils. The veil of safety I'd tried to wrap around my family felt thinner every day, but I couldn't predict where true safety might be found. Was the convent still secure? How much did the end of the Italian occupation matter? I was unable to sort out the circumstances, the way I once could. I came up with a weak rationale for keeping Annette in Grenoble.

Even the Nazis wouldn't dare go after nuns.

A FEW AFTERNOONS later, I was home alone when the knock came. My blood swept through my body in full alert. These days, unexpected visitors were to be feared.

"Sarah. It's me, Saul."

I drooped and opened the door.

"Saul. How nice to see you, but what a surprise! You should have written, or sent a telegram, to say you were coming."

"You'd better sit down. Where's Max?"

"Still at the factory. He'll be back soon. Tell me now. What is it? What's happened?'

"I should wait until Max is here."

"*Saul.* Tell me. *Now.*"

Saul was a much sterner character than his brother, but under my ferocious glare, he talked. "You need to take Annette out of that convent immediately. Tomorrow."

I laughed, little bubbles of relief. Annette had sent us dramatic, weepy letters every week, begging us to bring her home. Everything at the convent was beyond awful, according to our daughter.

"You came all the way here for *that*? Come on, Saul. Is she complaining about the food again? Or the stupidity of the other girls? Honestly. I expect Max to give in, but you? By the way, speaking of food, could I get you something to eat?" I asked, stepping toward the cupboard.

"Sarah! For God's sake! Just *listen* to me."

I stopped, frozen, with my hand in the air, reaching toward the cupboard.

"Annette was almost deported," he roared. "Everything's changed since the Germans took over the Italian zone."

Did he say deported, did I hear him say almost deported, please, please, I think I heard him say "almost." Saul took me by the elbow and guided me over to the couch.

"A crazy stroke of luck saved her," he said, shakily.

A year ago, even several months ago, I would have pressed him for every detail, then insisted we rush to see when the next train to Grenoble was, jumping on board, right then. Instead, I couldn't move.

Saul sat down next to me, and we stayed like that together, silently, that long, terrible September afternoon until Max came home.

"Saul. What are you . . . ?" Max looked from Saul to me and back again. "Why are you here?"

"It's Annette," he said. "No, no, she's fine. But we had a close call. Too close."

It dawned on me that although Saul had arrived hours ago, I hadn't yet heard the details of what had happened.

"I'd been visiting her every Sunday with the boys, just as you wanted us to. We'd fetch her at the convent and then go to a nearby farm. It's an old, rambling house with goats, chickens, gardens, and woods . . . a place for Jewish kids to just be free, to be themselves. About thirty children live there, kids whose parents have been . . . taken away. You know."

We did. Deported and likely dead.

"On Sundays, other Jewish kids hidden throughout the region would come and play with those who live there permanently. It is . . . was . . . a wonderful place. Lucien and Noah loved it and so did Annette . . . could I have something to drink?"

I gestured with my head to where the wine was, still not capable of speaking or moving. Saul filled his glass almost to the top.

"But last week, Lucien wasn't feeling well, so we didn't go to the Sunday House, as the children call it. We stayed home and I suppose Annette had a dreary day, being stuck at the convent instead of playing with her cousins." Saul took a swallow of wine, staring into his glass. "There was a raid at the Sunday House that day. All the children and their caregivers were put on trains and deported."

His voice flattened, but I heard beneath it his anguish, fury, and disgust.

"The person who revealed the location of the Jewish children's home was a neighboring farmer who wanted the land for himself. The raid was carried out by none other than Klaus Barbie. You know. The one they call The Butcher of Lyon."

IT WAS JUST six o'clock, but I went to bed. I walked unsteadily through the kitchen. *How could I have made such a terrible mistake?*

I lay on my back, my eyes wide open. If I closed them, I knew I would imagine the scene, of what *almost* happened: the Gestapo agents, their emotionless faces, prodding people with their guns if they hesitated at the train doors. Annette and her little cousins, pushed into a cattle car, screaming, crying. Saul, struggling with what he should do to protect the children, knowing that trying to run away with them would likely mean death, but that death could also be waiting at the other end of the line.

I was aware that Max and Saul talked well into the night, although I couldn't make out what they said. Hours later, I had finally begun dozing when the bed creaked with Max's long frame. He put his arm around me. We hadn't touched lately, and the familiar comfort of his gesture broke my silent shock.

"How could I have been so wrong?" I asked, barely recognizing my own ragged, weak words.

"Shush," he whispered. "I've been wrong, too."

"But it was my decision. I'm the one who found the convent. I'm the one who made the arrangements, with the nuns and with Saul and Sophie. I'm the one who brought her there . . . to the place where she could have *died*."

"Listen, my dove," he said, using my pet name for the first time in a very long time. "You were wrong this *one time*, perhaps . . . perhaps not. Many, many other families have sent their sons and daughters off, just as you did. But in terms of being wrong? I've been wrong for years. I've been drifting along, mired in my own despair. I've been so obsessed with the lovely life that we lost . . . with the insanity of what's happened to our country . . . with the danger that's everywhere . . . I've just been numb. I've left it all to my wife, my amazing, beautiful wife, to make rational choices in a world where nothing is rational."

He pulled me closer.

"I've always let you decide because . . . when I decide, I'm wrong. Throughout our lives together. Twenty years ago in Sedan, when our employee David robbed us? I hired him, but you didn't trust him from the start. When I lost Jacques in our escape from Alsace . . . there's no way you would have allowed that to happen. And remember in Nîmes, where I said we should register for the Jewish Census? I was so naïve. Imagine if you'd listened to me, what that might have meant for us to be on that list. I've always trusted your judgment . . . because I don't trust my own."

I heard the shame he'd been carrying for so long.

"Max," I said, facing him now. "It's not your fault. Annette was almost killed because of me. Not you. *Me*."

As I said these frightful words, I felt the crushing weight of their truth. But Max put his hands on my shoulders, sat me up on the bed, and lifted my chin.

"No. Not you," he said. "*Us*. And Saul gave me quite the lecture after you went to bed. He said we've all had to adapt and change during these hellish last four years, but that I've stayed in my pitiful little cave. And that it's well past time I came out. So, I'm sorry. For everything. I'm so, so sorry. But I'm here now, Sarah." He stroked my hair; in the old way he used to soothe me. "I'm right here."

Max and Saul took the morning's first train to Grenoble.

Chapter 28
GANGES, FRANCE
SPRING 1944. REVERSAL

LIBERATION AND DEATH were equally likely.

The war was shifting in the allies' favor. The Americans had landed in North Africa six months ago, taking control. Italy was in a state of civil war, with the North controlled by the Nazis and the South now fighting on the Allied side. The French Resistance was becoming bigger and bolder, bolstered by material support from the Allies and psychological support through the Free France broadcasts on Radio London. We didn't have a radio, although Jacques was delivering clandestine Resistance newspapers, which we burned after we read them. But both my sons ached to join what they considered the *real* Resistance, those dashing, daring *Maquisards*, who hid out in the forests and ravines of the Cévennes by day, conducting raids on Nazis and French collaborators at night. I forbade the boys from taking part. We'd come so far and endured so much.

Plus, we were Jewish. Yes, we had our false papers, but we could be denounced at any time and shipped off to the East. The Resistance press carried horrifying accounts of the camps now, reports from visiting refugee workers, humanitarian groups, and a few, rare escapees. French Jewish leaders were vociferously protesting to the puppet French government, presenting confirmed evidence that thousands of Jews had been murdered in Eastern Europe, and that the German government was not taking Jews for their labor but for the clear purpose of exterminating them.

Yet some people continued to believe the "work camp" fiction.

LATE MORNING ON June 6th, the racket began from our landlady's apartment on the second floor below. The complaint of heavy furniture being dragged. The slapping of windows being shut. The slamming and clacking of doors, being bolted. The frenetic snapping of high heels.

What on earth is going on down there?

It was a risk, but I decided to take it. I would pretend to be concerned about Claudine and go down to "check" on her.

I descended to the second floor and knocked on her door.

No answer. I knocked again, then spoke loudly, so she could hear me.

"Madame Paquette? It's Solange Seibert. Please do pardon me, but I've heard lots of bumping from your apartment. I'm just making sure you are all right? That you don't need any help?" Several more thumps and then I heard Claudine rush to the other side of the closed door.

"No, I certainly do not need anything from you, Madame Seibert. You could not *possibly* help me in any way"—Claudine choked—"with rampant lawlessness among our own people, Bolsheviks on the loose, the Anglos bombing elsewhere in France, who knows when they'll be here . . . and my son Giles out there, defending the nation . . ."

Now, she was becoming hysterical, and as much as I despised her politics, the mother in me understood her fears for her son. Claudine then pressed her mouth right up to the crack, her words muffled but her message clear. "Chief of State Pétain is due to address the nation at noon. He'll restore calm. Peace. Order. The way it used to be. That's all I want . . . an end to this insanity. So, go *away*, madame. And don't come check on me again."

Normally, I wouldn't pay attention to the official speeches, from Pétain or anyone else. Radio Vichy was pure government propaganda, dictated by the Germans. By 1944, fewer people were listening to it, and if they did, it was in disbelief. But my landlady's panic piqued my curiosity. Had her son tipped her off? Meanwhile, now that I thought about it, my own son André had hinted early this morning that "something big" was coming. *How does he know that?*

I decided to go to a café downtown, knowing there was a strong chance one of them would have a radio and would be broadcasting the address. I scrawled Max a note, saying I wouldn't be home for lunch and that he could open a can of soup and heat it up.

I found one tiny, empty table at a crowded café, in a tight corner. I said "excuse me" to some men at the next table, so I could get by. One of them stood up, allowing me to maneuver myself more easily. I recognized him from church, although I didn't remember his name.

"Madame Solange Seibert, I believe? It's a wonderful day, isn't it?" he said.

"Yes, it's beautiful out. I do especially love June here in the Cévennes."

The man leaned over, so I could hear him above the chatter and clatter of the café. "Aha, no, Madame, pardon me . . . but I am not talking about the weather. It's happened. *Le débarquement.*"

The Allied landings. The long hoped-for coming ashore of British, American, and Canadian troops. The man said it had taken place on the beaches of Normandy early that morning.

"That's why"—he made a face—"our *Chief* is speaking in a few minutes."

The café owner turned up the radio and called for quiet.

"People of France: The German and Anglo-Saxon armies are grappling on our soil. France has thus become a battlefield!" The familiar, tremulous gravel of Pétain's voice crackled through the speakers. "Civil servants, railway men, factory workers. Stand strong at your posts to maintain the life of the nation . . . obey the orders of the government . . . The circumstances of battle may lead the German army to take special dispensation, in the zones of combat. Accept this necessity . . ."

Pétain spoke for two minutes, his address finishing with the playing of the French national anthem. As the last stirring notes of the Marseillaise faded, the café exploded with patrons disputing, debating, analyzing what they'd just heard. Most people groaned at the speech's request for calm and cooperation, and they jeered at how canned, how generic it was. Pétain said nothing about Normandy or the invasion that had begun.

"He probably recorded it months ago," the man at the neighboring table said.

A few patrons slunk out of the cafe, their Vichy loyalties known. I raced home, hoping to catch Max before he returned to work. I turned the corner to our little alley of a street. I saw a man, but it wasn't Max.

It was Giles Paquette.

He'd replaced his conservatively cut Milice uniform with a comfortable-looking turtleneck, heavy brown pants, and hiking boots. A battered wool beret completed the classic clothing of a maquisard. A Resistance fighter. He stood outside his mother's first-floor rental office, as their elevated voices echoed off the buildings of the narrow alley. I stopped. Both Paquettes were eye-to-eye, so intent on each other, they didn't notice my presence.

"I know you're shocked, Maman," Giles was saying. "But when the Anglos get here, I want to be on the *winning* side. It's all over for Vichy, for the Nazis. Everyone knows it. I'm not the only one in law enforcement who's turned. Some of us have been carrying two . . . even three . . . different identity cards for months. Now, if I could please just come in, hide out here till dark, then I'll be on my way, to join my unit. We could have a little last visit, until the tide fully turns and the war is over. Wouldn't that be nice?"

Claudine gripped the door frame, as if she needed its help to stay upright.

"No, it would not be *nice* at all, Giles," she spat. "For these past four years of turmoil, of *hell*, my sole, constant, source of strength was the pride that my son was working on the *right* side. For law and order. For France. And now . . .who are you helping, Giles? Those crass, loud Americans? The stuck-up British, who've always looked down at us? Or worst of all . . . the godless Bolsheviks? Is that what you believe, Giles? In *Communism*?"

Giles put his hand on his mother's. In contrast to Claudine's wrath, he seemed content, even happy. "I can see you're upset, and maybe confused, too? Everything is changing so fast."

She slapped his hand away. "You are both right and wrong. Yes, I am upset. But no, I am not the least bit confused. You are a traitor, and you cannot stay in my house. Get out."

I admit, I was more than eavesdropping by then, as I witnessed this family drama from a few doors down, pressed up against a wall to make myself unnoticeable. Claudine and Giles had always been close. Whatever else one might say about him, he was known as a devoted son to his mother, especially after his father had died.

"You don't mean that, Maman," he said. "You're just all tangled up inside, I understand."

"No, you *don't* understand, Giles. If you did, you would return to your office, put your uniform back on, and defend your country. Or you would continue to wear that slovenly, ridiculous outfit and you would leave. Now."

It would be dangerous for him to be seen while it was still light. Whatever outfit he wore, he would be recognized, and both the Milice and the Resistance would not be forgiving of someone who'd been playing both sides. Mother and son regarded each other, their shared history about to change.

"All right, then," Giles said, and I heard the tenderness in his voice, despite what was about to happen. "*Au revoir,* Maman."

Claudine slammed the door in his face.

A few days later, we heard that Giles Paquette's body had been found in the Hérault River.

COMBATANTS WHO KNOW they are losing are the most dangerous enemy. It happened in Poland, when the Russians were losing ground during the Great War. Now, it was happening again.

After the Normandy landings, the allies pushed the Germans eastward. But as Nazi troops were forced back across France toward the Rhine, they exhaled their rage on civilians. In Mont Mouchet, they killed more than three hundred residents and Resistance fighters. In Tulle, the bodies of ninety-nine men were prominently hung around the town. Dozens of communities endured random, mass murders by the retreating troops.

Then there was Oradour-sur-Glane.

Even amid the soul-numbing tally of daily horrors, what happened in this quiet hamlet stood out. On June 10th, German forces killed almost the entire population: six hundred and forty-two men, women, and children were either shot or burned alive inside a church. There were seven survivors. A dozen of the soldiers involved were *Malgré Nous*—forcibly conscripted men from Alsace. As the Nazi's murderous withdrawal across France continued, I became more alert than ever to every minuscule, possible threat.

But there was one that I missed, right in our own home.

THE BEDSHEETS STUCK to me, on another humid, August night. I had just managed to doze when low voices from the kitchen yanked me out of sleep and into rigid awareness.

Were there police in our apartment? Middle-of-the-night arrests and kidnappings were always a possibility. The Milice liked to operate that way. Had Claudine Paquette discovered we were Jewish? Up until now, I had hoped that our landlady's crush on Max had prevented her from investigating us further. But perhaps her ardor had waned, with Max's lack of response. I rolled over in bed to alert him to the noise, and with horror saw he wasn't there. *Was he in the kitchen, talking with someone, bargaining with them, begging them not to take us away?*

But no, the voices sounded calm. I threw on a wrap and crept to the kitchen. Max. By himself. With one ear pressed up to a radio.

"Max. You gave me a fright. What on earth are you doing?"

"Shhh. Radio London. Listen. Good news."

"But how did you . . . ? When did you . . . ?"

I'd never seen this radio before, and it was illegal for any French person to listen to the broadcast Max had tuned into: the BBC.

"Shush, my dove. It doesn't matter where I got it. It's an old, old model that I fixed up with an extra wire here, a new bolt there. I learned that if you tune in very late at night, it's harder for them to jam the signals, and the French-language broadcasts from London come through more clearly. Listen. Come sit."

He pulled me into his lap, another small gesture suggesting the affectionate, tender man he'd been before. Little by little, since the near-catastrophe with Annette, I'd caught glimpses of my old husband coming back.

"Lean in closely," Max said very softly into my ear. "I can't increase the volume. Madame Paquette . . ."

He gestured toward the floor. If Claudine heard Radio London coming from our apartment, we knew she would promptly and happily turn us in. I bent over to listen through the static, to connect with that unseen human being, a real person talking to us, encouraging us, from all the way across the English Channel.

" . . . we repeat that, in the earliest hours this morning, August 15th, the American 7th Army and the Free French 1st Army landed on the French Riviera. Four German divisions were there to oppose them . . . it has been, by all accounts, an amazing success. And so, the Germans are now on the run toward their homeland in two directions: heading east from the Atlantic, and as of this morning, heading north from the Mediterranean . . ."

I snapped the radio off.

"But . . . why?" Max asked.

I stood up, our brief moment of reconnecting over. "Don't you see? This German retreat from the Mediterranean coast could spark the same cycle of killing as with the Atlantic retreat. Every southern town will be a target. We need to stay home; Annette and André won't like it, but they'll just have to endure. We'll tell Jacques he shouldn't come for dinner on Sunday, that he should stay in Issoire."

"But it *is* good news," he replied. "It might not be long now. Can you imagine being home, in Colmar? I'm starting to picture it. I don't dare, but then . . . I do."

"I picture Oradour-sur-Glane happening in Ganges."

"It could be different here. You heard what Radio London said, that the landings were an amazing success."

But he didn't push his point further, which I appreciated. I couldn't be hopeful. Not yet. Max and I retreated to our room, tiptoeing past André's closed bedroom door.

We didn't know that behind it, our son's bed was empty.

Chapter 29
GANGES, FRANCE
LATE AUGUST 1944. RESISTANCE

BY THE END of August, it seemed that Max would be right, we just might get that fairy-tale ending.

After the Mediterranean landings in mid-August, we listened to the radio every night, and every broadcast delivered thrilling news. The coming liberation of Paris. How town after town in southern France had been easily freed from German control. How in many southern communities, Nazi forces didn't even put up a fight, choosing instead to run east to protect their homeland. One evening in late August, the city of Ganges decided to celebrate.

"Sarah, let's go. We don't want to miss everything." Max bounced on the balls of his feet.

"Just let me fix my hair. Hold on. Where are my dress shoes? Is Annette ready?"

We entered the central square and were immediately pulled into a swirl of conversation, drinking, street music, and dancing. It was bewildering to be so happy. Annette ran off with some friends from church. André darted away as well, saying he also had friends to meet and that he'd be home much later, and that we shouldn't wait up for him.

"May I have this dance, *Mademoiselle?*" Max bowed low and held out his hand.

"Max, don't be silly," I said.

But I took his offer to dance, and allowed my mind to stop, for once. I let my body flow, to be captured by the warmth of the night, the music, the dancing, the reassuring familiarity of Max holding me. For the first time in years, I dared to savor the possibility of joy.

An improvised group of musicians had settled by the central fountain, and they began to play a slow waltz. Max guided me through the romantic tempo, and at our leisurely pace, I was able to take in the scene around us: the comforting, creamy silhouette of Ganges City Hall, the gnarled yet graceful sycamores, the contented faces of the townspeople watching those of us who were dancing. Among the spectators, I thought I saw them. But could it be? Yes, it was: Hector

De Beauville and his wife, Jo-Jo, sitting in a café, a bit removed from the center of activity. I stopped abruptly, stepping on Max's foot by mistake.

"Max, over there. The De Beauvilles are back."

"What? Oh, wonderful! We must go say hello."

We'd both been devastated by the De Beauville family's sudden disappearance from Ganges. We tried to convince ourselves that the family had fled before the unthinkable happened: that they hadn't been imprisoned, sent away to some unknown destination, or—just as possible—shot on sight. We remembered Hector talking about his partner in forgery, in Montpelier. Perhaps the De Beauvilles had sought refuge there, we told each other. Or, maybe they'd gone to Nîmes, a major city where it would be easy to go undercover and where Hector had many contacts. We invented these and other consoling possibilities, because not knowing the truth was excruciating. Now, we practically ran over to where Hector and Jo-Jo sat.

"Hector! Hector De Beauville," Max waved and called.

Hector waved back and stood up. He and Max embraced each other.

"And Jo-Jo, my goodness, welcome back," Max said, turning to Hector's wife, expecting her to stand so he could give her the same enthusiastic greeting.

But Jo-Jo did not rise. In fact, she seemed not to hear or see us. She held a bouquet of herbs in her left hand, twisting them. Her eyes were blank.

"Hector . . . ?" Max asked.

"They tortured her in prison," Hector said, flatly. "And she lost the baby."

It was then that I noticed Jo-Jo's arms were covered with red, infected insect bites, that she had no fingernails left, that there were bald patches on her scalp where the hair appeared to have been ripped out. And the baby . . . I imagined Jo-Jo, miscarrying her child, all alone in a prison cell, with no medical care, no comfort.

I tried not to stare, at this empty woman's body that once housed my friend's spirit. I remembered Jo-Jo's laugh, her herbal teas, how she and her husband adored each other . . . the shared glances, the little touches, the obvious delight they took in each other's presence. I shuddered, focusing on Hector. He didn't need to experience my rage right now. He had enough, I was sure, of his own.

"Hector," I said, as low and controlled as I could manage. "What happened?"

Hector put his hand on Jo-Jo's shoulder. She didn't appear to notice.

"It was a typical slow, summer morning at City Hall. Hot. Quiet. Then just before lunch, Giles Paquette raced in, yes—Giles, of all people. He warned me that the Milice were on their way to arrest me. I escaped out a back window, open because of the heat. I had to bicycle home, like I always do. But I thought I'd get there in time to warn her, because the Milice would likely spend a few minutes ransacking my office."

I imagined Hector, his legs pumping furiously up that giant hill from downtown, sweat pouring down his face, in the steaming heat, while his heart must have been exploding into a thousand shards of fear.

"Jo-Jo was in the kitchen when I arrived," he continued. "I knew I couldn't run far away because our house would be the next place they'd look. So, I said we should hide in our mausoleum, you remember, that brick structure in the yard? Remember how I explained that it locks from the inside? But Jo-Jo didn't like that idea at all. She said that the mausoleum was too obvious, and that once they found the house empty, they'd come out to the backyard and smash it, blow it up, destroy it somehow to get to me. 'I'll protect you,' she said. 'I'll pretend to be an innocent housewife, that I have no idea where you are. They won't dare touch me, Hector, I'm *pregnant*. The government *wants* women to have more babies, remember?'"

He stroked Jo-Jo's now ragged brown hair.

"We argued about it, but she insisted. Jo-Jo has always had her own mind. We heard their motorcycles grinding up the hill. We had to make a decision. I ran to the mausoleum. She stayed in the kitchen. I'll never forget that last moment. She kissed me, and gave me that sweet Jo-Jo smile. 'It will work, Hector,' she said. 'Don't worry, my darling.'"

Intent now on Hector, it took me a moment to realize that Jo-Jo had just said something. I leaned towards her barely moving lips. "I don't know," she said, rocking slightly back and forth. "I don't know."

"It's all right, my love," Hector said. "It's all right . . ."

He turned back to us. "From inside the mausoleum, I couldn't hear what was happening at the house. It almost killed me to stay there, when every part of me ached to dash out and be with her, to protect her. But I know how these Milice types work: they would shoot me immediately. And so, I stayed, locked inside my family's frigid tomb, praying to the God I've prayed to all my life: that Jo-Jo was right, that she'd play the role of naïve, pregnant wife, and that they'd leave her alone. A few minutes later, I heard the faint grumble of motorcycles departing. I crept out. The house was in perfect order, except for my locked desk in the library, which had been smashed open. And my wife was gone."

I pictured the cozy library, where we'd first met with Hector and Jo-Jo. I imagined Hector crumpled on the carpet, next to his shattered desk, bottomless sobs ripping him from inside.

"Hector," Max said, his eyes filling. "You don't have to . . ."

"No, I can finish. I . . . I'm almost . . . done." He took a breath. "She was taken to a Gestapo prison in Montpelier, which the Milice eventually took over.

A place with dungeons and torture rooms, where they . . . hurt prisoners who wouldn't talk. The Milice must have kept asking where I was, and she wouldn't tell them. Although I have wished every day since then . . . that she *did* tell them. Then maybe they would have taken me and left her alone."

I floundered, searching for the right words and finding none. "Hector. We are so very sorry."

"We're working with the best possible doctors," he said. "Maybe she'll get better."

But I could tell he was saying it for our benefit. Max and I stood there, awkwardly, as music and laughter from the community celebration swirled around us.

"What about your sons, Hector? Where are they? How are they?" Max finally asked.

"They're upset. Confused. They're staying with family nearby, while I tend to Jo-Jo."

I remembered Minou. "Tell them we have the cat. Minou is with us. Annette will hate to give him up, but of course . . ."

"Oh. I had wondered," he replied. "I'll tell the boys. We'll take Minou back, when we're ready. Thank you. Every small comfort I can offer them . . ."

The composure he'd somehow mustered to talk with us wavered, and he sat back down and took Jo-Jo's right hand. Her left hand continued to grip her herb bouquet.

"I don't know," she breathed. "I don't know . . ."

THUMP-THUMP-THUMP. Thump-thump-thump.

At five o'clock the next morning, I was still dead asleep after our late night at the downtown festivities. My subconscious processed the demanding thuds, creating a dream that I was back in Poland and that there were Russian soldiers at the door. The pounding continued, waking me fully up. *It must be a straggler from a fleeing unit of the Milice. Or what remained of the Gestapo. Or some other random, violent person with revenge on their minds and a gun in their hands.*

"Please Madame Seibert. Open the door!"

That sounded less threatening. The Milice and the Gestapo never said "please." Still, the war was not over yet.

"What should we do?" Max rasped.

"Tell Annette and André to hide in the backroom closet. I'll go to the door. If it's trouble, I'll try to fool them, or . . . talk my way around it somehow."

I grabbed my biggest kitchen knife and opened the door a crack, with the chain lock still engaged. Through the opening, I saw three young men, wearing ill-fitting clothes and battered boots. Their hair was unkempt; their faces were dirty. Under their jackets, I detected the outlines of impressive guns.

Maquisards. Resistance fighters.

"Madame Seibert," one of them said. "Our sincerest apologies for disturbing you so early, but it is of the utmost importance that you let us in."

I noted his excellent manners, despite his ragged appearance. And, of course, I would open to anyone involved in the Resistance. But before I unlatched the door, I asked, "How do you know my name?"

Max rushed into the kitchen. "André. He's not in his room."

"Yes," the young man said, peering through the space between the chain and the door. "André is one of us. A valued member of the group. He told us to come here, that you'd let us in. So, please, madame . . . ?"

I fully opened the door. "What's happening? Where is André?"

"He's fine," the Resistance fighter said, walking right by me, scanning our apartment. "Now, you must all leave. Immediately. You, your husband, and your little girl need to go somewhere else. We'll be using your apartment we *hope* just for today."

He strode to the living room windows. He appraised the view, overlooking the wide, dry bed of the Rieutord River. "Yes. Just as André said. Excellent."

The young man took his jacket off and checked over his gun.

"I'm sure you're curious . . . so let's just say that after a *scuffle* with our men a few hours ago, several thousand Nazi troops from the Toulouse Column will be trying again to retreat north through this region. We expect some might travel up the riverbed, and your living room window provides us the perfect vantage point. But beware, Monsieur and Madame Seibert. Although in some towns, the German withdrawal has been peaceful, in others it has not. This particular group of soldiers is furious. They know their country's cause is lost, and they have nothing left but anger. Anything they see moving, they'll shoot. You must stay indoors. Especially stay away from windows." He scanned the alley and riverbed below again. "We'll fire on them from up here. But please, go now. Before it becomes impossible."

Annette came into the kitchen in her nightgown. She gasped at the young men and their guns, and hid behind Max, who knelt and faced her as if he'd just had the best idea.

"Let's go over to your friend Joelle's this morning. Run along now and get ready."

"But, Papa. She won't be up, it's too early, and her parents won't like it."

"I'll explain everything to them. I just happen to know that Joelle especially wants to see you, right now, at this very moment. Let's go, Maideleh."

The other two maquisards joined their leader at the windows. They moved some furniture and pulled the drapes closed. One of them turned to me. He could not have been older than sixteen. *He's even younger than André.* It was sobering.

"Please. Go now, madame," he said. "Thank you for the apartment. We'll send word when it's safe for you to come back."

"But where's André?"

"André? Ah. Don't worry. He's close by. *Very* close," The youngest-looking one exchanged a knowing glance with his fellow maquisards. "He was downstairs with two others from our group, at your landlady's. The lower floor isn't quite as well-placed for shooting at retreating forces, but we'll use it for other purposes. However"—the young man grinned—"it's a safe bet that Madame Paquette was not as generous with her apartment as you are with yours."

Max laughed out loud and even I had to smile, despite the fact that there were three heavily armed Resistance fighters in our apartment, preparing to fire down upon German forces who would return fire upward. It was absurd, but I felt a bit better, knowing that André was involved with these polite, courageous, seemingly competent young men and that our son was just downstairs. I went to the kitchen and put on my apron.

"Madame?" one of the maquisards said.

"The Germans aren't here yet. In the meantime, you are all incredibly thin. I'm making you something to eat. Don't argue. André surely explained that with me, you're wasting your breath."

I set out bread, canned potatoes, and tinned meat. I scrambled some eggs. They gobbled it like it was a gourmet feast.

Gunshots echoed outside, muffled and still far away. But the maquisards pushed back from the table, changing from hungry boys to hardened fighters. The eldest gave me a forceful look, which I returned.

"I understand, young man. I'm leaving. I'll just go fetch André downstairs as I go, so he can come with us."

The leader shook his head. "No, madame. It's not worth your time. He was never intending to stay there long after the . . . uh . . . how should we call it? The *introductions* were made with Madame Paquette."

"But where is he? He's my son. There's a battle underway. You must tell me where he is, you *must*."

"I'm sorry, I cannot give you that information, madame. It would not be safe for you, or for him. Now please, I insist that you go."

DESPITE WHAT THE maquisards told us about the threat from this Toulouse Column, we arrived at Annette's friend's house in good spirits. Gathered around the family's dining room table for coffee, with the windows shuttered and the doors locked, everyone expected the Germans would slip away quickly and quietly, as they had in so many other communities. As noon approached, we told each other that the increasing gunfire cracking the air nearby was just angry Nazis letting off steam as they withdrew. But by mid-afternoon, we had to admit that there would be no gentle retreat through Ganges. There would be a battle. And as that day stretched on, with no word from André, I did what I do best: imagine the worst.

How did I not notice that André had been sneaking out? He'd always been drawn to stories of rebellion, from the Camisards of old to the Maquisards of today. I blamed myself for not paying more attention. The moment when liberation seemed possible, I'd shed my customary vigilance. I imagined my blue-eyed boy dead in a ravine somewhere, his legendary charm forever stilled.

By eight o'clock, Lise, the mother of Annette's friend, offered us dinner.

"No thank you," I managed to say, choking through my misery. "I just need to lie down, and to be alone."

"Of course," Lise said. "The guest room is there."

I closed the door, fell onto the bed, and into darkness.

I WAS BACK in Poland, with my brothers and sisters. We were packing a cart with all our belongings, fleeing again. We threw barrels and satchels and household items haphazardly into the back. It was winter, with snow and ice on the ground, but I was warm. My father and brothers settled in the front of the wagon. I climbed in the back with my sisters. But André was there too, wedged among bundles and baskets.

"Surprise, Maman," he said.

"Maman. Maman, wake up."

A small, moist palm patted my shoulder. Annette and Max stood by the guest bed. I chided myself for falling asleep. I was supposed to keep watch. For André.

"What time is it? Is it over? Are they gone? Have we heard from André?"

Max sat down next to me. "It's after ten o'clock. Yes, the battle is over. Yes, the Germans are gone. But no, we haven't heard from André."

I moaned and pressed my face into the pillow. It was Annette who managed to convince me to move.

"Maman. Let's go home. Don't be worried, you know André. He can do anything. I'll bet he's already there, waiting for us. Come on," she said.

The streets of Ganges were deserted. The smell of gunpowder still lingered in the air. We moved quickly, worried the fight might not truly be over, even though the stones of the central square echoed with the clapping of our heels. We approached our building, noticing that Madame Paquette's lights were off. That was fortunate. After André and the maquisards had "borrowed" our landlady's apartment, I was sure we'd have to move. We took our shoes off so we could pad up the stairs in our socks and avoid waking anyone. I opened the apartment door.

No André.

Max shooed Annette to bed. He and I sat at the kitchen table.

"You should eat," he said after a while. "Sit, I'll get it."

He was right, I was faint from consuming almost nothing all day. Max served me a little bread and goat cheese. I ate a few bites and had to vomit.

We moved to the living room, unsure what we should do. Eleven p.m. became midnight.

"I'll go find him," Max said. "I can't stand this."

"No. You could get yourself killed. There might still be German soldiers out there who got separated from their column. They'd like nothing better than to shoot at a male figure in the dark."

Midnight became one a.m. We were listless and alert at the same time. As two o'clock in the morning approached, our chins dropped to our chests. We dozed, jerked awake, then dozed again.

"Surprise, Maman . . ."

It must be my Poland dream, as I faded in and out of sleep.

"Maman, Papa. It's me."

André. His clothes and face were smeared with dirt and smoke. His hair stood stiffly in six directions. But there was no blood, no bruises, no apparent broken bones. In fact, he had never appeared happier. It took Max and I half an hour before we could stop crying and let go of him. André took a bath and slept till noon.

LATER THAT DAY at a very late lunch, André recounted his story, adding dramatic flair for his little sister. "Then, Mademoiselle, what do you think your brother did next?"

"Tell, André, tell!" Annette yelled.

"Well. After I 'introduced' my comrades, the other maquisards, to our landlady and her conveniently located apartment, I took off on my bicycle across town. Because I'm short, the Germans assumed I was just a kid. And they had other worries besides a boy on a bicycle."

André beamed as he chewed. He had cleaned up, combed his hair, and was talking as if he had just had a wonderful adventure. *Which it was, a deadly one.* But I was too relieved to be angry.

"About three thousand Germans called the Toulouse Column made it through the mountain pass in the wee hours of the morning," André continued with his mouth full. "They were in a terrific hurry to get across the New Bridge into Ganges, head east to Nîmes, and then get back up to Germany . . . which still includes Alsace."

His exuberance dimmed. We all knew there would be savage fighting once the Allies reached the province still under Nazi rule and still called *Elsass*.

"But the Germans won't get to the Rhine as quickly as they wanted." André returned to grand raconteur mode, giving Annette exactly what she needed: a tale starring one of her heroic big brothers. "Not after the fight *we* gave them. Traveling through Ganges was their fastest route, but we were not going to grant them that satisfaction. We stopped them at the New Bridge. Maquis groups eleven, thirteen, and twenty . . . all hidden in the shadows until the exact moment. Then we sprung upon them."

Annette cheered, as André basked in her admiration.

"Ha! Yes, it was just like the old Camisards of the Cévennes long ago. We showed them. My job was to keep the maquisards well-fed and well-armed. Our cache of food and ammunition was about a mile away from the battle itself, hidden behind a pile of wood at a bakery. The baker, of course, was on our side, like almost everyone in Ganges. All day, I rode back and forth, stuffing bullets, explosives, and food in my bike's side baskets, and then pedaling at a furious pace to where our guys were fighting. The shots were flying everywhere, but most of our men didn't get hit. We had the element of surprise on the offense, and knowing where to hide on the defense. Plus, when some of them tried to retreat another way, traveling up the Rieutord, well . . . as you already know, their troops were down low, and our men were up high. Including in our very own apartment. That gave us a huge advantage."

But there were some details André was leaving out of his merry little tale.

"*Most* of our men didn't get hit? How many people did you lose?" I asked.

"Um. Yes, Maman. Some maquisards and some civilians were shot. I don't know yet how many died. Perhaps more civilians than Resistance fighters, because they weren't trained like we were. It was a long day and night. But the Germans never did make it over that bridge. When they couldn't retreat that way like they wanted, some drove their tanks up the riverbed, like I said. Others, though, detoured through the village of Cazilhac, next door. At that point, the *Boches* were spitting mad because we'd blocked their fastest route. They entered Cazilhac and caused mayhem—looting stores and homes, grabbing food and wine, destroying buildings, and taking hostages. Probably killing some of them."

André's jolly recounting no longer seemed appropriate. He could have been among the dead.

But I could tell that for Annette, it was a magical storybook. Her wonderful big brother had helped deter the evil Nazis from Ganges.

Annette wriggled in her seat, then jumped up. "Let's go and see how the bridge is. I want to make sure Ganges is all right."

Going to the scene of battle where our son might have died was the last thing I wanted to do. However, it might reassure Annette to see that Ganges was unscathed. I was worried about our daughter. Unlike her brothers, who had more freedom during the war years, Annette had spent most of her time hidden, either at home or at the convent. Her social interactions were limited, and there had been long periods when she wasn't even able to go to school. While I knew that even in the best of times, twelve-year-old girls can be emotional—I often wondered if Annette's wartime upbringing made her especially so.

"Are you *sure* it's safe, André?" I asked.

"Yes, Maman. Positive. I was at the bridge. I watched them retreat to Cazilhac. The only Germans left at the Ganges town line are dead."

ALTHOUGH NAZI FORCES hadn't made it across the bridge alive, they had done so in death. Earlier that day, Ganges residents had carried the soldiers' bodies across the bridge to dispose of them, but also to check for food and money in their backpacks and pockets. Five years ago, that would have seemed grotesque. But we had suffered so much because of them.

We walked to the public square by the bridge. Annette took Max's hand, something she rarely did nowadays. On the sidewalks and in alleys, several bodies had been left, sometimes with their wallets beside them. These had been emptied of valuables by earlier passers-by, but the soldiers' identity cards and personal photos remained, items of value only to their loved ones far away. Annette picked up several of these. She read out loud:

"Gerhard Berger. Born 1924, Berlin. Felix Schafer. Born 1922, Heidelberg. Dieter Bauer. Born 1927, Keil." Annette gasped, staring at the papers. "He's only seventeen. He's younger than André and Jacques."

I was beginning to think it was a bad idea to come downtown. "Let's go back," I said.

But Annette had already gathered the papers and photos of a man who lay dead near a café. She scanned them, then threw the items down and rushed to Max, sobbing.

I picked them up. *Jost Hofmann. Born 1904, Munich.*

The man was just four years younger than Max. Photos in his wallet showed he also was a father of three children. He was tall, too, like Max, with the same luxurious black wavy hair. Max comforted Annette as she wept. I felt neither sadness nor vengeance. I felt nothing.

SOON AFTER THE battle of Ganges, the city of Nîmes was liberated. With huge regret, I decided we should move back there. We hated saying goodbye to Ganges. The feisty little community had welcomed us, protected us, and saved our lives. But there was more lucrative work for Max in a bigger city like Nîmes, and more apartments available for rent.

Because as expected, Claudine Paquette had terminated our lease.

Chapter 30
NÎMES, FRANCE
JANUARY 1945. ALMOST HOME

OUR FORMER LIVES dangled in front of us, teasing us with images of home. The colorful buildings of Colmar, with their gently sloping roofs. The curves of the Vosges Mountains and their abundant forests. The charming, well-kept villages surrounded by vineyards. We began to make plans. "When we go back, I can't wait to . . ." we would say to each other, afraid to hope but unable to stop.

But for now, returning was impossible. Six months of steady Allied success in France was now bogged down in town-by-town, street-by-street combat for parts of Alsace. Although Strasbourg had been liberated in November, the battles remained entrenched in an area dubbed "The Colmar Pocket." French and American forces fought together there, almost the last part of France to be freed. We had to stay in Nîmes.

One Sunday afternoon in January, Jacques and I remained at the kitchen table after we had finished our Sunday dinner, a mixture of potatoes, eggs, and bony chicken parts. Food was still scarce, as it had been throughout the war. For some women, this increased their inventiveness in the kitchen, as they took on the challenge of preparing meals despite key missing ingredients. For me, the shortages only enhanced my long disinterest in cooking. Or at least, they gave me an excellent excuse not to bother making an effort.

Jacques was in the French army. His unit was stationed nearby, and he'd been granted a day's leave to see his family. Now, the winter afternoon was darkening, and I knew he needed to report to his barracks. Still, I placed my hand on his, a quiet request to stay a moment longer.

"At the very end of the war, I hope you won't have to fight now, to liberate Colmar," I said. "Your friend Frédéric could be in those battles."

"Don't worry about me, Maman. They don't seem to have big plans for our group, we just march around and do drills. We're a brand-new unit, too inexperienced for them to put us in a tough fight like Alsace is right now."

"You know I'm going to worry."

Jacques stood to leave and gave me a quick kiss on the cheek. "I know, you can't help it. But don't fret about me, or Frédéric, either. He knows the Vosges and Colmar better than anyone. He's probably leading a battalion right now, singing 'God Bless America.'"

I laughed. "Yes, that's probably true."

As Jacques put on his coat, I noticed how tall he was. For the better part of his growing up, I had to focus only on survival. Now, in this odd, suspended time of "almost home," it often startled me to see my oldest son as an adult. Like me, he'd come of age during a war. But Jacques had also become a man amid an unprecedented, murderous campaign against European Jews. I wondered what impact this would have on him. He could become embittered and angry, paranoid and anxious, or simply depressed. But for the moment, I didn't see any of those qualities in my eldest son.

He's kind, I thought. *And grateful.*

ALSACE WAS LIBERATED in February, but still we waited to return. The province was just too close to the German border, and given the intense Allied bombardment of Germany, it would be too easy for a bomber pilot to make a mistake and drop his load on us. We hung on in southern France, ever more restless for home. I wrote to Adele, giving her our address in Nîmes and telling her we'd come back as soon as it was safe.

ON THE FIRST of May, I received a letter from Adele's son, René Chastain. I was afraid to open it.

> *Dear Sarah:*
>
> *I'm writing with regret to inform you that my mother and father passed away at the end of 1943. My mother died in November, collapsing early one morning outside the bakery. We believe it was a heart attack. My father lost his will to live shortly thereafter. I'm sorry they didn't live to see Alsace freed.*

Oh, Adele. My throat hurt. I put the letter down, remembering Adele as I first met her, in 1924. Her unadorned elegance, her gift of a box of croissants, the silver cross she always wore, which unsettled me at first, but which I'd come to realize symbolized the best of her faith: *Love Thy Neighbor.*

Adele hesitated only one second when I asked her in 1939 to buy our business, to hold it until we came home. She'd taken a crazy, enormous chance, hiding merchandise for us when the Nazi authorities in Alsace demanded people give up almost everything they had, to fuel the war. She'd risked a ferocious punishment that frigid winter night when she'd insisted that I stay at her home. Had she sensed then, that it might be our last visit? Even the hidden blueberry pie she'd served after supper was a humble act of rebellion. I savored the image of all the hateful, power-crazed men who controlled the province during annexation, and how a quiet, elderly woman outfoxed them, in ways that were perhaps small, given the scope of the war, but that were huge for my family. *Bravo, my friend. Thank you.* I went back to René's letter.

I apologize for taking so long to reply to the letter you sent my mother earlier this year. But until February, I was imprisoned at the Nazis' Schirmeck re-education camp for "un-cooperative" Alsatians, where they "re-educated" us through starvation, punishment and other types of abuse. I only recently have had the strength to write.

I regret that I have more bad news. I have not heard from my son Henri since he was conscripted into the German army more than two years ago. I can only assume that he was killed somewhere in Russia. My son died for a cause that my family abhors. At least my parents left this earth believing it was still possible that Henri might be alive.

But there is also some hope and light in my life that I must tell you about.

While my other son, Frédéric, was injured in combat, it's not serious. He got trench foot while serving with an American tank unit in the Vosges, as part of the battle for the Colmar Pocket. Frédéric has lost most of his toes, the fighting took place in sub-zero temperatures and several feet of snow. But he knows how lucky he is; he'll learn to walk again. Because of Frédéric's service with the U.S. army, he is being given American citizenship and will move there once he recovers. He plans to settle in a place I've never heard of, called "New Hampshire," a small northeastern state where several of his American army buddies are from. They tell him the landscape is a lot like Alsace, and that there are many French Canadians he can speak French with if he gets tired of speaking English.

Lastly, there is more good news. I am getting married again. To Claire Mueller. I know my mother never liked her, but perhaps your friend Adele is now smiling up in heaven at the irony of it. Claire has sold her clothing store and is working with me at Pain Pour Tous. She has a talent for baking that she never was able to realize, being saddled with running her parents' clothing store at such a young age.

So, our family and yours will once again be business neighbors on Rue Vauban. I look forward to that.
   René

ON MAY 8TH, at exactly three p.m., the sky above Nîmes exploded with the mad ringing of church bells, each instrument shouting its own song of joy, clashing yet harmonizing in crazed ecstasy with its fellow bells across the city. General de Gaulle had just announced Germany's surrender on the radio. Every city, town, village, and hamlet in France burst into rapturous celebration. My family and I rushed about, putting on our best clothes to join the festivities.

"Let's hold hands on the way," I said to my children.

While they were long past the age of holding hands with their parents, they did so. As we walked, we felt the warmth and pulse of each other's palms. It was a powerful reminder of life. The life we still had, for which we would be forever grateful. Together, we traversed the few blocks from our apartment to central Nîmes. Then we stopped short.

Everywhere people were dancing.

Makeshift orchestras had popped up, as people grabbed whatever instruments they had and played. Crowds danced in front of City Hall, on the university plaza, by the amphitheater, at every intersection where there was space. Friends, neighbors, and perfect strangers were hugging and kissing each other.

"What are we waiting for?" André shouted, and we plunged into the party.

Max and I danced with each other and with anyone, everyone. There were parades and speeches and drinking, then more speeches, more dancing, and lots of singing of the national anthem.

"It seems impossible to be so happy," I said, as we joined other waltzing couples, in an inebriated, joyous blur circling the massive fountain in Nîmes' central square, its white statues gleaming in the waning evening light.

"Anything's possible." Max stopped right next to the fountain and kissed me lightly. "Look at us. We made it. Thanks to *you*." His kiss deepened, stirring me to consider leaving the party, to be with him, alone. But it was a historic moment. I didn't want to miss a second of it.

We'll have time later. Lots of time.

The celebration continued all night and through dawn. My feet ached from dancing; my throat hurt from singing and cheering; I was drunk and exhilarated and exhausted. As daylight approached, I could no longer stand up. I told Max I was going home. I fell onto our bed, and into a chasm of welcome, profound sleep.

I was still dancing in my dreams.

Chapter 31
COLMAR, FRANCE
JUNE 1945. RETURN

OUR FAMILY GETS off the train in Colmar. I'm amazed that five years have passed, that we're really here. I look at Max and my children and see they're in the same state I am: elation, but muted by fear. At what we might find. At how different it might be. Then, Max emits a little cheer and puts his arm around Jacques, claps him on the shoulder. André and Annette hug each other.

I pick up my suitcase. "Let's go."

WHAT WE FIND on Rue Vauban is a miracle. Our building is untouched. The store below and our apartment above appear to be in the same condition as when I left in May of 1940. Meanwhile, my friend Adele had saved every piece of documentation showing us as the building's former owners, so it was easy for her son René to "sell" it back to us. His family's bakery, Pain Pour Tous, is still standing too, just across the street. I smile when I see that René has already re-labeled his business with its French name. The sign had read "Brot Für Alle" under annexation. At the same time, I dread going into the bakery for the first time. I'll look for Adele, expecting her to be at a table, waiting for me with coffee and pie. But she won't be there.

I close my eyes, holding her memory.

Other ghosts from the past five years also tap on my heart. Jo-Jo De Beauville.

Jo-Jo never recovered from being tortured. Hector tenderly took care of her, as I knew he would. But while he could have chosen bitterness, that's not who he was. When we said farewell in Ganges, he was already back at his City Hall desk. He even joked about running for mayor of Ganges someday. I can easily imagine Hector sitting in the mayor's office, doing his part to make the world a kinder, more decent place. Still, I wonder how he'll react if he sees Claudine Paquette about town. A local policeman told Hector that it was Claudine who denounced him. Jo-Jo had worried about that, but in the end, it was she who paid the price.

My eyes are still closed, now to block the tears. But today should be joyful, and I don't want to ruin it. I open my eyes.

I see my family before me. Max, now forty-five years with some grey streaking his black hair. He's thinner than before, but still the handsomest man in any room, still deeply loving and loyal. Jacques, a young man of twenty-one. His quiet intelligence, his steady nature have been strengthened by hardship. André, now nineteen, eager to regain whatever fun he can from his teenage years lost to war. He'll have many adventures, I think, but he'll be wise, too. And Annette, a little girl of eight when she left Colmar, clutching her doll. She's now thirteen, and taller than me. I already sense we'll have some intense mother-daughter battles as she enters fully into adolescence. But I know we'll be close, very close, after all we've endured together.

I pull the building's keys out of my purse.

"Come on," I say. "Let's begin."

A LETTER FROM LAURA

Thank you for sharing your time with *The Shopkeeper of Alsace*. If you enjoyed the novel, please consider leaving a short review, by scanning the QR code. I love connecting with readers and your review encourages others to consider my book. I'll keep you up to date on my next novels, set in fascinating locations you discovered in this book: Alsace and the Cévennes. And now . . .

THE REAL STORY BEHIND
THE STORY OF THE SHOPKEEPER OF ALSACE

This novel was sparked by a chance encounter.

In the mid-1980s, I was an American exchange student in Strasbourg, France, a lovely medium-sized city on the Rhine River bordering Germany and the capital of the province of Alsace. One winter weekend, my exchange program organized a weekend getaway in nearby Colmar for students, pairing us each with a family. I stayed with a woman named Annette. Yes, that Annette—the little girl in this novel.

Despite our differences in age and culture, Annette and I remained friends for more than thirty years. Over that time, she'd drop tiny scraps of her childhood war experience, mentioning that she was a "hidden child," for example, or telling a story about one of her brother's exploits. But she never offered much beyond a comment or two, and I didn't ask her to elaborate. To this day, I kick myself for that, especially since after college, I became a successful journalist. Perhaps I sensed that she was traumatized by what she'd endured and it would be best not to scratch too deeply. Or perhaps I didn't want to darken our rare, cross-Atlantic visits with her most frightening memories. Whatever the reason, when Annette passed away in 2015, I regretted not probing more. In the spring of 2018, I mentioned this to Annette's daughter, Brigitte, who had also become a close friend.

"I always wanted to tell your mother's story," I said, yelling over the table at a packed restaurant in New York City, "but now it's too late."

"But there's always my Uncle Jacques," she responded, also at top volume. "And he remembers everything!"

In the fall of 2018, I flew to France and spent an unforgettable November afternoon with then-ninety-five-year-old Jacques, who, as his niece promised, "remembered everything." An even wider picture of the family's story came from some cassettes made in 2005, when Jacques and his siblings, Annette and André, gathered to record their memories and read aloud letters from their mother. These recordings and a transcription of them were shared with me, and for months, I listened to and read the "Saga Seibert" countless times.

As my attachment to the story deepened, so did my awe for the family's matriarch, Sarah: her brashness, her courage, her foresight, and most of all, her huge heart. Her story felt too inspiring and too beautiful to be left untold.

But why a novel?

First, there are too many gaps in the narrative to write a cohesive work of nonfiction. As a novelist, I can fill in those spaces, as I imagine what might have happened, how people might have felt, what they might have said—although always, my conjecture is based on the saga itself, my conversations with family members, and my own historical research.

Second, there are others in this novel whose stories I felt needed to be understood. That includes both the people who helped Sarah's family—"Hector," "Jo-Jo," and "Adele" for example, as well as my villain, "Claudine." Each of these characters had their own backgrounds and motivations, and I thought their inclusion both expanded the novel's historical context and gave it more heart and soul.

Lastly, memory can be a tricky partner. There are key events in the family saga which each of the three children remembers differently. Whose version is "true?" Fiction allows me, as the author, to choose.

Still, many of the critical scenes in this book come straight from the family's history. That includes their flight from the village that the Jews called "Amshinov." The Polish name for the town is Mszczonow, but many early readers of my manuscript found the Polish name so distracting, I decided to go with the much easier-to-understand Jewish name. I have done my best to represent the village's fascinating history, including the prominent role Jews enjoyed there for many decades, and later, the terror that befell them.

All of Sarah's early life is as accurate as records and memories allow: her departure for France, her work in the family business in Metz where she met Melach, and the young couple's moves around the Alsace-Lorraine region. I've had to imagine some family dynamics, but these were always guided by both Sarah's letters and my own careful research, including interviews with several of the world's leading scholars on Jewish family life in that era, in Poland and France.

Sarah and Melach both came from large families, and all of their relatives described in the novel are fictional; brothers, sisters, aunts, uncles, parents, grandparents, etc.

Sarah's friend "Adele" comes from my interview with Jacques. More than once, he mentioned the importance of the bundles of merchandise his mother assembled—recalling how she packaged them up many months before France fell and then shepherded them down to southern France as the country was crumbling. He also mentioned her daring return trip (or trips) north, to collect the last of the merchandise. "It's those packages," he emphasized repeatedly, "that allowed us to survive the war." Clearly, this was a critical part of the family's survival strategy, so I did what any trained journalist does—I followed up:

"Who stored the goods for her?" I asked, "And how did your mother retrieve them?"

"There was a woman who helped," he said. "I'm not sure. I don't know."

As frustrating as it was, his answer made sense. Parents during WWII often told their children as little as possible, in order to protect them. So, I created "the woman who helped," Sarah's friend "Adele." Although the family saga indicates this woman met Sarah outside of Alsace to transfer the goods, I decided to set this scene inside the province, to give readers a sense of the extreme hardship Alsatians faced during the war years. I felt this was essential, because Alsace (and the annexed portions of Lorraine) experienced the war like no other part of France: As you've now learned, they were folded into Hitler's Reich. So, while the German occupation of northern France was brutal, and the fascist Vichy regime in southern France had its own cruel and capricious ways—there's a strong historical argument that Alsace and Lorraine suffered uniquely. Through Adele and her family, this novel opens a window to that Alsatian experience, one rarely covered in historical fiction.

One more historical note about that critical scene, when Sarah meets Adele back in Colmar: I have read dozens of articles and books and interviewed several French historians on how this encounter might have taken place, given the severe security at the Alsace-France border after 1940. The experts say that while these crossings were extremely difficult, they were not impossible. I've chosen to believe that if anyone could do it, it was Sarah Seibert.

Now, down to the characters in southern France. My novel's beautiful, heartbroken villain, "Claudine," is also based on a person mentioned by Sarah's children. All three remembered that their landlady in Ganges was devoted to the Vichy regime's Chief of State Pétain. Through extensive research, I've tried to paint a portrait of how Pétain's supporters might have felt, what influenced their thinking, and why some of them, like "Claudine," stood by the Vichy government till the very end, even at the expense of their own families.

The character of "Hector De Beauville" who forges the false identities for the Seibert family, was inspired by the real-life assistant mayor of Ganges during the war, Louis Monna. "Jo-Jo" is inspired by his wife, Henriette. The Seibert children all mention the Monnas in their recollections. Although the conversations and interactions I've written about the couple are invented, it's true that Henriette Monna was taken prisoner and tortured, due to her husband's illegal activities. Historical accounts (including the Seibert family's) also say that Henriette went "insane" or "mad" due to her torture. Despite the tragedy that struck his family, Louis Monna did go on to become a beloved, longtime mayor of Ganges. His name, and Henriette's, are placed on Israel's formal list honoring those non-Jews who helped Jews during the war, called "Righteous Among Nations."

The research undergirding this novel is massive. I absorbed books, newspaper articles, encyclopedias, municipal archives, videos, first-person accounts, museum exhibits, journals, and any other resources I could find, in French and English. I was greatly helped by researchers on both sides of the Atlantic who were extremely giving of their time.

Chief among them is Patrick Cabanel, whom I've come to refer to as "Mr. Cévennes." Professor Cabanel is one of France's leading experts on this region, with a packed schedule of teaching, writing, and traveling. And yet, he found time for me and this project. His generous, ongoing, enthusiastic help means the world to me. *Merci infiniment*, Patrick.

Second, a special *Merci* must go to two educators at the Alsace-Moselle Memorial in Shirmeck. For an entire afternoon, Delphine Pellenard and Marion Garcia-Paul answered my questions, directed me to other resources, and wholeheartedly shared their knowledge and passion for the history of Alsace. The memorial is a must-see if you are in the region.

On the American side, an enormous thanks goes to Tom White, former longtime educator with the Cohen Center for Holocaust and Genocide Studies at Keene State College. Tom was one of the earliest supporters of this novel, connecting me to a network of experts I couldn't have accessed on my own. My book, and our state of NH, are better for his work.

Many other researchers offered their wisdom, including: Antony Polonsky, Professor Emeritus at Brandeis University and one of the world's leading scholars on Polish Jews; Jakub Nowakowski, former Director of the Galicia Jewish Museum in Poland and currently Director of the Cape Town Holocaust and Genocide Centre in South Africa; Joanna Silwa, historian at the Conference on Jewish Material Claims Against Germany; Nancy Sinkoff, Professor of Jewish

Studies and History at Rutgers University; several archivists at the U.S. Holocaust Memorial Museum in Washington, D.C.; Nicolas Laugel, a historian based in Alsace; and Jan Darsa, head of Jewish Education at Facing History. I'm grateful for their time and insights. Of course, while these researchers did their best to inform me, any mistakes, contrivances, or misunderstandings are entirely mine.

Now, the personal thanks.

First to Annette, for befriending me all those years ago. This book would not exist without her. Deep thanks also go to her children, Brigitte, Jean-Michel, and Philippe, as well as her brothers Jacques and André, Jacques' daughter Martine, Annette's son-in-law Luc, and André's son Serge. *Merci*, a thousand times.

A giant thanks to my husband, Steve Winnett, for being this book's number one cheerleader, despite the many weekends and nights that I ignored him when I was deep in editing or writing mode. I could say "thank you" forever and it wouldn't be enough. Also, gratitude goes to my two sons, Isaiah and Abe, for putting up with my writing-related absences and for sharing their insights. In addition, this novel has three Fairy Godmothers—women who edited the manuscript at various stages, took my weepy phone calls, and insisted I continue after dozens of rejections. Margaret Porter, Ellen Grimm, and Suzanne Rico—I will love you forever for championing this book.

Thank you to my early readers for tolerating those initial, rough versions of my novel: Duncan Craig, Celia Rabinowitz, Sofia Thornblad, Margaret Porter, and Nicoletta Gullace. Your expertise was so valuable, and your encouragement of those first pages kept me going.

Others who strengthened this novel include Sonja Bolton, my social media expert, who makes my online presence classy, and my French teacher, Solenne Rivière, who polished my inquiry emails to French researchers so elegantly they just had to respond. Meg Chorlian, Tony Benson, and Stephanie Rico contributed insights and cheered me on. Kind support also came from others in NH's literary community: Masheri Chappelle, Robert Wheeler, Paul Brogan, Sarah McCraw Crowe, Cynthia Neale, Michael Hermann, Isabella Hardister, and the late Joe Monninger.

I'm grateful to my sisters, Sarah Jane and Pamela Jo, and my niece, Frannie, for remaining curious and supportive throughout the long cycle of writing, revision, rejection, repeat. I am a fortunate woman to have you all in my life.

Lastly, thank you to the incredible trio at Bedazzled Ink Publishing, for taking a chance on this debut author, for being wonderful publishing partners, and for their conviction that *The Shopkeeper of Alsace* is exactly the kind of novel we need right now.

Laura Knoy is one of New Hampshire's most well-known journalists. She was founding host of New Hampshire Public Radio's "The Exchange" which for 25 years was the state's most widely recognized and respected radio program. The show had 100,000 listeners across New Hampshire and extending in Vermont, Maine, and Massachusetts. She has worked at the national level as well; newscasting, hosting and reporting for NPR and other news outlets. She is the winner of many national and local journalism awards.

In mid-2021, Laura stepped down from the host's chair to pursue other interests, including writing fiction. Her skills in interviewing, moderating, narrating and public speaking are frequently called upon. In the fall of 2022, Laura joined the Warren B. Rudman Center at UNH-Franklin Pierce School of Law as its Director of Community Engagement. She's the host of three podcasts, including ReadLocalNH, which celebrates the literary community in her state. She's also the narrator of the award-winning children's book "Truffle," and has served as narrator for the travel app TravelStorys, and the Capitol Jazz Orchestra's annual Christmas concert.

She's the author of several magazine articles, in English and in French, as well as an essay in *Chicken Soup for the Soul: Tales of Christmas 2024*.

Laura graduated Phi Beta Kappa from George Washington University with a degree in International Affairs. She spends her free time reading or outdoors, while trying to avoid yard work and household chores. She and her husband are the parents of two young adult sons and one elderly cat.